D0390266

ARROW THE SKY HORSE

THE DISCOVERY

By

Melody Huttinger

THE DISCOVERY

Copyright ©2018 by Melody Huttinger

All rights reserved. No part of this book may be used or reproduced in any manner without the written permission of the author.

This book is a work of fiction. Except where noted, names, characters, places, and incidents are the product of the author's imagination or are use fictitiously.
Any resemblance to actual events, locales, or persons, living or dead is coincidental.

J BAR X PUBLISHING

Printed in the United States of America

ISBN-978-1-7328715-0-2

Cover Art by Maura Dorn

Edited by Heidi Thomas

Map art by Marilyn Wiley

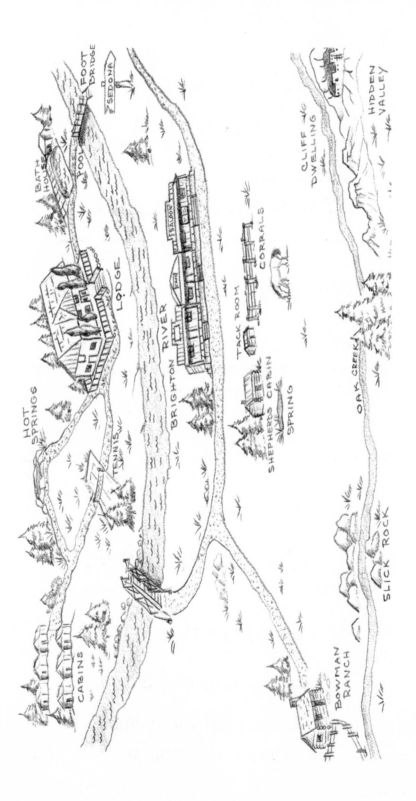

Contents

Chapter 1

The Move

Meadow Shepherd cracked the window and tried to take a deep breath without wheezing like a wind-broke horse. The fragrant scent of sage greeted her, sweet and spicy at the same time. Her father had told her the Indians used the sagebrush for healing and medicines. It must be nice to be able to heal someone with just a plant. She lay her forehead against the cool glass and suppressed a cough. How about a plant to heal this stupid asthma?

The scenery reminded her of an old western movie as it rolled by the truck's passenger window. She stared out, wondering who or what could live in such harsh conditions. With the exception of the brilliant blue sky, all she could see in every direction were varying shades of tan and the gray-green of the sage. It was beautiful in its own way. Stark, but beautiful. Who would have thought the desolate desert of Nevada would be so pretty?

The 1946 Chevy was fourteen years old that year, one year older than Meadow herself, and it groaned a little from the heavy load it carried. Even so, it managed to chug along at a fairly consistent forty-five miles per hour, hauling four horses, an electric range and a Singer sewing machine.

Her father, called Shep by everyone even though it wasn't his given name, drove with one arm casually draped over the back of the seat. Back home, he used to whistle his own unique melody when working around the horses. The horses seemed to like it and so did she, even though her mother claimed his whistle had no tune. Meadow wished he would whistle now. She hadn't heard anything so cheerful since they left on this trip.

Meadow felt a wet tongue on her hand and looked down at her black Kelpie dog trying to bring comfort. Kelsey seemed to sense her moods before she was aware of them herself. With a ghost of a smile, she stroked the dog.

The arrow-straight highway seemed to go on forever without another car in sight, and she couldn't imagine running across civilization any time soon. Lost in thought, she was surprised to find herself suddenly propelled upward, nearly smacking her head on the ceiling, when they hit a teeth-rattling pothole. Kelsey landed on the floor with an insulted look on her face.

"Easy, Gertie," her father said, patting the dashboard. "No more buckin'. I thought I had you broke better than that."

Meadow righted herself and quickly turned and peered through the rear window, trying to see the horses. She could only catch a glimpse of her father's tall gelding behind the partition separating them from the rest of their worldly goods.

Dad looked over at her and grinned. "Don't worry, sweetheart, they're fine."

"Are you sure, Daddy? That was a huge bump."

"We'll stop at the next filling station to see. Pretty sure your mother and the boys will be needing a break by then, anyway."

Checking the side view mirror, Meadow tried to find her mother's sea-foam green Ford Ranch Wagon. When she couldn't spot it, she settled back into her seat, and Kelsey crawled up next to her. She stroked her dog, and once again stared out of the passenger window, absently wondering if this country ever had clouds to mar the endless expanse of sky. At the home they left in Willamette Valley nearly a week ago, the cold drizzle that would continue throughout the long winter had already begun.

She'd thought they would never get out of Oregon, their progress constantly hampered by the many friends demanding they stay a couple of days. Not that *she* had any close friends she would miss, but her father seemed to know everyone. After some long, tearful goodbyes, they were on their way, headed south, for a brand new start in sunny Scottsdale, Arizona.

Does Scottsdale have any trees? Not only were there no cars on this road, there wasn't a tree in sight. In fact, they hadn't seen many trees since they passed through the Cascades into eastern Oregon. This was so different from Silverton. A little pang for the soft green hills they left behind skittered through Meadow's chest. She hoped this was all worth it. What if the desert air didn't cure her asthma?

She stole a glance at her father's strong profile, his cowboy hat shoved back on his head, a strand of dark hair escaping from underneath. He looked younger than his nearly fifty years, strong and fit from breaking colts and training horses. Even though he would never admit it, Meadow knew he must be worried, too. She had heard her older brothers talking about how hard it would be to make a living for the family in a place where he didn't know a soul. Poor Daddy.

As if feeling her eyes on him, he turned to her. "How are you doing today, sweetheart? You seem to be breathing all right."

"I'm fine, Daddy," Meadow lied. Her chest hurt with the effort to breathe, and she felt the weakness in her limbs, but she was so used to hiding the symptoms from her parents that it had become second nature.

She turned toward the window. Her reflection showed dark circles under her green eyes. Once again she had forgotten to brush her hair, and she ran her fingers through the long, dark mass, trying for some semblance of order in the wild array. Her mother would be after her at the next stop, saying she looked like one of those beatniks that hung out at coffee shops.

Oh forget it! Who cared about her dumb hair anyway? She rolled the window all the way down. The fresh air would help her breathing and mask the wheezing. As soon as the glass was down, Kelsey crowded across her lap, sticking her black muzzle out into the breeze.

Meadow laughed. "Hey, leave some room for me!" Kelsey turned and gave her a wet dog kiss. Poking her arm straight out the window, Meadow traced the silhouette of a far mountain as they chugged along. She gazed at the stark landscape, trying to breathe deeply as her doctor had instructed. Her attention turned to the front as her father spoke.

"There's a station up ahead. I'll pull in and we can check the horses and have lunch."

"Oh, good. I was beginning to think there was nothing out here at all."

Her father chuckled. "There's a lot more than you think."

Not long after they pulled up to the pump, the Ranch Wagon turned into the driveway, parking behind the truck. Her mother, Rose, got out from behind the wheel and stretched the kinks out of her legs, her pretty face tight with tension. Monty and Mike, her older brothers, continuing some argument, scrambled out and joined the rest of the family.

Meadow jumped out and headed for the back of the truck, hoisting herself up on the wheel well to see in. Her chestnut Arabian mare, Foxfire, gave a nicker of welcome and stuck her head over the rail.

"How are you doing, Foxy?" Meadow caressed the perfect star on her mare's forehead. "I hope you're not too jammed up back here."

The horses were behind a makeshift gate that separated them from the Hotpoint range and the sewing machine in the front of the truck bed. Even though her father wanted to travel light, her mother had put her foot down about leaving the range and sewing machine behind. Mom argued that the range was the only kitchen appliance she had ever owned, and she made all their clothes on the Singer, so it made no sense to leave either of them behind. Meadow could see her mother's point, but now the horses were fairly squished in the back.

The other three horses stamped and looked over, their eyes bright.

Meadow giggled. "Forget it you guys, I don't have any carrots." She quickly checked them.

Monty's rope horse, Elmer, shoved against Shadow, her father's gelding, who laid back his ears in warning. The pony, Blackjack, simply cocked one hind foot and closed his eyes, as if bored with the whole endeavor. Blackjack had been outgrown years ago, but none of them could bear the thought of leaving him behind.

"They're riding all right." Her father stepped up next to her. "We've got a few more hours before we stop for the night. There's a stockyard in Tonopah where we can unload."

They all took turns using the one bathroom at the station, then Dad bought them sodas to drink. Her mother pulled out peanut butter and jelly sandwiches she'd made before they'd left the last motel early that morning.

Mike made a face when he took his sandwich. "Man, will I be glad when we get there! I'm really sick of peanut butter. Can we at least buy some chips?"

"No chips." Mom's voice was firm as she handed out the rest of the sandwiches. "You know we have to be careful of our finances."

"I can't believe I had to leave all my friends to move to the stinking desert." Mike shot Meadow a dirty look and stomped over to a lonely picnic table. A pain gripped the pit of her stomach and she looked at Monty. He didn't say anything, but turned away from her. She sighed. He'd left behind a girl he was sweet on.

The queasiness increased and she walked off to sit by herself, Kelsey at her heels.

The sandwich lost what little appeal it might have had and she tossed it to her dog who made short work of it.

Mom soon found her way over to where she was sitting on the running board of the truck and sat beside her. "Pay no attention to Mike, honey. Everyone is cranky from the long drive. This move will turn out for the best. You'll see."

Meadow gave her mother a wan smile, not so sure. The family had left everyone and everything they held dear, all for her, because of her stupid asthma.

"Get down in front of me." Mom produced a hairbrush and rubber band from her bag.

She sat on the ground and leaned against her mother's knees while her thick hair was brushed out and fixed into a ponytail.

"That's better. You have such beautiful hair; you should pay as much attention to your grooming as you do Foxy's."

"Okay, everyone," her father announced, "pile in, we got miles to go before we sleep."

"My turn to ride with Dad." Mike tried to elbow Monty out of the way.

Monty shoved back, and soon the two of them were in an all-out fistfight. Their father strode over to the boys, and grabbing them by their collars, pulled them apart.

"That's enough fighting," he said. "Just for that, your sister gets to ride with me again. She'll be better company than either one of you ruffians."

Both brothers glared at her as she climbed up into the cab with Kelsey following closely. She agreed with them that it was more fun riding with Dad, since he was relaxed and told them yarns, while their mother, new to driving, usually sat silent with a death grip on the steering wheel. And sometimes her father let Monty drive even though he wouldn't be able to get his license till next month.

After settling in for another long haul, Dad glanced over when she gave a little sniff. She tried to hide it, but her whole world seemed to close in. Afraid to look at him, she kept her eyes fixed on the distant horizon.

"Do you see any mustangs out there?" he asked.

She turned toward her father with a grain of interest. "What? Mustangs?"

"Sure, there're still a few left around here. I used to catch them myself, in my younger days."

"Really, Daddy? Wild horses?" Unbidden, her eyes darted over the barren landscape in earnest. "I don't see any. Are you sure they're not all gone?"

"They're out there, all right. Things aren't always as they appear on the surface, sweetheart," her father replied. "Maybe Arrow the Sky Horse is out there somewhere."

"Who is Arrow the Sky Horse?"

"You remember my friend Nueme? The horseshoer? He moved back to the reservation last year."

"Oh yeah, now I remember." She nodded. "So we *will* know someone in Arizona."

How could she have forgotten Nueme? He was a real Shonto Indian, which to her meant romantic adventures in the Old West. Nueme didn't talk a lot, but sometimes she could get him to tell a story about his youth.

She pictured herself living free as a bird, unhampered by convention. "I wish I were an Indian."

Dad's response to her light-hearted comment came as a shock. "Be careful what you wish for," he said, sharply. Then, seeing her surprise, his face softened. "Anyway, Nueme won't be near us. He lives up north, but we might see him sometimes."

"But he told you about a wild horse?"

"Let me see if I remember." Her father wrinkled his brow. "It was years ago now that Nueme told me a legend called "Arrow the Sky Horse". I don't recall all the particulars, but it was about a wild stallion, a beautiful silver-colored horse that carried the dead to the Indian hunting ground. An Indian maiden loved the stallion and she was the only one that could tame him. I think there was some kind of magical amulet involved, too. It seems to me, according to the story, the Indians finally lost the stallion or he was stolen. Anyway, he disappeared without a trace. Maybe Arrow is still out there somewhere, roaming around. I wouldn't be a bit surprised."

The grain of interest sprouted, and Meadow imagined a silver stallion with an Indian girl riding him. "Oh, Daddy, will Nueme tell me the legend when we see him?"

"Well, he might. You know Nueme isn't much of a conversationalist, but he might tell you if he feels the time is right."

Meadow knew her father was just trying to distract her with the tale of Arrow, but strangely enough, it worked. The story kept revolving and expanding in her head. Wouldn't it be exciting to see a real wild horse? Especially a big silver stallion. What could be better than that?

Then a strange thing happened. At first it appeared as a ghostly form off in the shadow of the far mountains. Then gradually it came closer and closer, until it was near the roadway. It couldn't be, but there he was. She could see him clearly now. A beautiful stallion, galloping in the desert next to the road. No Indian girl, just the silver horse. He kept pace with them, jumping brush and flying across ravines and whatever else was in the way.

It was strangely comforting to have him accompany them through this foreign land, and as if by magic, Meadow could actually take a deep breath. For the first time, she looked forward to their arrival in Arizona. She couldn't wait to hear the whole legend, figuring there must be some truth to it. After all, weren't most stories based on some kind of facts?

From then on, the stallion would materialize whenever she was riding in the car or truck, and it didn't seem odd or unusual to see him galloping next to them, but she never told anyone, not even her father. It was too personal, and deep down, she knew he was there just for her. He was Arrow the Sky Horse.

Later that afternoon, with shadows growing long, they drove into the stockyards at the edge of the old mining town of Tonopah, Nevada. The cattle had already been shipped for the season, but unfortunately their odor lingered. All the pens were empty, so they picked a large one where the horses could get some exercise after being cooped up all day. The minute Foxfire's hooves touched the ground, she was off and running around the corral, snorting and kicking up her heels.

Meadow watched her for a moment then turned to her mother. "Can I take her for a ride? I'll walk to the motel afterwards. It's only across the street."

"Well, okay, but don't go too far," Mom said. "Maybe your brothers should go with you."

"Forget it," Mike said. "The last thing we want to do is ride around this ugly, rocky place, right, Monty?"

Monty nodded, but then looked a little guilty about letting his sister go alone. "You want me to come, Meadow?"

"No, I'll be fine." She spun Foxfire and cantered off, with Kelsey in hot pursuit.

Riding bareback, Meadow felt her mare's lengthening stride as she picked up speed. She leaned low over Foxfire's neck, and with her hair whipping behind like a flag, they galloped across the open desert for a mile or more.

Foxfire was barely breathing hard when Meadow reined her to a stop. Kelsey came panting from behind and immediately flopped onto the sand.

Meadow petted her horse and looked down at Kelsey. "What would I do without you two? You're the only ones who really understand me."

As if she *did* understand, Kelsey whined and returned the gaze, with her ears pointing straight up and her keen face alert.

"My brothers hate me for this move, but you guys always love me, no matter what."

After scanning the vista for a few moments in search of wild mustangs, she turned Foxfire back toward the stockyard. When she got there, Mike was filling the water trough. In the corral, Shadow, Elmer, and Blackjack were quickly scarfing down what was left of their evening meal.

"Too bad Foxy's late for dinner. Guess she'll have to go hungry." Mike had an ugly smirk on his face.

She frowned at her fourteen-year-old brother. "I'll throw her some more feed."

"You know you can't pick up alfalfa. It makes you sick, so Foxy's gonna starve tonight."

Meadow was well aware that handling hay caused her to break out in hives, wheeze and cough, sometimes with dire consequences, but she wasn't about to let Foxfire go without. After putting her in the pen, she started for the bale.

At the last moment, Mike shoved ahead and picked up the flake himself. "Don't be stupid. That's all I need, for you to keel over and die here in the middle of nowhere, and I'd get blamed. It's bad enough we have to move because of you."

"It wasn't my decision. Remember, Dad and Mom told us this would be a good opportunity for the whole family."

"That's a laugh. You're just naïve. Believe me, there's nothing for us in Arizona and we'll probably all end up in debtor's prison."

"Daddy will take care of us. He always has."

"He won't have any contacts there. You know his business is based on knowing everyone in the horse world. Like he did in

Oregon. Monty feels the same way. It's all your fault." With that, Mike turned on his heel and stalked off toward the motel.

Meadow watched him go, tears welling up and slipping down her cheeks. He was only one year older, and they'd always been close. Monty, at times, seemed a world away from them. But now it felt as if they were both against her.

The anticipation for the move slowly evaporated like a balloon with a pinprick hissing its air out. Her chest tightened again as she struggled for breath. Her legs suddenly weak, she slowly made her way over to the truck and sank down on the running board. The tears dried up when anger took over. She slammed her fist against her chest in frustration. It would have been better for everyone if she'd never been born.

Chapter 2

Best Friends

It was after dark by the time Meadow felt calm enough to walk over to the motel. Her mother was trying to air the room out with all the windows open. The worn carpet had a musty smell and Meadow's lungs protested. She gingerly sat on the edge of the roll-away cot, trying not to breathe too hard, and saw that someone had brought in her special foam rubber, dust-free pillow from the car. They would be pretty crammed up with her parents sharing one double bed, the boys in the other, and her on the cot.

"Where have you been? I was about to go look for you." Mom had that worried expression that seemed to be permanent on this trip.

"I was making sure the horses are okay."

Her mother sat down on one of the beds facing her. "Your father and the boys were hungry and went over to the café. I asked them to bring us a burger."

"Okay. I'm not really hungry anyway."

"You have to eat. You're way too thin."

Meadow lay back on the cot and stared at the grayish fly-specked ceiling. "Maybe I'll die of malnutrition, like Mike always says."

"Don't ever say such things!" Mom's voice was sharp, and Meadow felt a pang of regret for her words.

The door banged open and the three large males of the family filled the small space of the room, making it even more claustrophobic. To make her mother happy, she ate a few of the French fries and had a couple bites of the greasy burger before stuffing the rest back in the paper bag it had arrived in.

After dinner, they all read for a little while before retiring for the night. Meadow was reading *Thunderhead, Son of Flicka,* one of her favorite books, but it was hard to concentrate with her shortness of breath and wheezing.

Later in the night, she developed a persistent cough and tried to muffle it with her pillow, but in such close quarters that tactic wasn't very successful. She could hear Mike grumbling from his bed about being kept awake. Finally, in the wee hours, her mother gave her a dose of medicine, which did the trick and she eventually fell into a deep sleep. In that drug-induced slumber, she drifted pleasantly into a dream, riding the silver stallion through a backdrop of red cliffs. She felt light as air as he floated through the sheer crags like a bird on a gentle breeze. But gradually the horse turned into a giant black hawk with piercing yellow eyes and instead of on his back, she was clutched in his huge razor-sharp claws. When she twisted and screamed, he suddenly loosened his grip, and she fell toward a yawning crevasse.

She awoke with a start, feeling like she had just landed with a jolt onto the cot. The sun was full on her face through the open window. Still groggy from the after-effects of the medicine and lack of sleep, Meadow stumbled into the shower, and stood still, letting the pitiful stream of luke-warm water run over her head while she tried to soothe her still thumping heart.

Her mother poked her head into the bathroom.

"Hurry up, Meadow. Your father and Mike have already left."

She pulled on her jeans and followed her mother and Monty to the dingy café next door to the motel. Her mother watched with a frown as Meadow poked at her ham and eggs, not able to choke them down.

"Eat your breakfast, Meadow," her mother said. "It's time we got on the road."

"Okay, Mom." She took a bite of egg and quickly washed it down with juice. Her mother turned to talk to Monty, and she took the opportunity to wrap the ham in a napkin and stuff it into her jean pocket. "I'm done now."

Her mother looked skeptical when she inspected Meadow's plate, but didn't say anything.

She was glad it would be Monty riding in the Ranch Wagon with them. At least he would be quiet. And he didn't mind riding in the back seat where he could stretch out his long legs and read a book.

After sneaking the ham to Kelsey, Meadow put her in next to Monty, who was already sprawled out with his nose buried in *History of the Southwest*. Her mother wouldn't allow the dog up front because it was too distracting. Normally, Mom would require Kelsey to ride in the way back part of the station wagon, but it was already filled to the brim with clothes and household items. Meadow climbed into the front seat, settling in next to her mother.

"Are you feeling better, honey?" She frowned. "I noticed you didn't eat much breakfast. But I'm sure Kelsey was happy with the ham."

"I'm sorry, Mom. It's just that the medicine takes away my appetite. Gives me weird dreams, too."

"I know, honey. That's one reason we had no choice but to move. You can't stay on that medicine forever. Too many bad side effects."

Meadow nodded. She could feel herself sinking into a dark place, worrying about how the family would cope, all because of her miserable ailment.

Mom didn't usually chat while driving, but today she seemed to be trying to lighten the mood with conversation. Meadow didn't feel like talking, though, and wasn't very responsive to her mother's attempts to draw her out. She concentrated on trying to visualize Arrow, but even that wasn't working.

Her mother pressed down on the accelerator and before long, they saw the old truck up ahead. Foxfire had turned around and stuck her head over the back gate.

"Look, Meadow. I think Foxy is trying to see where you are. I'm glad your father decided to bring the horses, after all."

"Yeah, me too. I would have died without Foxy."

"Well, that's a bit dramatic, but I know you would have missed her. You two are certainly close, ever since your father brought her home." Mom chuckled. "And you thought your father had forgotten your seventh birthday."

A hint of a smile touched Meadow's lips. "I remember. I was so worried he wouldn't bring me anything and it turned out to be the absolute best birthday present I ever had. Foxy was so cute. Barely six months old."

Her mother tittered nervously, her hands still tight on the wheel. "I just couldn't believe your father traded a Shetland pony for a pure bred Arabian. That farmer apparently didn't know what he had."

"And I'll never forget how your father was so proud of himself that he led her clip-clopping right through the house and into the bathroom while you were in the tub with all those bubbles. I think I used the whole bottle of bubble-bath to cheer you up."

Meadow giggled along with her mother. "I know. Remember how Foxy tried to taste the bubbles and then sneezed really big and bubbles flew everywhere? Then when we laughed at her, she did a baby horse laugh right back at us! It was the funniest thing ever!"

They both laughed even harder, and her mother's hands gradually loosened their grip. By this time Meadow was making small hiccupping sounds, and her sides hurt from laughing. Her mother had tears running down her face. Every time they looked at each other, fresh peals of hilarity would erupt. They were just beginning to regain some semblance of control when they heard Monty gripe from the back seat.

"Geez, gimme a break. I'm trying to read!"

Meadow looked over at her mother and they both burst out into a fresh wave of uncontrollable mirth. Her mother pulled off the road to take a few deep breaths.

"Thanks, Mom, I needed that," Meadow managed to gasp at last.

"Believe me, I needed it as much as you, honey. This long drive has me strained to the limit."

Monty piped up from the back seat. "You want me to drive, Mom?"

"You know you aren't legal to drive yet."

"Oh, man." He rolled his eyes and stuck his nose back in his book.

Her mother put the Ranch Wagon into first gear and cautiously pulled back onto the road, even though there weren't any other cars for at least a hundred miles.

Meadow was still smiling. "Talking about when I first got Foxfire sure brings back a lot of good memories. We had a special bond from the start."

"Yes," Mom said. "It was love at first sight, for you both. I remember when she was little, she used to follow you around like a puppy. I felt sorry for her when you were too sick to go to the barn. She would just stand for hours in her corral, sadly watching the house for you to come and play with her."

"I know, and we still love each other the same. She was my first real horse. Before that, I had to make do with some pony Dad had around."

"I guess the boys used to run off and leave you behind when you rode with them."

"Until I got Foxy. Did I ever tell you about the first time we rode together?"

"Not that I recall," Mom replied. "Foxy was a two-year-old when you started riding her, and I thought you were too young to break a colt."

"I didn't break her. She let me climb on her back one day and that was that. Foxy liked it 'cuz we could go much faster and a lot farther that way."

"Yes, your father commented that she seemed to just train herself."

"Uh huh, it's true. Anyway, that day, Monty and Mike were exercising Jughead and Cricket for Dad." She turned around and faced the back seat. "Remember, Monty?"

"Mumph," was the only response she got.

She turned back around and made a face. "Well, when I had to ride a pony, they thought it was just so hilarious to ditch me."

"It was pretty funny to see how furious you would get." This time Monty sat up and leaned over the back of the front seat, probably to make sure Meadow got the story right.

"Well, I guess I showed you! That day riding Foxfire, no matter how fast you two galloped, she kept right up."

"That fat ole horse I was riding couldn't outrun a Billy goat."

"Yeah, but Mike was on Jughead. He wasn't any slouch. Mike was spurring him so hard to go faster that he started bucking."

"Then what happened?" her mother asked.

"Mike stuck one hand up like he was Casey Tibbs and kept on spurring until Jughead just plain quit. Mike had a big goofy grin on his face."

"That was supposed to be a secret, Meadow. You know how mad Dad gets about encouraging the trading stock to buck." Monty gave her a withering big brother look.

"That was years ago. I figured it was okay by now. Anyway, Mom won't tell Dad. Right, Mom?"

"I'm sworn to secrecy," her mother replied solemnly.

Probably feeling left out, Kelsey put her front paws on the back of Meadow's seat and tried to crawl over.

"No, Kelsey, you have to stay in the back." Her dog slunk back down, looking wounded.

"You have a way with animals. Not so much with people." Monty patted Kelsey. "Remember when you found this silly mutt? You were out on one of your solitary rides."

"That's right," Mom said. "I used to really worry about you riding alone, but thank goodness Foxy never threw you. What were you, about ten?"

"Yeah, I mostly rode alone because the kids from school never really liked me, they just liked the ponies Dad always had around. Nobody wanted to hang out with the *sick kid*."

"You did miss a lot of school," Her mother's hands tightened again. "Where did you go the day you found Kelsey?"

"Out one of the old logging roads. I stuffed some of your famous oatmeal cookies in my pocket in case Foxy or I got hungry. They came in handy when I ran across a starving puppy."

Monty showed some interest now. "You found her at one of those abandoned logging camps?"

"Yeah, hiding behind a building. She was pretty scared, but came to me in the end." Meadow turned around, reached into the back seat, and fondled Kelsey's ears.

"You want to trade seats now?" Monty asked. "I'd like to sit up front for a while."

"Okay, let's switch." She scooted over the seat to the back and then her brother scrambled up front. Kelsey showed her approval with the new arrangement by promptly putting her head in Meadow's lap.

"Oh, Kelsey, I'm so glad I found you that day. I'll bet you remember it, too." She lay back and closed her eyes, her hand on Kelsey's sleek black coat. "What kind of person abuses and starves a defenseless animal?"

"I know you didn't want to give her up, even though she didn't belong to us. I was afraid she was valuable and someone would claim her and break your heart." Her mother spoke softly.

Meadow's face hardened as she thought of Kelsey's first owner. The kids all called him the trash dump guy because his ramshackle house was surrounded by a yard full of broken bottles, old tires, and useless car parts. She still shuddered when she remembered what a close call she had that day.

It was getting near to dusk and Meadow had fallen into a road-trip stupor when she was roused by her mother's voice.

"Good heavens, look at that!"

Meadow jerked up and peered through the front windshield to see what her mother was talking about. Rising out of nowhere was an endless array of light. The whole desert seemed to be on fire.

Chapter 3

High Stakes Poker

The competing sights and sounds of Las Vegas were overwhelming. With the flashing neon signs and the din of traffic so foreign, Meadow didn't know which direction to look next. She gawked at the throngs of people, many of them wearing gaudy clothing that threatened to outshine the bright lights.

Beads of perspiration arose on her mother's forehead as she concentrated on maneuvering the Ranch Wagon through the crowded streets, trying not to lose sight of the truck. With a sigh of relief, she followed as the truck finally turned into a property with a large sign that read "Twin Lakes Lodge". They drove down a long lane shaded by palm trees. The two small lakes they passed were filled with ducks making circular patterns on the otherwise smooth surface of the water. It was almost dark, but they could see fish swimming from the underwater illuminations.

"Just like a picture post card," her mother said, her voice not quite normal.

"Look at the fancy stable. Foxy will love it here." Meadow rolled down the window and Kelsey pushed her head out, sniffing the air.

Monty glanced over at Mom. "This is a lot nicer than our usual motel. I wonder how much it costs?"

Mom didn't say anything, but pulled in and parked next to the truck. Her father, as he stepped down off the running board, had a triumphant look on his face.

"Shep, are you sure we can afford this?" Mom's little pucker between her brows deepened.

"Darlin' Rose, I think we all deserve a break. There's a pool for the kids to play in, and adjoining rooms so we can have some privacy and maybe do a little playing ourselves." He winked at her.

She rewarded him with a faint smile. "How did you know about this place?"

"Al Cooper comes to Vegas to rodeo and told me we should stay here. You know Al never gives me a bum steer. He also told me about a game I could get in on."

"Poker?" Her mother got that worried look again.

He put his arm around her. "Don't worry, darlin'. Nothin' I can't handle. Monty, you're in charge of unloading the horses." They strolled toward the office, their heads close together.

The stable was a shed row style with stalls facing out toward the lakes. After Monty unloaded the horses, Mike led them to individual stalls, a real novelty for the horses used to being all together in one corral.

Meadow took Foxfire's rope and hopped on to give her a gallop around the grounds before bedding her down. She was relieved the mare seemed fine with riding in the truck and being in different stables every night, as long as she got some exercise every day. As they passed one of the lakes, Kelsey splashed in after the ducks, and was midway in the water when Meadow heard the frantic quacking.

"No, Kelsey! Do you want to get us thrown out of here?"

Kelsey came gamboling back, as happy as Foxfire to have a run.

"We'd better get back now anyway. C'mon, Kelsey, stay with us."

Returning to the stable, she led Foxfire into the stall where someone had already put feed in the bin. Kelsey had followed her in and now gave a tremendous shake, flinging water over them. Meadow giggled and gave her a pat on the head, then turned to go out. Kelsey tried to follow.

"Sorry, girl. Mom says you have to stay with Foxy. This motel doesn't allow dogs." Resigned to her fate, Kelsey flopped down on the fresh straw.

On her way back to the motel room to find her family, Meadow saw that her brothers were already in the enormous resort swimming pool. It must have been a half acre in size and had an island in the middle with a high diving board. Even though it was Halloween day, the weather was warm compared to where they had come from, and she watched enviously as the boys had a raucous splashing contest.

She peeked her head into the motel room. "Mom, can I go swimming, too?"

"I don't know, honey." Her mother peered at her closely. "How do you feel?"

"I'm fine, Mom. Really."

"Well, okay, for a little while. Since you won't get any trick or treating in around here, I guess you have to have some fun."

"Geez Mom, I'm too old for trick or treating anyway." Meadow hurried past her mother.

She flung off her jeans, slipped into a swim suit and raced to join Monty and Mike before Mom could change her mind. They were the only ones swimming, and it was glorious to have the gigantic pool all to themselves. After being cooped up in the car for so many days, they had plenty of energy to spare, and proved it with splashing, diving off the board, and playing Marco Polo. Mom and Dad came out to poolside, sipping on drinks. They pulled up lawn chairs to enjoy the show.

Meadow was floating on her back when a little ferret-faced man appeared, puffing and waving his arms around.

"The pool is closed for the season. Get those kids out of there!"

Her father looked at him and frowned, then stood up, towering over the much smaller man. "And just who the hell are you?"

"I'm the manager!" His face grew red with the apparent effort of trying to appear bigger.

Dad's voice became a low growl, which wasn't a good omen. "What d' you mean? I don't see any sign that says pool closed for the season. You think I would pay the outrageous sum of ten dollars a night for these accommodations if you didn't have a pool for the kids to play in?"

The manger got the message and edged backwards. "Well, maybe I can make an exception this time, but have them out by ten p.m."

"I'll do that." Her father smiled pleasantly as the manager slunk away.

Meadow and her brothers stayed in the pool until they were blue and shivering. It seemed a miracle to her, but even after all the swimming, she didn't get short of breath. She didn't notice when, but sometime while they were swimming, her father had disappeared.

The next day, they were all sad to leave the wonderful resort, but Dad was in an even better mood than usual. Meadow figured he must have won at the poker game last night. They said goodbye to the city of lights and were on their way.

After a lunch break, it was her turn to ride in the truck. Kelsey snuggled up next to her, putting her muzzle in her lap.

"Daddy, yesterday I was thinking about how we got Kelsey. Remember?"

"Yes I do. She was one lucky dog that day. I know your mother made you ride to all the neighbors and ask if she belonged to them."

"Yeah, it was pretty scary going to the trash dump guy." Meadow shivered. What a horrible man.

"I'll bet. It took a lot of nerve to confront him. You never did tell me what happened that day."

She shrugged. "I never told you because I was afraid of what you would do to him."

Her father looked at her sharply. "Why? Did he touch you? What'd he do?"

"Just came after me and shoved me down when I tried to save Kelsey. He backed off when Foxy got between us and laid back her ears and pawed at him."

"Why, that low-life piece of crap was even worse than I figured!" His face darkened. "Good thing I didn't know about it, or they would have found him in a pool of his own blood."

"Exactly why I never told you. But the next day, Kelsey was back at our ranch. How did you arrange that?"

"Your mother accosted me as soon as I got home that night, going on about the poor helpless puppy in the hands of that animal abuser. First thing the next morning, I went to see the trash dump fella."

"What happened?"

"Well, he wasn't overly friendly at first, but once I brought out my friend Jack, he got a whole lot more receptive."

"Your friend Jack?"

"Jack Daniels."

"Ohhh, now I see. You plied him with whiskey."

"Yeah, and when I suggested a game of poker, his eyes just sorta lit up." Her father chuckled. "We played for a while, and I kept pouring out of that ole bottle, and he kept drinkin'. Pretty soon, he was fairly sloshed."

"Then what happened?"

"Until then, we were just playing for quarters, so I upped the ante. We had a hand going and the pot was getting pretty rich. I threw in another fifth of Jack and he said he didn't have any more money to put in, but he was really eyeing that bottle. I said how about throwing in that scrawny pup cowering in the corner, winner take all?"

Meadow laughed. "He obviously didn't know what he was doing, trying to beat you at poker."

"He lost the hand all right, and I won Kelsey fair and square. But I gave him the booze, anyway. And he was mighty happy to give me the pup."

"That was the best poker pot you ever won." She gave Kelsey a little kiss.

He patted her dog. "I think so, too, sweetheart."

They spent the night in Wickenburg, Arizona and her father announced it would be the last night on the road before arriving at their destination. By this time, Meadow was pretty bored with traveling and couldn't wait to get there. The only one still grousing about the trip was Mike. He took every opportunity to make Meadow's life miserable by making snide comments when he knew their parents weren't watching. She dreaded having to ride in the Ranch Wagon with him on the final leg of the journey.

The next morning, Mike sat up front next to their mother, and Meadow busily scribbled on a tablet in the backseat. She heard him going on and on about what he called the "ugly wasteland" they were moving to. All the negative comments finally defeated her creativity and she put aside the poem she had been working on about Arrow. She lay back and feigned sleep.

After her mother had glanced into the back seat, she started in on her brother. "Mike, I'm really tired of hearing how bad everything is here." Her mother sounded exasperated. "Try to concentrate on the positive aspects of this move."

"Like what?" he grumbled.

"Like the fact that your sister hasn't been sick since we got into the lower desert. Don't you remember how bad her asthma was last winter? She almost died."

"Yeah, I guess she was pretty sick," he said. "She never ate, and I was sure she was going to die of malnutrition, like the poor starving natives in Africa."

"You wouldn't be hungry either if you were getting steroid shots twice a week."

"But she wasn't close to dying," he argued.

"She did almost die!" Peeking out of one eye, Meadow could see her mother's tense posture. "And I want you to quit torturing you sister, not to mention the rest of us!"

Mike didn't say anything else, but his profile was etched in stone as he stared out the window.

Meadow's insides were churning like simmering oatmeal. Why was she always the center of quarrels in their family? Oh well, at least Mike was quiet for a change. She sat up, stretched, and yawned loudly. She picked up her writing tablet and looked out the window for inspiration.

Before long, the ghostly form of the Sky Horse appeared and the next thing she knew he was racing in the desert near the car. This time he looked over and she could see his dark, liquid eyes, as if he were telling her everything would be all right. Her stomach quit aching and she started writing furiously, putting down everything that came to mind. She was so lost in the poem that she didn't even notice where they were until Mike's voice broke in.

"Look, we're entering Phoenix city limits. Isn't that close to Scottsdale?"

Her mother heaved a breath. "Yes, thank goodness we're almost there. I'm so tired of driving I could scream."

"Hey, that's something positive about this move!" Mike sounded almost like his old self. "You finally learned how to drive."

"That's true." Her mother smiled. "I had no choice about that if we were going to bring the horses. Your father and I discussed trading the truck for a car that could fit us all, but in the end neither one of us could stand to leave our favorite horses . . . and of course, my appliances."

For the first time in days the black cloud lifted from Mike's face. "Well, it was really funny when Dad traded that ole mule team for this car and made you learn to drive out in the horse pasture. It sure took you a long time to get the hang of the clutch. You must have killed the motor at least a hundred times." He laughed.

"Don't rub it in."

Meadow giggled. "It *was* pretty funny, Mom."

"Well, I'm a good driver now. That's all that counts." Her mother raised her chin defiantly. Just then, a car passed them, honking at their slow pace. She paled and her death grip on the steering wheel increased along with the city traffic.

Mike looked back at Meadow and rolled his eyes. She stifled another giggle.

Chapter 4

Arizona

It was the first week of November and the weather was warm, almost too warm from Meadow's point of view. Their destination of Scottsdale, Arizona was in sight. Her father turned onto the main road, and her mother followed close behind.

As they drove down the street, Meadow was amazed at the Old West style town. Every shop had a western façade, including a hitching rail, but what she really liked was that the city fathers had seen fit to leave enough room on the side of the streets to incorporate horse-riding trails.

Her father kept driving until he found a good sized stable where they could stop. A sign out front advertised horse boarding by the month. Everyone piled out of the two vehicles.

"Well, here we are in sunny Scottsdale, all in one piece," Dad announced, putting his arm around Mom and kissing her full on the lips.

"Shep!" Mom straightened her blouse and recovered her composure. "What a trip! I really hope we never have to do anything like that again."

"You did great, darlin'. Didn't run off the road once, although I was a little worried a couple of times." He grinned.

"Yeah, me too," Mike added, and their mother cuffed him playfully.

"What a neat place, Daddy!" Meadow smiled up at him. "I think this town is great. Did you see all the trails around town?"

"I did. Of course, we won't be right in town when we find a place to rent. But until then, you can ride Foxy right down Main Street. Just no patronizing the local saloons, young lady."

Meadow giggled and her brothers groaned.

"I'd better go check with the manager to see if there's enough room for all the horses." Her father strode toward the office.

It turned out there was an open corral big enough for them all, and the price on it was much less than individual stalls in the barn. They wouldn't have any shelter, but her father said they didn't need any because it was so much warmer here. He also made a deal with the manager to help feed and clean the stalls for the other boarders, which reduced the cost even more.

The stable manager even suggested a cheap motel nearby. It was only five dollars a night. When Meadow saw the pink stucco on the outside, she couldn't believe anyone would paint something that color on purpose. But it got even better when they accepted the key from an older lady with pink-tinted hair and wearing a frilly pink dress. Going over to the assigned room, they unlocked the door and pushed it open.

She examined the room with her mouth agape. "Mom, this place is *all* pink!" And it was—pink walls, pink carpet, pink curtains and two beds with pink tufted bedspreads.

Mike ventured into the bathroom. "Yikes!"

Meadow poked her head in. Sure enough—it was adorned with pink and white tiles, a pink bathtub, a pink toilet and a pink sink. It even had pink gardenia soap.

Mike made a face as he sniffed the soap. "I hearby dub thee 'Stinky Pink Motel'." Meadow and their mom laughed. But it was clean and the price was right, so they decided to stay until they found a place to rent.

Her mother and father decided the kids could wait to enroll in school until a rental house was found. Meadow breathed a sigh of relief that she had a few more days of freedom before the agony of being the new kid at school began. Along with her brothers, she spent the time exploring the town.

One day Monty stayed home to read while Meadow and Mike were riding. They found themselves near the greens of a golf course.

Mike got a sly grin. "Let's go ride on the golf course."

She chewed on her lip. "It does look fun, but we better not."

"Come on. No one will see us. Are you afraid?"

"No." She could feel her face getting warm. Mike always knew how to push her buttons.

"Then let's do it." He started across the course at a canter.

Meadow urged Foxfire forward and she soon passed Mike. It was heavenly riding on grass again. Just like Oregon, green and springy underfoot. They came up over a rise and suddenly a sprinkler head was there, shooting an undulating spray of water over them. They both shrieked and rode back and forth, laughing, with wild abandon over the wet green. They didn't hear the approaching golf cart, but clearly heard an angry voice shouting at them.

"What do you think you're doing? I'm getting the authorities. Come with me!" The man was wearing banana yellow pants and a matching shirt. Meadow had never seen a man in that particular color before.

Mike patted Elmer and put on his most charming face. "Sorry mister. We didn't mean any harm. We just moved here from Oregon and it's so hot here the horses needed to cool off a little."

The banana man wasn't entirely convinced. "Who's going to pay for the damage to the green?"

"Gosh, I don't know. My dad hasn't found a job yet. Maybe I could work for the golf course to pay for the damage."

"Me, too." Meadow tried to look like she was about to cry.

"Don't you two go to school?"

"Yeah, we'll be starting soon, but we could work after school. We're really sorry about the damage," Mike said, while Meadow nodded.

Banana man started to soften. "Well, I'll let you off the hook this time, but don't let me catch you here again."

"Don't worry, we've learned our lesson."

They waited until they were off the course and out of sight before busting up in laughter.

After a week of diligently searching, her father found a place they could afford that would accommodate the family and the horses. The house was vacant, so they were able to move in right away. None of them were sad to leave Stinky Pink. Meadow vowed she'd never own anything pink, and her mother said she couldn't wait to have a normal smelling place again.

Meadow and her father loaded the horses in the truck, while her mother and brothers put their clothes into the Ranch Wagon and then they all made the short drive to the rental property. The house was set back off a gravel road on a five-acre parcel to the west of Scottsdale. It wasn't long before they were pulling into the driveway that circled to the back, where her father parked next to the barn. Mom stopped near the house.

"Look, Mom. It's made of adobe." Monty got out of the car. "That's what the indigenous people used to build with."

"It has a flat roof. That's sorta weird." Mike had to add his two cents worth. "Good thing it doesn't rain much here. It would probably leak."

Meadow had already dismissed the house as not very interesting and headed for the barn, a large airy structure, with slatted sides and a center aisle-way. On both sides of the aisle were stalls with corrals attached so the horses could go in or out. At the far end was a double stall with a huge corral.

"Daddy, I love this barn. It's so spacious, and not even closed in."

"It's not for keeping them warm. Mostly for shade so the horses don't get too hot in the summer," her father said.

"I get dibs on this one for Foxy!" She stood in front of the largest corral.

"Okay, let's get them unloaded. I'm sure they've all had enough riding in the back of the truck for a long while."

Foxfire immediately trotted around her new stall, exploring the whole thing with Kelsey at her heels.

The adobe house was the same color as the surrounding sand and had foot-thick walls and tile floors. A big front yard had a strange broad leaf kind of grass the landlord said was from Africa, and orange, lemon and grapefruit trees grew around the sides of it. The place was like an oasis surrounded by desert, and Meadow soon discovered she could ride out in any direction. She avoided the pockets of new housing developments with models that all looked exactly alike. Who would want to live all crammed together like that?

The next Monday, they were enrolled in school. After only a couple of days, Meadow decided that the kids were snooty. She stomped into the kitchen, letting the screen door bang and slammed her books onto the table.

"Mom, I think my junior high is even worse than the school I left!"

"Well remember, in Oregon last year, you were still in grammar school. It's different in junior high."

"Yeah, different because ninth graders think they're so cool and grown-up, wearing make-up and painting their nails. I hate them all." She yanked out a chair and flopped down.

"Don't worry, you'll start making friends. Aren't there any girls your age who ride?"

"Yeah, but they only ride in arenas. With their trainers. That's just dumb."

"Not all parents let their kids ride all over the country with no supervision." Her mother said pointedly. "Maybe Monty and Mike will ride with you."

"No, they're way too busy with homework. Don't worry, Mom. You know I like riding by myself."

"You *are* a bit of a loner. Just be careful of rattlesnakes."

One reason Meadow didn't mind riding alone was that she was hoping to get a glimpse of Arrow again. Was he just a flight of her imagination on the trip out here? She just didn't—just couldn't—believe that. He had been so real. With the flurry of moving into the new house and starting school, she was too busy to really worry about not seeing him, but he was always flitting around on the edge of her mind.

Just as her mother predicted, she saw a rattlesnake one day. It was the color of the desert, with a diamond pattern on its back and rattled its tail at them, then slithered away. Kelsey started to go after it, but when Meadow told her to let it be, thankfully, her dog obeyed. She didn't tell Mom about the encounter, not wanting to worry her.

The landscape was so different from what Meadow was used to that she felt as if she were in a whole different country. She was amazed by the huge Saguaro cacti, with their arms pointing up or down, like giant sentinels. When she rode down a dry wash, Meadow couldn't figure out why it had a sign that read "Roaring Creek".

In January she found out when it rained for two days straight, and the normally dry creek bed had more than two feet of water rushing down it. Mom told her to stay out of any washes if it had been raining, because sometimes flash floods came and swept people and even cars away.

The desert was such a strange place—dry for months on end and then when it did rain, it flooded. But after the rain stopped and the sun came out, the land immediately turned green with sprigs of grass and later an array of tiny red, blue and yellow flowers emerged. It was as if they knew the opportunity to grow wouldn't last long.

One spring day when Meadow was riding, searching in vain for the silver horse, she suddenly felt weighted down with loss. Where was he? She was a stranger in a strange land—had he abandoned her there? She searched for him everywhere she rode. Even though she still had Foxfire and Kelsey, Meadow had a strong sense that a piece of an important puzzle was missing in her life.

It was a miserable school year. Meadow had been a good student before, but for the first time flunked a subject. Arizona history! How was she supposed to know anything about Arizona? Her brothers had a hard time, too. Monty was even quieter than usual, and Mike had gotten into a couple of fistfights. It seemed they missed their friends back home.

The only good part was that she wasn't sick. It was wonderful being able to breathe, and if she did have an asthma attack, it was mild. Her new doctor thought the attacks would go away altogether in a year or even less.

In April, the weather started getting hot. Really hot. She broke out in sweat just stepping foot outside. Imagine getting hot in April! It was too much for her father, and he decided they had to go to the mountains. He told his family that right after school was out they were moving to the high country. The trading business had gotten off to a slow start, so he was ready for a change of scenery.

Meadow was excited about the plan, and that night dreamed about the silver horse for the first time in months.

Chapter 5

Brighten Hot Springs

Meadow went with her father to the weekly horse auction that Saturday. She always loved auctions, the excitement of the bidding, the smell of horses mingled with sawdust, and her father coolly nodding to the auctioneer when he saw a horse he wanted.

She adored her father and loved doing anything with him. He was just about perfect, a tall and handsome cowboy, with black hair and a ready grin. Today he looked as if he had just stepped out of a John Wayne movie with jeans, boots and a cowboy hat. And he was the best horseman she had ever seen. He seemed to know how to speak their language and soon had even the wild ones as gentle as lambs. With people he was friendly and personable, and a shrewd judge of character. Meadow had inherited his hazel-green eyes and his affinity for horses.

The week before at the auction, her father had met a wealthy rancher by the name of Bill Bowman. Bill and Dad had hit it off immediately. Now, spotting Bill near the announcers stand, he brought Meadow over to introduce them.

"This is my charming daughter, Meadow."

Bill responded just as gallantly. "My, what a pretty name for a pretty girl. I have a daughter, too, but she's a little older than you. Her name is Linda."

"How old?" Meadow asked.

"Well, now, let me think." He rubbed his forehead. "She must be eighteen now, just graduated from high school. She's going to ASU next fall to study archeology."

To Meadow, this seemed pretty exotic. "Wow, I hope I meet her sometime."

"Oh, you will. I have a fifteen-year-old son, too. You'll soon meet the whole family." Bill Bowman went on to explain. "Your dad has agreed to run a dude string for me this year up at my resort, Brighten Hot Springs."

"You mean we will rent out horses to rich city people who don't know how to ride?"

The man chuckled at Meadow's expression of horror. "Yes, that's right. I think it will help us both out by enticing *more rich city people* to Brighten."

Meadow studied Bill Bowman for a moment and decided she liked him. He was a big man, although not as tall as her father, and had gray hair and a nice smile. He wore fancy boots she thought must be alligator or maybe ostrich hide.

"But Dad . . . horse rentals . . . to dudes?"

Her father put his arm around her shoulders. "It's just for the summer. At this point, I'm ready to try anything to make a few bucks, so I agreed to take it on for the season."

"A resort in the mountains sounds fun, but I'm not so sure about the dude thing," she said.

"Like I said, we're just trying it."

Her father purchased a big paint horse and a smaller bay at the auction, and after loading them and saying their goodbyes to Mr. Bowman, they headed for home.

"I think I'll name them Spot and Brandy." Meadow looked at her father for approval.

"Whatever you think sounds good to me."

She couldn't wait to go north for the summer. "What's the resort like, Dad?"

"It's set up as a frontier town, with a boardwalk, a general store, and a little café. It even has an old-time saloon. Off in the woods, there are cabins for people to stay in. There's a hotel, too, for the ones that don't like to rough it," he said.

She began picturing the resort. "Why is it called Hot Springs?"

"That's the main attraction. Hot spring water bubbling out of the ground. There are foot baths and a steam room and a big swimming pool filled with the hot spring water. They have to put in some river water, too, or it would be too hot to swim in. And people like to drink the darn stuff."

"They drink the hot spring water? Yuk!"

"It's supposed to have all sorts of minerals that are good for you."

"Sounds awful . . . where will we live when we get there? In the hotel?" It would be really neat to live in a hotel. Ordering room service every day and a maid to clean up.

"No, not in the hotel. We have our own cabin. Fairly rustic, but we'll make do."

For the first time, it hit Meadow that this was a pretty big step for her family. "What if it doesn't pay off?"

"It's a risk, but if you don't take risks in life, you'll never make anything happen."

Meadow's stomach tightened a little.

Her father was a flurry of activity the next few weeks before school let out, buying gentle horses and various size saddles to accommodate the dudes that would be coming to the stable for trail rides. The barn was crammed full by this time and Foxfire had to share her large corral with the three horses that accompanied her from Oregon. Meadow wondered how he was paying for it all. Probably using every penny he had worked day and night for before the move. Her mother would just look at each load of horses coming in and shake her head.

Mom arranged to have them take their final exams in advance, so Meadow and her brothers got out of school a little early, much to their delight. In the second week of May, they moved to Brighten Hot Springs in the Arizona mountains, roughly twenty miles north of Sedona.

Her father had made the trip to the stable several times already, transporting the dude horses, but for the rest of the family it was all new. Monty got to ride with Dad in the truck, while Meadow and Mike rode with their mother.

As they drove toward the high country, Meadow was struck by the changing scenery. The Sonoran landscape gradually changed to high desert, with just a few cacti; then they drew near the red rock country of Sedona. The town itself was small, but the setting was spectacular, with the surrounding vermillion cliffs soaring against a backdrop of azure blue sky. It reminded her of the dream she had where she was riding the silver horse through red canyons. Maybe, just maybe, she would see him again soon.

They drove on through Sedona, gaining in elevation and were soon in the pine forest. Proceeding along a gravel road, before long, they pulled in to the little frontier town at Brighten Hot Springs. Her mother parked the Ranch Wagon next to the truck in front of the general store.

A short, rotund man hurried out to greet them. He was nearly bald, with just a few wispy hairs sticking straight out of his shiny pate.

"Hello, Shep." Then he turned to the rest of them. "I'm Wendell Halstead, the general manager. You must be Shep's family. Bill Bowman phoned to let me know you were arriving today." He waddled like a penguin across the boardwalk with his hand out.

Her father introduced the family to him, and Wendell shook hands with all of them in turn. When he took Meadow's hand, his limp, sweaty palm made her want to gag. As soon as he let go, she quickly wiped it on the back of her jeans.

"My wife, Lucy, is in Sedona today getting supplies." Wendell turned and went back across the boardwalk and opened the door. They all filed into the large room. "Lucy runs this store and the post office back there."

The store was set up like an old time general mercantile, and the wood floor creaked beneath Meadow's feet as she explored. It was stocked with various items the resort guests might need to make them comfortable during their stay, including souvenirs so they would be sure to never forget Brighten Hot Springs. In the back of the store, she saw the post office, consisting of a counter with some pigeon holes behind it. The saloon had not yet opened for the season, but Wendell told them a gala dance was being planned for sometime within the next three weeks.

Wendell drove them across the bridge, over the river, and around the grounds so they could see the Brighten Lodge, the hot springs, and swimming pool.

"How large is the resort?" Mom asked.

"We can accommodate forty guests in the hotel and we have another thirty cabins that sleep four each," Wendell replied. "But the resort is only a fraction of the land Bill Bowman owns. The surrounding ten thousand acres belong to him, too. It's a working cattle ranch. The Bowmans stay out in their ranch house a few miles from here during the summer."

"Let's go see the stable now," Dad said.

The stable was located back across the river on the opposite side of the street from the general store and saloon. It was a ways off the road in a lovely setting of tall pine trees.

When Meadow first saw the stables and cabin, she could hardly restrain herself from shouting her approval. This was more like it! Beautiful, with red rocks and Ponderosa Pines. The stables had several large corrals with shelters for the horses and a huge tack room for all their saddles and gear. Her mother wouldn't be able to use her electric range, though. No electricity to the cabin or running water.

Wendell led them across the porch of the old log cabin, which he told them was the oldest building on the ranch dating from the 1880s. Meadow stepped inside behind the adults and scanned the interior. One room was a large kitchen with a big wood cooking stove, an ice box to keep food cool, and a dining table. The other, somewhat smaller room, was a combination sitting room and bedroom and had a double bed for Mom and Dad.

She spotted a ladder and climbed up. "Can I have the loft?"

Mike immediately countered. "No way. We get the loft, right, Mom?"

"I'm sorry, Meadow. There're two of them and no room down here. You'll have to sleep on the cot in the kitchen."

At first she was irritated. Why did she always get the crummy cot? But after sitting on it all tucked up against the window, she looked out to see Foxfire's corral right across the stable yard. She could be up with the sun in the morning and sneak out for an early ride. Meadow smiled. "It's perfect."

"Where's the sink? How do we get water in here?" Monty asked.

"Uh, there's no water to the cabin, but there is a spring down that little trail in the back." Wendell led the way to the back deck.

"Where's the bathroom?" Mike asked.

"There's an outhouse, down that way." Wendell pointed the opposite direction from the spring. "But you know you can use the bathhouse at any time."

"The pool, too?" Meadow asked.

"Yes, of course. All the amenities are at your disposal."

With Wendell still talking to her parents, Meadow wandered down to the spring and was happy to find it had cold water and not the hot mineral variety. After contemplating it for a few moments, she walked on the opposite trail, where Wendell said the outhouse was. Finding the shed-like building, she opened the door and frowned at the double holes. That's weird. Who would want to take a friend with them to the outhouse?

In spite of the rustic surroundings, Meadow sighed in pure bliss. She was going to love this place. A special kind of belonging overwhelmed her, like she had lived here before. But no, that wasn't possible. Still, the strong feeling persisted—something wonderful was going to happen here.

Chapter 6

An Elusive Vision

Meadow awoke to the sound of a whinny. In that moment between sleep and wakefulness, she thought the sound came from her all-too-real dream. In it, she had been an Indian maiden, riding the beautiful silver horse, flying like a rocket through the air. The wind whipped her hair and her fingers entangled in his mane stung slightly as she clung to his back. She had been thrilled and a little frightened, but the reason for her fear eluded her.

Another whinny brought her fully awake and she sat up with a smile. Looking out the cabin window, she saw Foxfire trot around her corral, and then stop and rear up on her hind legs. The mare jumped and kicked up her heels, and then broke into a gallop. She raced to the fence and slid to a halt, and then spun and galloped back. Meadow grinned. Her mare was feeling pretty frisky.

Pulling on her jeans, she crept barefoot through the dark cabin where her family was still sleeping. Since their arrival at Brighten a week ago, they had established a routine, and she knew her mother would be up at any moment wanting her to get wood for the stove. She slipped through the door, and was outside with the sun barely peeking over the trees.

Kelsey rose from where she had been resting on the back deck, and stretched. Giving her a pat on the head in passing, Meadow skipped down the steps on the way to get Foxfire. Kelsey wriggled in anticipation and bounded ahead. Meadow followed her across the riding stable yard, with the other twenty horses eyeing her expectantly, looking for their breakfast. "You guys can wait a while."

She snatched her mare's bridle from the tack room and rushed toward her corral. It wasn't an easy job taking care of the horses and wrangling dudes all day, but it was making the family some badly needed money. The guests had started arriving at the resort three days after they moved in. Meadow and her family barely had time to learn the trails before going out on guided trips. By now it seemed like old hat, taking various dudes out for an hour or two at a time. Whenever she could, Meadow sneaked in a solitary ride to explore the vast forest and rim country.

As she approached the corral, Foxfire pricked her ears and came trotting over to the gate, anxious to get going. She lowered her head and accepted the bit willingly, then waited while Meadow grabbed her long mane with both hands and swung onto her back. Foxfire minced along until they reached the edge of the stable yard, as if sensing the need for stealth. "Let's go!" Meadow whispered, leaning over.

Foxfire didn't need any more encouragement and broke into a canter, lengthening her stride until she was in a full gallop. Kelsey sped along behind, occasionally detouring after a furry varmint that needed chasing.

Meadow crouched low over her mare's neck, pretending to be a jockey, her dark hair flowing behind. The trail was narrow and winding with deep woods on both sides. At a full gallop, she rounded a corner, and saw a large ponderosa pine lying across the trail ahead that must have fallen the night before.

Instead of slowing her horse, she urged her on. "Come on girl, we can do it!"

With total trust in Meadow, Foxfire galloped straight on toward the log. Lifting off at the last moment, she tucked her legs and sailed over the obstacle. They landed as one on the other side, in perfect balance. Meadow had a wide grin on her face, the rush of adrenaline making her lightheaded, and they cantered on with a harmony that most riders could only envy.

She sat up, slowing Foxfire to a walk and they moved along sedately, enjoying the fresh early morning air and the sweet chirps and trills of a Purple Martin. Meadow tossed her head like a filly and shook her thick mane of hair back off her face. "What a bother!" All this hair, but her father wouldn't hear of her cutting it. How nice it would be to have really short hair, like a boy.

Deep down, Meadow wanted to be as wild and free as the creatures she so enjoyed watching in the woods. She felt the cool sunshine of late spring, and smelled the heavenly scent of pine in the air. Inhaling deeply, she remembered it hadn't been all that long since she could breathe this well. The asthma hadn't bothered her since they'd moved to Brighten.

Stroking Foxfire's warm, silky neck and loving the feel of her, Meadow was reminded of the dream the night before that seemed so real. She couldn't put her finger on it, but knew that it was somehow more than a dream, and an uneasy feeling marred the perfect day. It wasn't riding the wonderful silver horse that worried her, but something more.

Something was just not right . . . it was almost evil. It seemed strange that she'd been having such vivid and powerful dreams since they'd moved to Arizona. She didn't remember having dreams before that were hard to tell from reality. Maybe she was cracking up. Meadow brooded over the whole thing for a moment, and then tried to shrug it off.

She was still lost in her thoughts when Foxfire threw her head up, staring intently down the trail. Meadow searched for what had startled her mare and caught a glimpse of silver fading through the trees. Was that a horse?

Her heart pounded, and gathering up her loose reins, she cantered to where the animal had vanished. As she arrived, Meadow saw what looked like a silver horse melt into the trees. She again followed. This happened several times, and before long she found they had arrived in Hidden Valley, where the old timers said the wild horses lived.

It was one of her favorite places, with thick grass and a little stream running through the middle. Deep forest surrounded the valley, protected by the mountainous approach.

Meadow blinked her eyes. How did we get here so fast? She vaguely remembered crossing Oak Creek and heading up the canyon, but had been so intent on chasing the elusive animal that she had lost all track of where they were.

Quickly scanning the valley, she saw no horses in sight. She wouldn't chase an illusion any longer. Sighing, Meadow slipped off Foxfire to let her graze, since her mare had missed breakfast that morning.

She lay down in the thick carpet of grass, and gazed up at the cobalt blue, cloudless sky, enjoying the perfect day. But then the feeling of unease crept in again. It was hard to put her finger on what was bothering her—maybe guilt about being the cause of her family having to move? She knew her brothers and parents missed friends back home.

Kelsey came and flopped down next to her, resting her head on Meadow's chest. As if vying for attention, Foxfire ambled over and nuzzled her affectionately. She smiled. How could she feel down when surrounded by her favorite companions?

She lay back and closed her eyes, and was just drifting off when she heard a loud, trumpeting neigh. Foxfire's head swung up with flaring nostrils to catch the scent. Meadow jumped to her feet, and tried to see the horse that had called. On the far side of the valley, she saw a silver tail disappearing through the trees.

A thrill ran through her. It must be Arrow, the Sky Horse! She desperately wanted to go chasing after the mysterious animal, but knew she should get back to work at the stable. She struggled with her conscience for a moment, but couldn't resist the impulse, and jumping on Foxfire, galloped towards the far side of the valley.

She got to the spot where she had seen him and searched, but there was no trace of any hoof prints. He had simply disappeared like the early morning mist.

Her shoulders sagged as she turned Foxfire toward home. What if she never saw him again? She pondered the legend her father had told her on the drive down from Oregon. She hadn't seen Nueme yet, but was anxious to hear the rest of the story. It probably *was* just a story, but in her heart she hoped it was true.

Chapter 7

The Bowmans

When Meadow finally made it back to the cabin, she gobbled a bowl of cereal and then went out to help with the dude rides. Her parents weren't as strict about her working as they were the boys. Monty and Mike were somewhat resentful at times that she got away with goofing off, but they cut her some slack because she was the youngest and, after all, just a girl.

The stable had a busy, profitable day, and the Shepherds were all feeling pretty good about the endeavor. They were to meet the rest of the Bowman family later at the pool. The Bowmans were driving from their Scottsdale home, and would arrive at Brighten that evening. Meadow was looking forward to meeting the daughter, Linda. It would be fun to have another girl around. She wasn't so sure about their fifteen-year-old son. He was around her brothers' age, and they were a real pain sometimes.

They would also be meeting with the resort manager and his wife, Wendell and Lucy Halstead. They had already met Wendell to get the layout of the resort, finding out that it was part of a larger cattle ranch that the Bowmans owned. Meadow and her brothers had been working so hard, they hadn't even had a chance to really explore the resort, and this evening would be their first introduction to Lucy Halstead.

After dinner, Meadow and her family gathered their clean clothes and headed to the bathhouse. It was a short walk past the main street of the frontier town, on the other side of Brighten River.

As they walked across the suspended foot bridge, high above the river, Mike started swaying it back and forth. The bridge groaned and creaked.

"Knock it off, Mike." Dad looked down at the swiftly moving water. "I'm not so sure how sturdy this thing is and the river is still pretty high with spring run-off."

They continued across the bridge and arrived at the bathhouse, next to the pool.

Usually, every evening after the chores were done, all of them had a mineral bath, then a swim. It was a huge pool with a depth of twelve feet at the deep end. Meadow had been practicing diving to the bottom to see how long she could hold her breath. She was proud of the fact that her lungs were so strong now that she could stay under water longer than her brothers.

Mom reminded them that tonight since they were meeting the Bowmans, they wouldn't have time for a swim. Meadow looked with longing at the clear water lapping gently against the sides.

After they entered the ladies' bathhouse, Meadow and her mother picked out one of the large tubs, pulled the curtain around it and turned the faucets on full blast.

They left their dirty clothes in a hamper, inside a bag marked *Stable,* which would be picked up by a hotel laundry worker. The next day a staff member would deliver their clean clothes to them. Meadow stepped into one of the giant tubs, sitting at the far end from her mother.

"We'll have to go bra shopping before school starts," Mom said.

Meadow's face grew hot and she sank a little farther into the tub. "Yeah, I guess so."

Her mother lay back and closed her eyes. "Isn't this mineral water heavenly? It feels so good to soak after a long day in the saddle. There are some nice benefits to living here."

Meadow grinned. "Yeah, we have our very own swimming pool."

"Yeah, that too."

After their relaxing bath, Meadow and her mother joined Dad and the boys at poolside. Instead of their usual swimsuits, they were all neatly dressed in jeans and western shirts. The pool was still open for resort patrons, but the daytime crowd had thinned out and only a few people were still swimming.

Her father found a large empty table under a cabana with enough chairs for everyone. A family sat at the table next to theirs and the cute blonde girl kept glancing over at the boys. Mike got antsy and went to check out the snack bar, and Meadow saw the girl get up and follow him. Soon they began talking, but she wasn't close enough to hear the conversation. Mike could talk to *anyone.* She forgot about them when the Bowman family showed up, and her father waved Mike back to their table.

Bill Bowman, dressed like a western banker, expansively greeted everyone by doffing his Stetson. Her father stood and introduced his family to them. Bill's wife, Mary, was tall, with graying blonde hair. She held out her hand to Dad and nodded to everyone else. Her long skirt was held in place by a silver Concho belt. Bill Bowman introduced his children.

His daughter, Linda, was one of the most beautiful girls Meadow had ever seen. She was also wearing a skirt, but it was a fashionable shorter length. With her waist-length honey blonde hair and long, tanned legs, she looked more like a movie star than an archeologist. She definitely didn't look like someone who would want to dig around in the dirt for a living.

Meadow had to admit their son, Brett, would be pretty good-looking, too, if it hadn't been for the somewhat sullen, bored expression on his face. He was tall like his sister and was wearing preppy looking clothes. His startling slate blue eyes seemed to take them all in with a slightly disapproving look.

Mr. Bowman ordered refreshments for everyone and before long, a pool boy appeared with the drinks and placed them on the table. The rancher took a sip of his beer.

"I've been in telephone contact with my general manager, Wendell Halstead, and he said that the stable has gotten off to a good start. He and his wife will be joining us a little later." He glanced at Mom. "I hope you are comfortable in the old cabin. It's not very luxurious, I'm afraid."

Dad answered. "Oh, it's fine. We've lived in worse, right, Rose?"

"Especially when we were first married. I think we camped out until the kids started coming along," her mother said, only half kidding.

Mrs. Bowman looked at Mom like she was a rare specimen that needed to be dissected.

"Please tell us about how you and Shep met," she asked. "I always like to know all about the people who work for us."

"They don't actually work for us, Mary," Bill said. "They are running the stable as an independent enterprise, which will no doubt benefit the resort as well as them. But I, too, would like to know more about you both." He smiled at Mom.

It seemed as if Mom had lost her tongue in front of these people. "Well, I . . . "

She turned to Dad for help.

He stepped right in. "Well, to really know Rose, you have to know her real name. It's Velma Rose, but I called her just Rose from the moment I saw her pitching hay onto the wagon at old Bess Brown's place." Her father launched into a story Meadow was very familiar with.

"Old lady Brown was a trading buddy of mine, and this girl was working for her." He nodded toward Mom. "And she could ride and pitch hay as good as any man. I took one look at her dark hair, porcelain skin, and cornflower blue eyes, and decided I would call her just Rose. Such delicate beauty deserved a fitting name, I thought. I'm pretty sure it was love at first sight for both of us."

Mom turned the color of her namesake as Dad told the story.

"She was only nineteen, and I was thirty back then. And I was worried about our age difference, but Rose said it didn't matter if we loved each other."

"I wasn't about to let him get away," Mom said. "He was the best thing that ever happened to me."

Linda seemed to hang on every word. "What a romantic story. Please go on, I'd love to hear more."

"Tell them about Pegleg," Mike said.

"Pegleg? Yeah, I'd like to hear about Pegleg," Brett said, looking bored.

Meadow caught his tone, and frowned at him. He looked back at her with one eyebrow slightly raised, as though daring her to say anything. She met his stare, lifting her chin.

"Pegleg, huh? Well okay, if you really want to hear about her." Dad smiled a little. "When Rose and I were first married, we used to go to a lot of fairs and rodeos to trade horses. I usually had an ole horse that could run a little, so I would enter it in the match races they always had going on."

Brett perked up at the mention of match races.

Dad went on. "Rose was a perfect jockey. Look at her, even after three kids, she's about a hundred pounds soaking wet."

Brett turned to Mom. "Wow, that's pretty neat that you rode in races."

Mom smiled at him, and then stole a glance at Mrs. Bowman. Brett's mother had her lips pursed and didn't seem to be enjoying the story as much as everyone else.

Meadow wiggled in her seat. She was pretty sure her father was aware of the dynamics at the table, but he continued anyway. In fact, he seemed to be kind of dragging it out on purpose.

"I just happened to come across this lanky bay mare that had a distinct limp when she walked. She wasn't in pain, she just walked with a strange up and down motion, like she had one wooden leg, so we called her Pegleg. She would buck when she was cantered slowly, but loved to run full out. After Pegleg got going, she ran like Sea Biscuit, so I decided to enter her in the county fair race in Coos Bay."

Meadow fidgeted. Come on, Dad, wrap it up!

"Well, I found plenty of folks willing to race their horses against Pegleg, just by them looking at her walk with her funny lopsided gait. So I made quite a few side bets that day. When it was time for the race, Rose climbed on Pegleg and rode to the starting line."

"How exciting!" Linda said.

"True to form, when the horses took off, Pegleg bucked, with Rose sticking like glue, until she hit her stride. Then the mare shot forward and easily passed all the challengers to win the race by a good five lengths."

Brett's face lit up. "Wow, that's cool!"

Just when Meadow was heaving a sigh of relief that her father was finally finished, he kept on talking.

"There was only one problem, once Pegleg got going, it was almost impossible to stop her, so she just kept on running around the track. I was too busy collecting money to notice her going past for the second . . . and third time. Poor Rose was pulling and yanking, but the mare just kept on running." Her father shook his head.

"What happened?" Brett asked.

"Someone from the sidelines finally yelled, 'Turn her head to the outside rail.' Rose did as she was told and the mare slowed right down."

Mom nodded. "Pegleg finally stopped, but it was a wild ride until then."

Meadow squirmed, but her father kept talking. "Afterwards when Rose talked to the man, it turned out he was an old racehorse trainer from Santa Anita. He told Rose that racehorses were all trained to stop when they were turned to the outside rail. Then the man pulled up Pegleg's upper lip and sure enough, she had a racing tattoo."

Bill Bowman nodded. "That's right. Racehorses are all tattooed before they are allowed to race on a recognized track."

"What finally happened to Pegleg?" Linda asked.

"I made money hand over fist that day when some fella decided he just couldn't live without ole Pegleg, and made me an offer I couldn't refuse." Dad's face took on a deadpan look.

Bill, Linda, and Brett laughed with appreciation, but Mrs. Bowman's face remained stony.

"What a great story!" Brett said, his bored look totally gone. "I'd sure like to ride some match races."

"Well, son, you're a little too tall to be a jockey, but you could probably do roping or bulldogging all right," Dad said.

Mary Bowman scowled and shook her head emphatically. "No, Brett. I certainly don't want you participating in a rough sport like rodeo."

"Why not?" Mike spoke up. "Monty and I both do it. It's a lot of fun . . . ."

Dad gave Mike a look and her brother broke off mid-sentence. "Why don't you boys go get yourselves a candy bar?" Dad started digging around in his pocket for some change and handed the money to Monty.

Mr. Bowman nodded in agreement and the three boys headed toward the snack bar, with Brett appearing relieved to be off his mother's radar.

Linda scooted her chair a little closer to Meadow. "I love learning about your family." She was speaking so quietly that Meadow had to lean over to hear her clearly. "I can't remember my parents ever telling us about how they met. And they never say anything about what they did before Brett and I came along."

"Oh, really?" Meadow had a hard time imagining her parents not talking about their courtship and early marriage. Didn't all families talk about those things? Maybe it was safer not to pursue that subject with Linda. "It must be nice to be out of high school."

"Yes, but I start ASU in the fall and then the real work starts," Linda said.

"Your dad told me that you are going to be an archeologist. How did you get interested in that?"

Linda's face grew intense. "I went with a friend on a dig on the Shonto reservation last summer. I found it so fascinating that I want learn all I can about Indians."

"We have a Shonto friend here. He's our horseshoer, but he's been up in Flagstaff working, so we haven't seen him yet," Meadow said. She hoped he'd get back soon, so he could tell her the legend of Arrow.

Their conversation was cut short when Wendell Halstead and his wife walked up to their table. Bill stood to greet them.

"Hello, Wendell, I'm glad you and Lucy could join us this evening. Wendell, I know you've met the family, but Lucy hasn't.

Lucy, this is Shep, Rose, and their daughter Meadow. Their sons, Monty and Mike are standing over by the snack bar."

"Lucy runs the post office and store," Mrs. Bowman said.

While everyone greeted them, Meadow looked Lucy over. She was almost a head taller than her husband, had jet black hair and was very full-figured, almost bursting out of her shirt.

"Wendell and Lucy have only been with the resort since April, but have really caught on quickly," Bill said.

"Very pleased to meet you, I'm sure." Lucy's speech had a strange inflection.

Meadow wasn't positive, but she thought it might be a New Jersey accent. Lucy favored them with a toothy grin and plopped down in the nearest chair.

After Wendell was seated, Bill made an announcement. "I wanted everyone to meet here this evening to let you know that I will be out of the country for the next few weeks. Wendell will be taking care of the books, and Shep, if you have any problems, let him know. He should be able to handle everything while I am gone."

Wendell bobbed his head vigorously. "That's right, Mr. Bowman. I will make sure everything runs smoothly. You have nothing to worry about."

Bill clapped him on the shoulder. "Okay, that's fine. As soon as my family gets settled at the ranch, I will be off."

"Where are you going?" Dad asked.

"I will be in Spain this time," he replied. "I also own an import business, so I will be purchasing some architectural details and artifacts for resale here in the States."

Meadow caught Linda looking sadly at Mr. Bowman when he said he'd be out of the country for a few weeks. She was glad her own father only went for overnight trips and not weeks at a time.

Linda turned to Mrs. Bowman. "Mom, you won't be running off to your gallery while he's gone, will you?"

"No, dear, I will be here for at least part of the summer." Mrs. Bowman turned to Mom. "I'm afraid my children are tired of housekeepers and nannies. Both Bill and I have our own businesses to run, and that keeps us away from them at times."

"Oh, I'm glad you'll be here," Mom said. "Shep and I are taking a group on a two-night pack trip starting tomorrow. I'm sure the kids will do fine alone though." She looked at Meadow and smiled.

Meadow smiled back, figuring she and her brothers could take care of themselves for a couple of days with no mishaps.

Before long, the adults brought the evening to a conclusion, all of them tired from the day's activities. Mike complained about leaving since they were having such a good time swapping stories with Brett, who, in turn, said he was happy to have a couple of boys his own age living close by for the summer. Meadow said her goodbyes to Linda, excited that maybe she had found a friend here. All in all, it was shaping up to be a fun summer, especially if she could track down Arrow.

Chapter 8

The Stallion

Meadow sat on a rock, dangling her feet into a pool of water, long hair partially covering her face. She'd gone with Mike to the creek after the day's rides were finished. He wanted to try his luck at catching some trout and his efforts were being duly rewarded.

She sighed, still disappointed that the wild horse she chased yesterday had eluded her. Had he been real? How had he disappeared so quickly without even leaving tracks?

Her mind went to last night's events at the pool. She had felt an instant connection with Linda, but still wasn't so sure about Brett. He seemed a little stuck on himself. Oh well, her brothers had gotten along with him okay. But would they ever have time to really get to know Linda and Brett?

All they had been doing since they got to Brighten was work, work, and more work. She was so sick of dudes she could just scream. Since her parents had left on the pack trip, Meadow and her brothers were even busier, all three working from early morning till the long summer day was done. She came with Mike to the fishing hole for a change in routine. It was better than gathering firewood.

She glanced over at her brother who was casting his fishing line into the rushing creek. "Mike, did you really see the mustangs in Hidden Valley today?"

Meadow knew he sometimes embellished his stories to get attention. She hadn't told anyone about her earlier experience, not being sure it had even been real. Had she really heard the stallion and chased him, or was it her imaginary horse again?

"You know I would tell *you* if it wasn't true," Mike answered softly, not wanting to scare the fish.

"I thought I saw a wild horse yesterday morning too, but I wasn't sure, it happened so fast," she said.

"Shhh, you'll scare all the fish away. Oh forget it, they've quit biting now anyway." Mike reeled in his line and after taking the bait off, he picked up his string of trout. "At least we have enough for dinner."

"Did you really see them?" she asked again.

"Yeah, I saw them all right. And there was something really strange about the herd."

Meadow leaned in. "Like what?"

"I told you about the stallion, the big, beautiful dapple grey stallion that was with them. The strange thing was, he must have been over sixteen hands tall. You know mustangs are never that big. It was really weird."

She stared off into space. "That is strange."

"I didn't say anything about that before, 'cuz I knew no one would believe me. Mustangs are usually pretty scrawny."

"How close were you to the herd?" she asked. "Maybe he just looked big from a distance."

"No, he was big, he was right next to the mares and they looked puny compared to him. I would sure like to catch that stallion. What a prize!"

Her voice took on a determined tone as she pictured the big, beautiful stallion. "I don't think anyone should catch him. He should always be free."

Mike looked at her and just shook his head. "Come on, goofball. We need to get back to the cabin with these fish." He turned and started off down the trail.

She followed slowly, still thinking about the wild horses.

The next day, Meadow stood near the hitching rail with a scowl on her face. Her parents had taken a group up to the Mogollon Rim for two nights, with Dad guiding the trip and Mom along to do the cooking. They told Monty he was in charge while they were gone.

Earlier that morning a family had come by the stable to look over the horses and book a ride. Meadow recognized the daughter as the same blonde girl who had spoken to Mike by the pool when they met the Bowman's.

Meadow's frown deepened as Monty tried to ignore her, busily getting the saddles out of the tack room.

"But why does she have to ride Foxy?" Her voice had an edge to it. "You know Foxy doesn't like anyone to ride her but me."

Monty placed a saddle on the rail near Meadow, then turned and faced her.

"I know, Med, but we are short a horse for the ride and the daughter doesn't want to ride a pony."

"How do you know she can handle Foxy?"

"She's been taking riding lessons and when I told her you always ride bareback, she said her trainer makes them ride bareback for learning balance." She could tell Monty was trying to be patient with her. "So she's not even using a saddle. That should make you happy."

Meadow stubbornly rejected Monty's attempt to placate her. "Well, I still think she should ride Blackjack."

Blackjack was a fourteen hand Welsh pony and they only used him for smaller, timid guests and children.

"I *told* you, she doesn't want to ride a pony. She's kinda spoiled, I think. You know Dad left me in charge and all the horses have to earn their keep, even Foxy. We need all the money we can get right now."

"I don't care." Her fists became tight knots at her side, knowing she was losing. "She's not me and will probably pull on Foxy's mouth and jab her in the side!"

"Too bad, you can ride along on Blackjack and watch her then!" Monty's voice ratcheted up. "You're a spoiled brat, too!" He slammed the tack room door with a loud bang.

Meadow could feel herself spinning out of control. "I'm not riding a stupid pony! I hate you and I hate that girl, too!" She stormed away, blood pounding in her head.

By the time the group arrived, Meadow had cooled off enough to get her mare ready for the ride. She lovingly brushed her glossy red coat and combed out her long mane and tail.

It was a family of four—an overweight boy of about Monty's age, the blonde girl, and their parents.

The father swaggered over to Monty and stuck out his hand.

"Hello," he said. "Remember me? I spoke with you earlier about the rental? We're the Markowitz family, from Scottsdale. I'm Ben, my wife Marge, my daughter Cynthia, and my son Ralph."

Monty shifted his feet uncomfortably, and Meadow knew he would rather be reading a book than dealing with customers. He finally shook the man's hand, mumbled something, and then turned back to the horse he was saddling.

Ben Markowitz rattled on about how he always took time off from his law practice in the summer to bring his family up to Brighten Hot Springs. "I'm not crazy about riding myself, but Marge and Cynthia kept pestering me to take them. I guess it's good practice for Cynthia. After all, I'm spending a fortune for her riding lessons."

Meadow decided the man must want everyone to know his entire history. Monty still had his back to him, but the man apparently loved to hear himself talk. Must be a lawyer thing.

"I personally like to golf, but Cynthia wanted to fit in with her friends, I think. I'm not sure she really loves riding."

Cynthia had been listening to her father and got a petulant look on her face. "That's not true, Daddy! I simply adore horses and riding!" She walked to where Monty was busy tacking up Spot and began patting the big horse as if to make her point.

Ben Markowitz glanced at his daughter and then continued talking to no one in particular. "Anyway, as I was saying, Cynthia rides, I golf, and Marge goes to lunch. I'm not sure what Ralph does . . ." He paused and frowned at his son for a moment, before turning to Meadow.

"Your brother told me this is your horse," he said. "Don't worry, little girl, my Cynthia will take good care of her."

Meadow, afraid he might actually pat her consolingly on the head, took a step back. Cynthia had come up next to her and she noted her too tight jeans and shirttails tied at the waist.

"Just make sure you keep Foxfire at a walk. She loves to run and can be a handful."

Cynthia raised her chin and looked down her pert little nose. "I've been taking lessons on Jumpers, so I'm sure I can handle your kiddie horse."

Meadow felt like smacking her, but tightened her jaw and held her tongue. She *would* go along on Blackjack to keep an eye on Foxfire. She gave Cynthia a boost up onto the mare's back, noticing how she tensed and laid her ears back. Meadow stroked her neck. "It's okay, girl." Foxfire relaxed some, but her ears stayed back.

Cynthia tittered a little, glancing at the ground. "Isn't she big for an Arabian? Not as big as the thoroughbred I ride, of course, but kinda tall."

"She's 15.2 hands."

"Much better than a pony." The blonde girl smirked, rubbing it in.

Meadow gritted her teeth and helped her brother get the rest of the family on their horses. Monty swung into his saddle, and took his position in front of the group. Cynthia watched him go by, practically drooling. He glanced back at the riders, quickly checking to see if they were ready to go. The horses stood patiently, awaiting yet another forced march down the trail carrying insensitive and uncaring tourists.

Cynthia tossed her blonde curls and flashed Monty a smile, showing off her small, perfect white teeth. "We're all set. Let's go!" Her voice rang with enthusiasm.

Monty rarely spoke to the patrons except to give needed directions, and so he nodded to the girl and started out slowly to lead the group.

The horses obediently fell in behind the leader, walking head to tail and keeping some distance between them as they had been taught, except for Foxfire. Without any urging, Foxfire closed in on Monty's big, bay quarter horse.

"Cyndi, honey, don't get too close to his heels," her mother cautioned.

Cynthia ignored her mother, trying to get near Monty. "I'm so glad your sister let me ride her special horse, she's beautiful." She rode right up next to Monty.

"It definitely wasn't her idea," he muttered.

"Your brother Mike told me that Foxfire is a purebred Arabian, and that your sister got her when she was a weanling. Is that true?"

"Yep," Monty replied.

Cynthia kept trying, but Meadow saw with satisfaction that Monty wasn't paying any attention to her. His answers to her silly questions were always short yeps and nopes.

"Isn't this nice, dear?"Marge Markowitz asked her husband. "We're finally having a family outing all together."

"I just hope this darned ride isn't too long," Ben Markowitz said. "I wouldn't want to lose the tennis court I have booked."

"And I can see why Cynthia likes that Monty. So nice and polite, but not much of a talker." Marge's rate of chatter rivaled her husband. "Maybe he'll be at the dance Saturday night. I wonder what we should wear. . . ." She went on, but Meadow tuned her out, just like her husband seemed to.

Meadow slowed down to get behind Ralph who was bringing up the rear on Spot. Kelsey started to follow Foxfire, but then decided to stay with Blackjack. Ralph pulled out a Big Hunk candy bar and unwrapped it.

"Do you take riding lessons, too, Ralph?" Meadow asked, trying to keep her mind off her annoyance with Cynthia.

"Nah." He answered in between bites. "I don't like horses, and the only reason I'm here is that my parents made me come. Anything Cynthia wants to do is what we have to do. When she saw your brothers at the pool the other night, she decided she wanted to go riding. She's boy crazy."

"I don't think she'll get anywhere with Monty. He's a bookworm and not interested in girls." This wasn't strictly true, especially the latter part, but Meadow didn't want to encourage anything between her brother and Ralph's sister.

"He only does this job 'cuz my parents need his help with the stable," she added.

By now, Ralph was squirming in the saddle. "Where are your parents? And why are you riding a pony?"

"They took some people on a pack trip up to the Rim," she explained. "They have all the other horses with them, except for the ones my other brother took out earlier today. He has six riders with him. The only one left was Blackjack. He's a good pony, but I like to ride my mare."

"How long will your parents be gone? I can't believe they left you alone. That's not very responsible of them."

Jeez, he was as bad as his sister.

"We're not exactly alone," she snapped. "There are at least fifty people staying at the Hot Springs right now. And we're good friends with the owners. Besides Monty is sixteen, and that's old enough to stay alone!"

"Well, I'm sixteen, and my parents would never let *us* stay alone." Ralph finished the candy bar and dropped the wrapper on the trail.

That explains everything, Meadow thought in disgust, getting off to retrieve the paper. She caught up with Ralph just as he complained, "Oww, my thighs are getting rubbed raw."

"You shouldn't have worn shorts!" What kind of dope shows up to ride dressed like that?

Not in the mood to put up with Ralph any longer, Meadow urged Blackjack past the rest of the family, until she was right behind Cynthia again. Might as well enjoy the beautiful day. Her face raised, she felt the sun's warmth between the dappled shadows of the giant ponderosa pines. It was early in the season and the trail was still covered with pine needles, not yet as dusty as it would be later in the summer. She enjoyed the steady clopping of hooves on the soft cushioned surface and the sound of the whispered breeze high in the treetops.

About an hour into the ride Cynthia tired of Monty's inattention. "I've been taking riding lessons twice a week. How do you think I'm doing?"

"You're doing okay for bareback, I guess," Monty answered, not looking at her.

Cynthia clucked for the mare to go faster. Foxfire trotted out smartly.

"Let's race!" The girl called as she passed by Monty. Foxfire's extended trot soon left the other riders far behind.

"Cynthia, pull her up!" Meadow yelled. She rode up next to Monty, who had checked his bay. She could see that he was furious.

"That silly brat! Now I'll catch hell from Dad!"

"I'll ride after her and try to the catch Foxy." Meadow was already urging Blackjack forward.

"Okay, I'll keep the group together. Foxy might really stampede if we all run after her."

As Meadow cantered forward, she could hear Marge Markowitz screaming, "Cynthia, come back!" Then she heard Ben Markowitz yelling at Monty, asking him what he was going to do.

Blackjack was trying his best, but he was no match for Foxfire, and Meadow lost sight of them in the trees. As she rounded the corner, Meadow could clearly see Foxfire trotting down the trail ahead with her long floating gait. The mare's ears were flicking back and forth and she was switching her tail, indicating she was irritated with her rider.

Darn! They'd soon be in Hidden Valley and Foxy might really take off. Afraid for Cynthia, Meadow urged the pony on faster.

By the time she arrived at the opening to the valley, Foxfire had broken into a canter and was midway into the grassy expanse. Cynthia was hunched over and pulling on the reins with both hands. Foxfire tossed her head, pulling the reins out of the girl's grip, and then ran even faster, finally into a full gallop.

Cynthia let the reins dangle and clung to Foxfire's long mane, while her heels dug into the mare's side. Meadow knew Foxfire had never felt digging heels before, and would keep running to get away from the unpleasant feeling. Cynthia appeared to be totally out of control, and off balance, slipping around on the mare's sleek back.

Meadow felt a sinking feeling. "Foxy, Foxy!"

She knew Foxfire was too upset to heed her, if she could even hear her at that distance, but she had to try something.

Kelsey whined, wanting to chase after the fleeing horse.

"No, Kelsey. You'll just make it worse. Foxy!" she called in vain.

A loud whinny rang out. Foxfire snorted and skidded to an abrupt halt, sending Cynthia flying over her head. Meadow winced as the girl landed on her back with a thud. She gave a weak moan and then lay still. Foxfire looked over at Cynthia, then threw her tail up over her back and raced toward the tree line on the opposite side of the valley.

Meadow stared into the distance, her pulse pounding wildly. She couldn't believe her eyes. This time she was sure, it *was* the silver stallion. And Foxfire was going with him! Her stomach did flip-flops as she watched the horses disappear into the forest. Where were they going? She wanted to race after them, but the blonde girl was still on her back.

She hurried Blackjack toward her. "Are you okay, Cynthia?" She jumped off the pony, and ran to the girl's side, who was covered in dirt with a ripped shirt.

"Are you hurt?" Meadow took her hand and patted it.

Cynthia slowly sat up and shook her head groggily. "I don't know." Her voice quivered and tears streaked her face.

The rest of the group arrived with Cynthia's mother and father looking distressed, and her brother, Ralph, grimacing from the long trot on Spot.

"Cynthia! Is anything broken?" Her mother fumbled with the reins and looked confused about whether to get off or not.

"Don't move." Ben Markowitz dismounted and went to his daughter.

"I think I'm okay," Cynthia said. "I don't feel like anything is broken, I'm just a little dizzy."

"Probably a concussion." Ben Markowitz looked accusingly at Monty. He supported his daughter as she got to her feet.

"I really think I'm all right, now," Cynthia said. "Wow that was scary. Foxy is fast! You were right about her liking to run, but where did she go?"

"What about me?" Ralph whined. "Cynthia is fine, but my thighs are totally raw, and nobody even cares!"

Everyone had forgotten about Ralph with all the excitement. Monty and Meadow exchanged glances, stifling snickers at how pathetic he sounded.

"We have to head back to the stable instead of going on anyway," Monty said. "Cynthia, you will have to ride behind me on Elmer."

"Your horse's name is Elmer? What a cute name!" Cynthia choked back a giggle.

Monty turned red and smiled bashfully.

Her father frowned. "Maybe Cyndi should ride behind me."

"No," Monty said firmly. "You aren't a good enough rider to go double. What if something spooked your horse? You'd both be on the ground."

The furrows between Markowitz's eyes deepened, but he reluctantly helped Cynthia up behind Monty.

"I'm still pretty dizzy." She leaned her head on Monty's back and wrapped her arms around his waist.

At first, Monty stiffened, but soon relaxed into his usual easy riding position, and smiled.

Meadow held Markowitz's horse while he remounted, then when everyone was all set to go, she made an announcement to the group. "I'm riding after the wild herd. I have to go and find Foxy."

"Well, if you don't find her, head home before dark," Monty said, with a sigh.

Meadow knew he would figure it was useless trying to forbid her to go and he was well aware that she could take care of herself. After all, she had ridden all over these mountains alone. But she was glad he had the dudes to worry about, so there was no argument.

She watched as the group started back down the trail, then trotted Blackjack toward the far side of the valley, determined to find Foxfire.

Chapter 9

The Cliff House

Meadow urged Blackjack forward, acutely aware of the differences between the pony and Foxfire. Blackjack was tough and eager to please but couldn't maintain a fast pace for long. She would have to take it easy and not push him too hard.

They got to the place where Foxfire had met up with the stallion and Meadow saw her bridle laying on the ground. How did she get that off? She dismounted and retrieved it. Thank goodness it wasn't broken. It was a single ear-loop style bridle without a throat latch, so the stallion must have pulled it off over her head. She tied Foxfire's bridle to the back of Blackjack's saddle, glad for once not to be riding bareback.

After finding the tracks that were many shapes and sizes, she realized it wasn't just the stallion and Foxfire.

"Look, Jack. We're going to be following a whole herd. Good thing, too. They'll be easier to find."

Meadow remounted and rode as quickly as Blackjack was able, trying to follow the herd's hoof prints but losing them once in a while. Since the horses were all unshod, the prints were not as obvious on this rough ground.

Even Foxfire was barefoot and had never needed horseshoes, because she had such hard hooves. Nueme always commented on her perfect Arabian feet whenever he trimmed her.

She wished Nueme was with her today since he was an expert tracker. It was a slow process, and oftentimes she would have to double back to try to pick up the prints again. She was leaning over looking intently for tracks when Blackjack stumbled, almost going down.

"You silly pony, pick up your feet." Then, feeling sorry for him, she dismounted to give him a break.

With the footing getting rockier, it was easier to follow the tracks while afoot, so Meadow walked, leading Blackjack. They had already traveled for about an hour looking for the herd, and the hoof prints were leading them up into a narrow canyon. When they crossed over a creek, Blackjack dropped his head and took a long drink.

"That's enough, boy. I don't want you getting sick from this cold water."She remounted and they continued going up.

The grade became steeper. They'd been climbing steadily for twenty minutes or so and now the pony was winded, puffing. Blackjack was willing and sweet natured, but he wasn't young anymore.

Meadow sighed. The pony was pretty tired, his black coat swirled with sweat. She reined him to the shade of a gnarled old mesquite tree near some big boulders to give him a rest. After dismounting, she took off his bridle and tied him to the tree with the halter underneath. She loosened his girth and waited until he cooled down before gathering some mesquite beans hanging in long pods from the tree. Meadow put the pods in a mound for Blackjack to eat.

Seeming glad for the reprieve, the pony let out his breath and munched on the mesquite beans, crunching noisily. She stroked his neck affectionately.

"What a good boy you are, Jack. This is a hard trail and you've been a real trooper for an old guy."

Blackjack nickered to her softly, butting his head against her, and she kissed him on his soft nose. She knew the pony would work for her until he gave out, and she didn't want that.

Meadow was especially fond of Blackjack, who was one of the chosen horses that had made the long trip from Oregon with them. All three of the children in the Shepherd family had learned to ride on him when they were just little tots.

They all graduated to more challenging horses, but her father had kept Blackjack around for their school friends to ride. When her father made the decision to bring the horses to Arizona, naturally the pony was included. Since Foxfire and Monty's rope horse, Elmer, were brought along, too, she wondered if Mike had felt left out. But Dad told him he was such a good colt breaker that he could ride all the rough ones. Mike always liked to top off a bronc.

Meadow turned from the pony and looked around for Kelsey. She saw her sniffing and pawing in an area of some piled up brush. All of a sudden her dog gave a surprised yelp and dropped out of sight.

"Kelsey!" she screamed, running toward the brush pile.

She tried looking down into the dark hole, but there was too much brush in the way. Meadow hastily cleared away the debris and lay down, peering into the abyss. She could barely see Kelsey at the bottom.

As her eyes adjusted to the dim light, she could make out some stalagmites and stalactites protruding from the bottom and top of a cave, receding into the darkness. She had learned about those formations in her science class last year but couldn't remember which was which. Kelsey was several feet below and tried to climb up to her, but the sides of the opening were too steep.

How in the world could she get her out?

"Kelsey, come on." Her encouragement prompted Kelsey to jump, but she fell back when the shale rock gave way. Meadow reached down to try and help her. She slid down a little, so she could reach further. Kelsey whined and wagged her tail.

Just a little farther . . . then as if earth opened, the side gave way under her weight and Meadow slid head first toward the floor of the cave. She grabbed frantically at the sides, trying to get a handhold but it was useless, the momentum was too great. Just like when she fell off a horse, she tucked her head, but felt the sudden impact and the sharp pain that followed.

Meadow lay still, with her eyes closed, trying to catch her breath and assess the damage before she moved. Slowly she became aware of something warm surrounding her. The feeling intensified, and she felt a presence nearby. There was a soft halo of light and she looked up to see a face.

A lovely Indian maiden with dark doe eyes smiled and held out her hand. Meadow reached to meet her hand and felt a warm grasp. The young woman took Meadow's hand and placed it on a pendant that she wore around her neck. It was a beautiful silver inverted crescent with turquoise around the edges and a sparkling crystal suspended in the middle. On each end of the crescent were tiny hands, and in the center of the crystal, she could make out a horse.

"This is my people's place. You are the chosen one. You must—" Before the Indian girl finished speaking, everything went dark, and Meadow didn't catch the rest of her words.

She felt something wet and opened her eyes to Kelsey licking her face, and emitting little whines. Meadow shook her head, trying to clear the fog that surrounded her brain, and looked around. She and her dog were alone in the cave.

"What happened?" Kelsey whined again, and cocked her head, staring intently at Meadow.

She knew she must have dreamed the Indian girl, but couldn't shake off the feeling that the incident was somehow real. After all, she wasn't knocked out . . . or was she?

Instead of being frightened, she sensed the girl was good and meant her no harm. But she was confused. What had the Indian girl meant by her words? She sat for a few minutes trying to sort it out and gradually became aware of the beauty of the formations around her.

Meadow looked up at the sheer sides of the opening above her and felt a prickle of fear. It would be impossible to climb up. Was there another way out somewhere? She got up, feeling a little wobbly, and started through the cave into a narrow passageway. It was fairly dark, and Meadow crept along, her hand feeling the way on the side wall. The path wound through the mountain for what seemed like a long distance, and she squinted to see, cautiously sidling forward.

Eventually, Meadow saw a bit of light ahead. Her pulse quickened. Had she found another way out? She hurried toward the light and suddenly the passage opened up and to reveal a large chamber formed into the cliff wall. She sucked in her breath. This must be an Indian cliff dwelling.

One side was open to the canyon and Meadow edged over to look, then gasped and quickly stepped back. They were high up the canyon wall and the vertical drop down was hundreds of feet.

Darn, no one could enter or get out of the dwelling from this point without wings.

She turned back to survey her surroundings. In the middle of the room, under a canopy of draping rock formations, was a large fire pit with decorated clay pots that must have been ancient cooking vessels. On the walls beautiful portrayals of Indians, horses, deer and other animals depicted everyday life and hunting scenes. It was like being in a museum of Indian culture, with a display of vibrantly colored paintings and carvings etched directly into the rock. Meadow traced her fingers over a spiral symbol.

Then she noticed smaller rooms off the main one. Going into one, she found a bed, complete with Indian blankets and next to it woven baskets of different sizes. Another room had an arsenal of bows and arrows and what looked like axes with stone heads. It looked as though the inhabitants had hurried off, leaving behind their belongings.

She kept walking in sort of a daze until she found steps leading down to another chamber. The light in the passageway was dim, but she heard water dripping on rocks. Before long, the cave opened up again into a large room and she saw shafts of sunlight filtering through from openings up above.

In the center of the chamber was a large pool of water, the result of an underground stream. She looked into the perfectly clear pond, and could see down into what appeared to be enormously deep canyons. It seemed to be a whole kingdom of rugged terrain beneath the surface.

She put her hand into the water and discovered it was less than a foot deep. The illusion was caused by the reflection in the water from the formations hanging from the ceiling. As if in a trance, Meadow sank down and gazed at the water, envisioning the life of the ancient people who had lived there.

She didn't realize it was getting late until Kelsey came up to her and stuck her wet nose in her hand. Meadow shook her head to clear it.

"You're right, Kelsey. We better get going before they send the posse out." Meadow really wanted to explore some more but knew her brothers would be worried if she were gone much longer. She left everything as she'd found it. It seemed important to not disturb a thing.

She wound through the tunnel to the original opening. Maybe she'd missed a way out. But no, the sides were just too steep to climb. Her shoulders slumped.

A few minutes passed before Meadow snapped to attention. She hurried back to the main room, remembering a ladder lashed together with rawhide leaning against a wall. After retrieving it, she dragged it along the passageway to where she and Kelsey had fallen in.

Meadow propped the ladder at the opening and boosted Kelsey midway up, and from there the dog clambered to the top. She followed her out into the waning light of dusk. Blackjack was waiting patiently, one back foot cocked, half asleep after his mesquite bean snack.

"Good boy, Jack." She patted him, then slipped his bridle on, and tightened the cinch to his saddle.

Blackjack was revived and eager to go. Just as she was about to mount him, he whipped his head up and whinnied. Through the brush, up the canyon, Meadow could make out a dark horse with a rider. The rider was bareback and dressed in buckskin, with feathers woven into his shoulder-length hair. For a minute she thought she was hallucinating again. But Blackjack had seen them, too, hadn't he?

Meadow jumped on and trotted to where she had thought she had seen the Indian, but there was no sign of him. And there was no time to look. She had to get home before Monty became furious with her.

She was worried about Foxfire, but figured her mare would be all right with the wild herd for the night. As she hurried Blackjack down the trail, her thoughts kept wandering to the day's strange events. She was positive the cliff dwelling existed, but wasn't so sure about the encounter with the Indian girl or the brave she had thought she'd seen. Maybe those things were a result of the bump on her head, but they seemed so real to her.

Just as she got to the main trail home, she saw a rider trotting toward her. It was Mike, mounted on a handsome buckskin gelding he was breaking. Mike had hopes he might keep this horse as his own and had put a lot of time into his training. The buckskin was lathered with sweat and breathing heavily from the long trot. Mike reined him in.

"Whoa, Rowdy." He stopped the gelding next to Meadow. "Where've you been?" He sounded irritated. "It's getting dark! Monty is pretty mad. What happened to you? You're all covered in dirt!"

Meadow fairly bubbled with excitement. "I found something really amazing, but you have to promise not to tell anyone."

"What did you find?" Mike asked.

"Do you promise?"

"Yeah, yeah. I won't tell anyone. What'd you find?"

"I found a big Indian cliff house with a bunch of Indian stuff. I mean a whole bunch of Indian stuff—pots and blankets and clothes and weapons and everything! It's as if they just left and didn't take anything with them. You wouldn't believe how wonderful and beautiful it is. It feels like you're in a whole different world."

She purposely omitted the part about the Indian rider and the vision of the Indian maiden with the beautiful pendant. She wanted to think more about those things before she told anyone.

"Wow, that's really neat. How did you find it?"

Meadow described how Kelsey had actually found it.

"Are you sure you can find it again?"

"Yeah, I know where I was tracking the horses, but it is definitely off the beaten path. I think the entrance was camouflaged on purpose so no one could find it. I can't wait to go back and explore some more. Do you think those Indian things are worth anything?"

Mike nodded his head. "Probably. There has to be someone that likes old Indian junk. We can go back and look at it tomorrow, okay?" He paused for a moment. "Oh wait, we can't go tomorrow, I have a big group that booked a ride to the gorge, and then Mom and Dad will be home in the afternoon."

"Tomorrow I have to look for Foxy anyway."

"No, you have to help me with the group, a bunch of bigwigs from Phoenix. I plan on raking in some good tips from them."

Mike was the polar opposite of Monty, loving to meet new people and engage them in conversation and although not as tall as his older brother, he was more muscular. He always pulled in the most tips from the guests. Meadow felt a little pang of jealousy that she never seemed to get as many. But then Mike didn't have an easy relationship with their father. They're too much alike, her mother always said.

"What about looking for Foxy?"

Mike snickered. "Oh, she'll be all right. I'm sure she's having fun with that stallion!"

"Oh, yeah." She hadn't thought of that. "We'll probably have a new foal about this time next year, huh?"

"No doubt."

They rode on toward home, and she shivered with excitement at the prospect of a new foal. An Indian ruin, a foal next spring, what else would this summer have in store for her?

That night, Meadow fell asleep with a smile on her face and had muddled dreams of silver stallions, Indians, and baby horses.

Chapter 10

The River

The next morning, Meadow finished bridling Rex, while Mike grabbed his saddle and heaved it up on Rowdy. Monty was nearby getting Spot ready for the ride. Seven other horses were tied along the fence awaiting the group of eight that would be arriving at any time.

Monty adjusted the stirrups and turned to Mike. "Do you think it's a good idea to cross the river with dudes today? It's still pretty high with spring runoff."

"It'll be okay. If they're scared to ride they can always walk over on the log bridge and Med and I can herd their horses across."

Monty frowned. "Make sure everyone *does* walk across the bridge. We don't want any more mishaps while Mom and Dad are gone."

"Okay, sure," Mike replied. "They'll love the gorge trail and it's long enough to tell them some good stories."

"No doubt to get some big tips. Just make sure you pay attention to safety."

"Yeah, yeah."

Pretty soon the group arrived and introduced themselves. They said they were staying in the lodge, which made perfect sense. None of them looked like the type that would like to rough it.

A beefy man with a ruddy complexion said he was Bob Rawlins, the CEO of the company. He brushed by Meadow as if she weren't there and spoke to Mike. "We're having a sales meeting here at Brighten, so I'm giving the staff a treat. You know what they say about all work and no play."

Mike nodded and handed him Trooper's reins. "Everyone will have a good time on this ride, sir. I'll make sure of it."

"Well, son, you're pretty young for so much responsibility. What are you, about sixteen?"

Mike's chest swelled a little. "No, sir. I'm fourteen, but I've been riding all my life, so it comes pretty easy for me. I even trained this horse myself." He nodded toward Rowdy. "He's only three years old and can already slide stop and spin on a dime."

The man standing next to Bob Rawlins listened to the conversation with a sour look on his face. He was a youngish man with slightly protruding front teeth. His face screwed up at Mike's words. "How hard can it be to train a horse, anyway? They're just dumb animals. You just force them to do what you want, right?"

Mike snorted. "I'd like to see you try and force a twelve hundred pound animal to do anything."

The man opened his mouth to reply when his boss, Bob Rawlins gave a warning look.

"Back off, Paul. The kid's done a great job." Bob smiled apologetically at Mike. "Paul Misner's new to my sales team, but he'll get the hang of diplomacy before long." He gave Paul another look." Right, Paul?"

Misner's thin laugh was unconvincing. "Just joking around with you, kid. I'm sure it's really hard to train a horse."

Meadow helped the guests mount. Paul Misner sat hunched and grabbed onto the horn as if Brandy would bolt any moment. His tense posture was a dead giveaway he was intimidated with the large animal. He kept wiping his hand across his forehead, even though it was still cool out.

She climbed up on Rex, and turned him to get behind the last horse in line. As they plodded along, her mind kept wandering to the dapple gray stallion and her chestnut mare. She wasn't so much worried about Foxfire, but she really missed her.

When Meadow wasn't thinking about the horses, her mind went to the cliff dwelling. Why had the Indians left in such a hurry without taking anything? And what did her vision about the Indian girl mean? It had been so real. It was a puzzle, but maybe she would never know the answers.

She pulled her thoughts back to the task at hand when Paul Misner turned and spoke to the large lady riding directly in front of Meadow. His voice sounded annoyed. "Why did he require a sales meeting out here in the middle of the wilderness, anyway?"

The woman gazed at the trees surrounding her. "I think it's beautiful." She turned in her saddle to include Meadow. "Don't you think so, dear?"

Meadow smiled. "Yes, this is one of my favorite trails."

The gorge trail, following alongside the Brighten River, was deeply trenched with high banks from the many horses and hikers that had used it through the years. Near the river, it was thickly wooded with pea green grape vines clinging to the trees and hanging down from branches like forgotten party streamers.

Spot's wide rear end moved up the trail, with the large lady's butt bumping along in the saddle, almost a match for his. Meadow sighed. Poor Spot. He was so big and patient, he always had to carry the most weight and the worst riders.

The woman was friendly and talkative, and enlightened Meadow about the finer points of their earlier sales meeting. The woman had kind of a squeaky voice, and that seemed strange given her ample girth. Meadow was only half listening, her thoughts often wandering to Foxfire and the cliff dwelling. The climb up the trail became quite steep at one point and, with the extra effort, Spot suddenly passed gas noisily which made the woman to pause in her recital.

"Please excuse me and my horse!" she squeaked loudly to the group.

Meadow burst out giggling, and the woman turned around and joined her with a great squeaking laugh.

The Brighten River was swollen from the melting snow higher in the mountains, and as they approached the ford, Paul held up his reins and glanced around, like he was looking for a different way across the water.

Mike stopped before the crossing and had everyone gather around him. "Whoever wants to ride across, just stay put. The rest of you can walk on the footbridge."

Meadow frowned at Mike's disregard for Monty's instructions. She could only hope he knew what he's doing.

Everyone except Bob Rawlins and Paul Misner opted to walk across the footbridge that was suspended high over the water for hikers. Paul's face was taut, looking at the angry river.

Bob looked at Paul, daring him. "It's okay if you walk across, Paul."

Paul grabbed the horn firmly. "No, no, I enjoy taking risks." His voice was higher than normal. "I'm no sissy."

Mike gave some final advice. "Just stay in the middle of your horse and don't throw him off balance."

Paul looked down at the swollen torrent, chewing on his lip, his face white. Mike and Meadow hazed over the rider-less horses, and then Bob rode across.

Bob yelled back at Paul. "Come on, it's a piece of cake!"

Paul hesitated, as if frozen in place. Mike rode back into the middle of the river, gesturing for him to proceed.

After Paul took a deep breath, he started forward. The large, rounded rocks in the bottom of the river made the footing slippery and the horse went side to side making his way across.

Brandy was slipping and sliding, with Paul trying his best to stay centered. Then the horse went down onto one knee. Paul lost his stirrups and slid to one side.

He grabbed desperately at the saddle. "Oh my God!"

Mike called to him. "Pull yourself back up, he won't go down!"

Brandy scrambled to regain his footing, but instead of pulling himself back onto the middle of the saddle, Paul panicked, let go and fell headlong into the murky, raging waters.

Meadow recoiled in horror as he was swept downriver end-over-end, gasping for breath with his arms flailing. She jumped Rex into the river, but Mike was ahead of her, already spurring Rowdy into action. His colt leapt forward and plunged through the torrent to get ahead of Paul, with Meadow coming from the other side. The floundering man hit a submerged tree and frantically grabbed onto a branch.

Seconds later, Mike and Rowdy made it to the tree, the water chest high on the colt. Mike reached down with his hand. "Grab on and I'll pull you up behind me."

Meadow couldn't believe it, when instead of grabbing Mike's hand, Paul whimpered. "No, I can't let go." He blinked repeatedly and she couldn't tell if it was the rivulets of water from the dunking, or tears that were streaking his colorless face.

Just then, the branch let go and Paul was again taken by the violent flow. Mike was ready when the limb broke loose. He quickly thrust Rowdy in front of Paul to block his way and reached down to grab hold of his arm. Rowdy planted his feet, his flanks quivering with exertion, and he braced himself against the current, standing steady. Mike lifted Paul's lean body and pulled him up behind his saddle. Brandy had already made it to the far bank and Meadow joined him and the rest of the group there.

Mike arrived and deposited his rescued passenger onto the ground with an unceremonious thump. Paul's legs gave out and he fell into a heap. His skinny, dripping body shook, but he was otherwise unhurt. The group broke out into a spontaneous cheer and applause. Mike dismounted to give Rowdy a breather, patting him affectionately.

"Mike, you're a hero!" Bob Rawlins slapped him on his back. "And that buckskin is a fantastic animal! Do you want to sell him? I'll give you a good price."

Mike stiffened and replied shortly, "No, he's not for sale."

But Meadow knew all the colts Mike broke for her father were for sale. Her heart went out to him. He was especially fond of Rowdy. How would she feel if her father sold Foxfire?

Mike hastily changed the subject. "Do you want to continue the ride? We're at least half an hour from the gorge."

Bob Rawlins made a quick decision. "Sure, let's go on. No use spoiling a fine day because of a little mishap. Paul will dry out."

Paul Misner frowned, but shakily climbed back on Brandy while Meadow held the reins. His teeth chattered from the icy dunking and his hair was plastered against his skull. Spot's lady took pity on him, offering her sweatshirt, which he accepted with a brief nod.

They reached the gorge and the group all seemed suitably awed, judging by their comments. It *was* an awe inspiring sight with the waterfall rushing down a narrow chasm, and the spray sprinkling over them where they stood peering over the side. The dark green moss-covered boulders, with water roiling and gushing up and around them, gave the impression the whole area was from another, more pristine age. Meadow felt privileged to see such beauty. It was a magical place, like the cave she had found. She wondered if the Indians that had lived there had also frequented this place. It had the same special feel about it.

A faint trail led down to a crystal clear, reflective pool. Someone long ago had put a nail in a nearby tree and hung a tin drinking cup on it. Everyone sampled the water and declared it the sweetest they had ever drunk.

The hotel had provided box lunches for the riders, so they pulled them out of their saddle bags and found various rocks and logs to sit on to enjoy their repast. Spot's lady was the only female in the group, so Meadow found a place near her and sat down. Her lunch wasn't quite as fancy as what the hotel had packed, but she was happy with her peanut butter sandwich. Kelsey sat eyeing it, and she tossed her half.

The rest of the group were all together, chatting and laughing, but Paul sat by himself in the oversized sweatshirt, looking miserable.

"You know Paul brings all his problems on himself." Spot's lady said conspiratorially. "He's always negative and doesn't make a lot of friends."

Meadow nodded. "He's not very nice."

"He was an accountant, but decided he'd like to try sales. I heard it was because he finally has a girlfriend and is trying to impress her. I think he's upset because he didn't make his bonus." The woman chattered some more, and then got up to speak with her boss.

When the woman showed up, Mike moved from his spot near Bob Rawlins and sat down next to Paul. He must be trying to smooth things over, Meadow thought. She got up and came closer to them, thinking she might be able to help. Dad would be livid about the river incident.

Mike worked on Paul. "You know, you were doing real well crossing the river until that darn horse almost went down. Shoot. That accident could have happened to anyone."

Paul just glared at him.

Mike sat for a moment, and then tried a different approach. "See those mounds over there on the right?" He pointed to some lumpy areas near where they were sitting. "They're Indian burial grounds."

"Really?" Paul perked up a little. "Do you know which tribe?"

"Apache, I guess, or maybe Shonto. I'm not sure. All I know is that the graves have been robbed and now the sheriff keeps a pretty sharp eye out for pot hunters." Mike was on a roll. "But I know of a place that has lots of artifacts that are all intact."

Meadow sucked in her breath, but now Paul was all ears. "Where might that be?" His nose wrinkled slightly, like he was catching a good scent.

She stared daggers at her brother, willing him to be quiet.

Mike saw her reaction and became evasive. "Oh, it's a day's ride from here. Near where we take the pack trips." He turned to the rest of the group. "Did any of you know there are wild horses around here?"

Spot's lady lit up. "Where are they? Will we see them?"

"Not today, probably. I've seen them plenty of times, though. They're led by a giant silver stallion. Some say he's a phantom horse." He turned to Meadow. "Tell them the poem you wrote."

Meadow felt her face flush, and she gave him a furious look. She had written the poem after her father told her the legend, thinking he was an imaginary horse, but she knew now he was real. She certainly didn't want to share it with a bunch of strangers.

Seeing that Meadow wasn't about to cooperate, Mike forged ahead. "I remember some of it . . ." He began to recite:

They called him Arrow and 'twas a good name
For a beautiful wild horse that no one could tame.
He ran like the wind, was wild as waves on the sea
The only thing that he wanted was to always run free.

Mike thought for a minute, then shrugged. "I don't know the rest, but it ends up with Arrow getting trapped by the horse hunters and jumping off a cliff to his death instead of being captured. But there are some people who still see him running on the plains when there's a full moon. Something like that . . . I thought it was pretty good for a kid. And it really describes that stallion perfectly." Mike beamed at his rapt audience.

Meadow had grown cold, but could feel a trickle of sweat run down her back. What a jerk—he'd do anything to make a good tip. She vowed to never tell him anything again.

Spot's lady apparently saw how embarrassed she was. "I think it's a beautiful poem." She patted Meadow's shoulder.

Meadow offered a shy smile and felt a little better.

After entertaining the group, Mike became businesslike. "Okay, everyone, time to mount up and head for home."

This time when they crossed the river, everyone walked across the bridge and they arrived back at the stable without any further problems. The riders dismounted and Monty helped tend to the horses. All the male riders except Paul handed Mike a nice tip for his heroism and entertaining stories. Spot's lady handed Meadow a dollar, which was the most she'd ever made on a tip.

Meadow saw that her mother was back from the pack trip and went to greet her with a hug. "I'm so glad you're back, Mom." She looked around. "Where's Daddy?"

"He went to the resort office to settle the account with Wendell." Mom's brow puckered. "What is wrong with that man?"

"He's mad 'cuz he fell into the river."

Her mother paled. "What!" She hurried over to where Bob Rawlins and Paul Misner stood and asked them what happened.

Bob Rawlins, ignoring Paul's dark look, enthusiastically told her about the exciting events. "That was by far the best trail ride I've ever been on! Your son is a hero, rescuing Paul here from the river."

Her mother sucked in a breath. "Are you all right?"

Paul was about to answer, but Bob's loud voice boomed out again.

"And your son's nice buckskin horse, why, I offered to buy him, but Mike said he wasn't for sale. Here's my card in case you change your mind. If I could get that buckskin, I would buy horses for my whole family."

Meadow's stomach twinged. Mom looked a little strained, but she took the card. "I'll give this to Shep when he gets back." She turned to Paul. "Are you okay, now? I'm so sorry about what happened."

Paul gave her a sickly smile. "I'm fine. I found out some interesting things about the Indians who used to live here."

Meadow couldn't stand it anymore and went in search of her father at the general store. If he wasn't done with his meeting yet, she would wait and walk home with him. When she got there, the sign said closed, but she tried the door and it was unlocked. Quietly entering the store, she could hear her father and Wendell talking in the office behind the sales counter. Some of the tourist trinkets were fascinating to her and she tiptoed over to them. The voices carried to where she stood, checking out the dolls dressed in Indian attire.

Her father was speaking. "It seemed like a good deal when I talked it over with Bill, but with the cut you say he wants of the profits, we'll barely make ends meet."

Wendell's tone was smooth. "Just wait until the 4th of July. You'll have so many riders, you'll have to add more horses. And this Saturday, we're having the saloon dance. With more people around for that, you're sure to pick up customers."

"Actually, we have quite a few customers, but Bill never mentioned it would be a twenty-five percent cut to the resort when I signed on for the summer. I figured he would want something, but that seems a little steep to me." Her father sounded angry.

"Don't worry, Shep. It'll work out. Mr. Bowman wants me to handle the financial details for the resort. After all, you're getting a free cabin and the stables included in the deal."

"It better work out. I spent every last penny on buying horses and tack to get this thing running. When is Bill getting back?"

"Any time now. Like I said, don't worry, it will work out."

Meadow could hear the chairs move and then her father came out. She rushed over to him and flung herself in his arms. "Daddy! I'm so happy you're back!"

He squeezed her to him. "I missed you too, sweetheart. Let's go home."

The sun was behind the ponderosas by the time they walked into the stable yard. As they entered the small cabin, Meadow smelled the aroma of pork chops her mother was frying on the wood stove. Monty was reading by the light of a kerosene lamp, and Mike was lolling on her cot.

Her father planted a kiss on her mother's cheek, and sat down at the table, looking stern.

"Monty told me about the girl getting dumped off Foxy."

Foxfire had been gone a whole day now and a chill passed through Meadow. "We have to find her."

Her father smiled reassuringly. "Foxy will come home. I'll bet she's back by Saturday."

"Do you really think so?"

"I'm positive. She doesn't want to be a wild horse. She wants to see you and have cookies all the time." He winked at her, and she smiled in relief.

"I can't wait till she's back, I miss her sooo much."

Her mother served dinner and after they all gathered around the table, she mentioned the mishap with Paul Misner. Dad's face took on that dangerous look, and he didn't hold back.

"Two customers off their horses in two days. That's not good. We have to do better than that or we can't stay in this business. Your mother and I should never have both gone on that pack trip and left you kids to run the stable. Foxy will never be suitable for a dude horse, and Mike, you should never have crossed the river with guests this early in the season."

He gave the boys a thunderous look. They shifted in their seats and looked down at their plates uncomfortably.

Then Meadow spoke up. "You should have seen that guy Paul, though. He looked just like a drowned rat!" She made a face with her lips curled and her teeth sticking out. Even her father laughed at that. But her mother gave her a severe look. "Meadow, you mustn't make fun of how people look."

Meadow didn't say anything, but Mike kicked her under the table, and slyly stuck out his front teeth. She suppressed a giggle.

"Oh, that reminds me." Her mother pulled a card out of her back pocket. "Bob Rawlins gave me his card. He's interested in buying Rowdy and three more horses for the rest of his family."

"Rowdy's pretty young for an inexperienced rider." Her father frowned, taking the card.

"Yes, that's what I thought, too. Maybe you can interest him in one of the older horses." Mom sounded hopeful, glancing at Mike.

Mike sat perfectly still, holding his breath.

Dad cut his meat. "We'll see."

Meadow saw Mike's face tighten, and for once he didn't have anything to say.

After dinner, the family was quiet, each lost in their own world, as they walked across the footbridge to the pool.

Meadow bit her lip. Surely her father would find a different horse to sell to Bob Rawlins so Mike could keep Rowdy.

It was Thursday. Only one more day to wait until Foxy would be home!

Chapter 11

The Dance

Meadow sprang out of bed at the sound of a whinny. Foxy!

Not bothering to pull on her jeans, she rushed outside into the dawning light in her knee-length tee-shirt. Foxfire trotted to the porch and put her head down to nuzzle Meadow affectionately.

Tears of happiness streamed down her face. "Oh, Foxy, I missed you so much!" After checking her mare over, she poured out a big bucket of oats and led her to the corral. She was sitting on the fence watching Foxfire eat when her father came out of the cabin and ambled over.

"Didn't I tell you she'd be back by Saturday?"

Meadow looked at him with wonder. "How did you know?"

"Horses are creatures of habit. Once she got done with her little adventure, she started missing her family here. So she came home. Of course, that stallion may try to lure her back. Stallions don't like to lose mares."

Meadow nodded.

Her father went on. "And by the way, I saw Brett and he told me the so-called wild stallion is really from the Bowman Ranch. Bill recently imported him from Mexico to improve his remuda of ranch horses. The stallion is a purebred Andalusian that was raised on a huge Mexican Rancho. A few weeks ago he jumped out of his corral and joined the mustangs up on the range."

Meadow felt a little pang. "Really?" She didn't want her father to know she thought the stallion was Arrow.

"What's an Andalusian?" she asked. Being horse crazy, she knew most of the breeds, but hadn't heard of that one.

"It's an ancient Spanish breed. They were originally bred as war horses, but now are used for bullfighting and are often highly trained for dressage. Very similar to Lippizans."

"Oh, yeah, I've seen pictures of them rearing on their hind legs and kicking out. I read that was how they were trained to intimidate their enemies by jumping high and kicking. Aren't they always white?"

"Not always, but most of the ones they use as show horses are. Actually they're black when they're born, but gradually turn gray and then white by the time they are trained enough for the show ring."

Meadow spoke without thinking. "So the dapple grey stallion must be pretty young, he's still dark with a silver mane and tail."

Dad raised his eyebrows. "I didn't know you saw him that clearly. Brett said he's only six years old, same as Foxy."

"Wow, Foxy's going to have a beautiful baby. Half Andalusian and half Arabian."

"Yes, it should be a beauty. But I wonder how Bill feels about his prized stallion breeding with our mare."

Her father left to get some firewood for the stove, doing Meadow's chore to allow her a few more minutes alone with Foxfire. It made her smile to picture the stallion and her mare frolicking and racing across the valley together, and a foal coming in spring. She couldn't help feeling a little let down, though, that the stallion didn't appear to be Arrow after all. It seemed her imagination had gotten the best of her again. Oh, well, she had Foxy back and that's all that really mattered. When Mom called her for breakfast, she reluctantly got down from the fence. Ugh, another work day, but at least she had something to look forward to. Tonight was the first dance of the season at the saloon.

After a busy day of horse rides, they all marched to the bathhouse earlier than usual, excitement in the air. Meadow couldn't wait to see Linda again, and maybe even Brett. It would be fun to listen to some music, and maybe dance, if anyone asked her. The band would be playing rock and roll as well as country western, so there should be something fun to dance to.

For this special event, they all put on their fancy western garb. Her father wore his good Stetson and calf-skin boots that he had traded a pony for, and her mother was all dolled up in a square-dancing skirt with lots of petticoats. The boys had on new fancy western shirts their mother had sewn for them the winter before.

Even Meadow had on a skirt, which felt strange to her. She never wore anything but jeans or shorts in the summertime. She hoped no one noticed her legs that were scraped and scratched from exploring and bushwhacking through the brambles. She held up a small mirror and brushed her hair until it glistened and then tied it back with a red ribbon.

The family walked together from the bathhouse to the boardwalk of the old west town. It was mainly a façade of storefronts made to look old for the amusement of the resort guests. Meadow loved it because she enjoyed pretending she was living in a Zane Grey novel. They made their way to the saloon and went through the double swinging doors.

Meadow hadn't been in the saloon before and looked around with interest. The hardwood floors were strewn with sawdust and a large open dance area was surrounded by small tables. A raised bandstand took up one end of the room, and adorning the other end was a massive fireplace with an enormous buffalo head presiding over it. The buffalo's glowering look made her think he was mad about being hung on a wall instead of alive and roaming the hills.

The long antique bar with high stools had patrons already sitting at it, some drinking beer, others with Cokes. Behind the bar was an immense mirror encased in a beautiful ornately carved frame. Meadow loved the old west paintings and western artifacts hanging on the walls. It seemed Bill Bowman had spared no expense to give the guests a good time and make them feel like they were living in a bygone era.

The band was already playing and a few dancers were on the floor.

Wendell Halstead and his wife, Lucy, came over to greet them. The last time they had seen Lucy, her hair had been jet black. Tonight, her hair was an amazing shade of orange-red. Meadow couldn't help staring. It looked kind of like a bonfire on top of her head. Her mother finally gave her a little nudge to show she was being rude.

Wendell showed them to a table. "You folks are looking mighty spiffy tonight."

Lucy grinned, showing all her big teeth. "I'm so glad you could make it." She wore bright blue eye shadow and intense orange-red lipstick to match her hair.

Wendell and Lucy sat down with them at a table not too close to the band, but where they had a good view of the dancers. Wendell told them this was their first season at the resort, too. They had taken over when the previous manager had retired, and Wendell went on to say how much more profit the resort was making, now that he and Lucy had assumed responsibility.

The Bowman family was all there, except for Bill, who was still away on business. Meadow hadn't seen Mrs. Bowman since the introduction at the pool. She had seen Linda and Brett occasionally in passing, but with dude rides taking up all her time, hadn't had a chance to talk much.

She really liked Linda, who had lively brown eyes and a sweet smile. It was too bad they weren't closer in age. She was so interesting. Meadow watched as a line of suitors waited to dance with her. Must be nice to be so popular. Linda picked an attractive young man from the line that Meadow didn't know.

Linda was nice, but her brother, Brett, was a different story. Fifteen, good looking, and full of himself. He was polite to her, but she could tell he thought she was just a kid and didn't deserve much attention. Like his sister, he was tall and had sandy blonde hair, but his eyes were a deep blue. Meadow felt like she swallowed a lemon when she saw him head for their table. He pulled out a chair and sat next to her.

He looked her up and down. "So you *do* have legs. I've never seen you in a dress before, and you finally brushed your hair. A remarkable improvement."

Meadow could feel a hot blush suffuse her face.

"I heard your mare came home. I'm glad you got her back." Brett looked around the rest of the table. "And just to let everyone know, Dad is offering a thousand dollar reward for the safe return of our stallion, Diablo. After I help move some cows to summer range, I'm going to look for him. Anyone that wants to come along is welcome."

Before Meadow could say she would love to go look for the stallion, Mary Bowman approached the table. She was wearing an elegant cocktail dress and an expensive looking necklace with red stones.

"Hello, everyone, I hope you're all having a good time," she said.

Her father stood up. "Hello, Mary, would you like to join us?"

"No, thank you, I'm sitting with them." She nodded toward some people that looked like resort guests. "I came over to invite Meadow and the boys to help with the cattle drive, if they would like to."

Her father grinned broadly. "Well, that's a fine offer and we appreciate you thinking of the kids. Unfortunately, the boys can't help out, they have to work at the stable. We could probably spare Meadow, though."

"Oh boy, I get to go on a cattle drive—I've always wanted to do that!" Meadow bounced in her seat, then embarrassed at her outburst, clamped her lips.

Brett snorted amusement, and Mrs. Bowman smiled at her. "Yes, you can come up to the ranch tomorrow and stay for a few days. Linda will be delighted that you can visit. It gets pretty lonely out at the ranch sometimes." From her expression, Meadow wasn't sure if she was talking about herself or Linda.

Mrs. Bowman looked around for her daughter, and her jaw tightened as she saw Linda still dancing with the same attractive young man. The song ended and Linda brought her dance partner over to the table.

"This is Dave Redland. He's the new deputy assigned to Brighten." Linda still held onto his hand.

Dave seemed a little older than Linda and was tanned, as though he spent a lot of time outdoors. His dark hair was carefully smoothed down and combed for the dance.

"Hello, nice to meet you." He stood back a little and Linda pulled him forward.

"This is my mother, Mary Bowman."

Mrs. Bowman offered him her hand, but her face was stern. "I see you've been monopolizing my daughter. I think you had better give the other young men a chance to dance with her."

Dave glanced around at the other men still waiting in the wings for Linda. "Oh, I guess you're right." He didn't relinquish her hand, though.

A popular Elvis tune, "Love me Tender", started to play and Linda smiled at Dave as he steered her to the dance floor. They brushed by a sleazy looking man who seemed to be about to approach her. He was the same man Meadow had noticed speaking at length with Wendell, so she guessed they knew each other. But for the last few minutes he had just been hanging around Linda, obviously smitten.

The man was wearing a black leather jacket, tight black jeans and had longish, greasy-looking hair. He stood watching Dave and Linda dance, with an unpleasant sneer on his face. Meadow thought he looked out of place here, but then her attention was diverted by her father.

"May I have this dance, young lady?" Dad bowed in front of her.

Meadow giggled. "Yes, you may."

Mrs. Bowman rejoined the group of guests she had been sitting with, and Lucy went in search of an adult beverage at the bar.

Wendell asked Mom to dance, and they went out onto the floor, next to Meadow and her father. She noticed Wendell was rather light on his feet given that he looked something like a bowling pin with legs.

After the dance, Meadow came back to the table where Brett, Monty, and Mike were discussing the new Corvette that had just come out of Detroit. They were interrupted by a cute blonde girl in a flouncy dress bouncing up to the table.

"Hi Monty!" Cynthia beamed at him.

"Oh, hi, Cynthia," he mumbled.

"Aren't you going to ask me to dance?"

"Yeah, sure." Monty rose stiffly, and took her proffered hand. They began dancing right next to the table.

Mike and Brett looked at each other and snickered.

After a few minutes, Cynthia's father stalked over to the dancing couple.

"Cynthia! What do you think you're doing? I said you could come to the dance, but you're supposed to sit quietly and watch. You know you have a head injury and still get dizzy spells." Ben Markowitz did not look at all happy.

"Oh, Daddy, please, just this one dance? I promise to sit after this. It's a slow one."

"I'll bring her right back after this dance." Monty actually seemed to be enjoying himself.

Ben Markowitz agreed to let them finish the dance, grumbling to himself as he walked away. The ditzy blond smiled happily and put her head on Monty's shoulder. After the dance, they sat down together before Cynthia went back to her table.

"We're leaving tomorrow." She batted her long lashes and turned her mouth down at the corners.

Monty's surprise showed on his face. "I thought you were here for another week."

"We're leaving early because of the accident. Daddy wants me to go to a specialist for my dizzy spells."

"But you saw Dr. Weaver right after the fall and he said you are fine. Nothing to worry about."

"Well, you know how Daddy is. He doesn't think anyone knows anything unless they're from Scottsdale. I feel fine, I'm sure there's nothing wrong with me. And, I hate to leave early. I'm having such a good time this year. Better than any other year we've come here." Her lashes fluttered again.

Monty's face turned crimson. "I'm having a good time, too. I wish you weren't going."

"Will you write to me?"

"Sure, I guess so." Monty got a worried expression. "But I'm not much of a letter writer."

"Oh, any letter will do. I'd better go back now." They stood and she tucked her hand into the crook of Monty's arm as he escorted her back to her parents' table.

Cynthia smiled sweetly. "'Bye, Monty. Remember your promise."

Markowitz glared at Monty.

The band kept playing and the dancing continued into the night. Brett finally asked Meadow to dance. She thought his mother had probably told him he *had* to ask her. It was a fast country swing and he was a good partner. He seemed a little surprised that she kept up with him so well. He twirled her and she spun out and back, never missing a step.

"Hey, you're a pretty good dancer, for a kid," Brett said when the music stopped.

"Thanks, you too."

Meadow danced with some of the other young people, but none executed the steps as well as Brett. She was disappointed he didn't ask her again, but saw that he had plenty of other partners.

As the night wore on, more and more people arrived, until the saloon was filled, including the patio area to the rear. Meadow wandered out to get some fresh air and recognized the group from the gorge ride seated with several tables pulled together.

Lucy was sitting with them, laughing too loudly, and regaling them with boisterous stories. Off to one side, Wendell was speaking with Paul Misner, the man who had fallen into the river.

Meadow maneuvered her way back inside in time to see Linda finishing up a dance with the unsavory man in the black jacket. Linda was probably just being polite, because it was clear that now she was trying to get away from him.

He kept trying to engage her in conversation and she would answer, but then turn to the other young people. It was obvious he'd been drinking too much. Dave was keeping an eye on him, apparently not liking his surly demeanor. The man finally pushed the limit by grabbing Linda's arm and pulling her towards the dance floor again.

"Come on, sweet lady, it's my turn." He started forward, towing her along.

Linda tried to twist away from him. "Let go of me!"

In an instant, Dave Redland was at her side and shoved the man away. The man stumbled and then swiftly turned and punched Dave square in the stomach. Dave gasped and hunched over in pain. Taking a deep breath, he recovered quickly, and as he rose up, he sent a hard right to the stranger's jaw. The man went reeling backward and Dave dove onto him as they both went to the floor, each struggling to gain dominance over the other.

Everyone in the saloon gathered around, watching the young men thrash about. Dad strode over to intervene. "Hey, you young pups, what's all this about?" He grabbed the stranger by his leather jacket and pulled him away from Dave.

"That's enough fighting. You boys simmer down and act like adults." Dad chastised them as he would Monty and Mike, whose fights he had broken up many times. His words calmed the situation, and the stranger glowered at Dave, but stalked off in silence. Dave was puffing and his face was red as he watched the other man retreat. He turned to Dad.

"Thanks, Shep. I'm glad you broke it up. The sheriff will be pretty mad at me if he finds out about this."

"Oh, I doubt he'll find out." Dad glanced around the room. "Nobody here will say anything, right? After all, you were just helping a lady in distress."

Everyone nodded and murmured their agreement with that.

Dad called over to the lead guitarist. "How about some music, boys?"

The band started playing again and the dancing resumed.

Linda smiled at Dave and they danced, heads close. Meadow smiled dreamily. What a wonderful couple, so sweet together. They didn't even notice the black jacketed man shoving his way through the crowd, on through to the back patio, but Meadow did.

He's up to no good, she thought, and followed him out. When she got outside, he was having an angry discussion with Wendell and Paul Misner. Meadow couldn't hear the exact words, but it was something about keeping a low profile. Wendell was waving his short arms around and getting funny red splotches on his face. Before long, the man in the black jacket slunk away. Wendell and Paul sat down at a table and pulled their chairs close. It was pretty weird that they all knew each other. Definitely three of a kind.

When Meadow made her way back inside she saw that Mike and Brett were having a competition to see how many girls they could each dance with. She wrinkled her nose. It was disgusting how they were carrying on. She swallowed hard, and plopped down morosely next to her parents.

"Don't worry, honey," Mom consoled her, "your time will come. Don't try to grow up too fast."

"Well, I think you're the prettiest gal here, except for your mother, of course. In another couple of years, you'll be the belle of the ball," her father added.

Meadow tried to smile, but didn't feel much like it. She'd even brushed her hair.

Monty was also sitting at their table looking down in the mouth. He'd apparently decided not to dance anymore since Cynthia had been firmly escorted away by her father.

It was past midnight when Dad declared the kids had enough partying for one night. He rounded up Mike, who protested vehemently, and they all headed for the cabin.

Meadow was ready to leave. It had been a little disappointing that she didn't get to dance more. But she couldn't wait for her visit to the Bowman Ranch the next day. A real cattle drive!

After she was in bed that night, her thoughts went to the silver stallion. She was still convinced there must be something special about him. She just had to discover what it was.

Chapter 12

The Ranch

The next morning dawned sunny and warm, with Meadow up early and waiting impatiently for Linda to pick her up. Linda had insisted on bringing the horse trailer, even though Meadow told her she could just ride out to the ranch.

It was after eleven when Linda finally arrived. "Sorry I'm so late. I didn't get to bed until three a.m."

Meadow noticed her faraway look. "That's okay, you must have been having a good time."

"Yes, I had a wonderful time."

After Meadow loaded Foxfire into the trailer, Kelsey jumped into the back of the pickup, intending to go along. "Kelsey, you weren't invited." She was about to get her out, when Linda put her hand on her arm.

"Oh, let her come, I'll bet she's a good cow dog."

Before they left, Meadow poked her head into the cabin.

"'Bye, Mom, we're leaving now. And so you don't worry, Kelsey is coming along."

Her mother laughed. "What a surprise. 'Bye honey, have a good time."

Meadow put her small suitcase in the back of the truck, and they headed out on the five-mile drive to the Bowman Ranch headquarters, due east from the Brighten Resort. It was pretty slow going on the gravel road, and in places they had to cross washouts. Linda drove carefully so she wouldn't jar Foxfire too much.

Meadow squirmed. It would have been faster to ride out.

Wondering if Linda wanted to talk about her new beau, Meadow tested the waters. "Dave seems like a nice guy."

"He's the most interesting guy I've ever met in these parts. We just talked and talked last night." Linda got that swoony look again, but then her face turned serious. "But I don't think Mother approves of him. She's originally from New York City and can be a trifle stuffy. She thinks I need a proper husband that's a doctor or a lawyer. I plan on choosing my own boyfriends, though."

This was a different side of Linda that Meadow hadn't seen before, and she looked at her with new respect.

"Well, I'm on your side. I think Dave is great. Just look how he defended you last night. Not every guy will punch someone for you."

Linda's face broke into a grin. "That's for sure."

They drove along through beautiful scenery, with tall pines interspersed with some oaks and cottonwoods near the streams. Then the trees opened up to a pretty valley and Meadow saw the ranch house in the center of it on a small knoll. Off to the side sat a large barn and various size corrals.

They drove through the ranch gate under a hanging sign proclaiming it to be the Bowman Ranch, with the Lazy B brand next to the name. The house was a southwestern style hacienda made of adobe, with blossoming shrubs and trees all around it for shade. Meadow immediately felt like she belonged at the ranch and thought how lucky she was that the older girl liked her. Linda drove on to the barn. It was built in the same style adobe as the house and had stalls with paddocks off them.

They unloaded Foxfire, and led her into the barn. Linda showed Meadow a stall all prepared with fresh straw for her horse. As soon as she was loose, Foxfire trotted out into her paddock to investigate her surroundings.

"I just love your ranch, it's so wonderful," Meadow said.

"Yes, I love it, too. We've been coming up here in the summer since I was ten years old. But it's always nice to share it with someone, so I'm really happy you're here."

"Thanks, I know I'll have a great time."

"Yes, we will." Linda put her arm around Meadow. "Let me show you the house."

"Okay." Meadow turned to her dog. "Kelsey, stay with Foxy. Good girl."

The girls left Foxfire, with Kelsey to keep her company, and went to the house. It was shaped like a U, with the living room, dining room and kitchen in the middle, and bedrooms off to both sides. In the center of the U was a tranquil courtyard with beautiful flowering lavender, honeysuckle and other plants, and a huge fountain, with water splashing through it. Most of the rooms of the home opened into the courtyard.

Meadow was entranced by the house, which was luxurious in an understated way. The furnishings were different than any she was familiar with. "I've never seen a house that looks like this, it's beautiful."

"Mother is an interior decorator, besides owning an art gallery. She picked out all of the pieces in here. Dad has an import business, and he gets in a lot of items from Spain and Mexico,"

"Your family is soo interesting." Meadow gazed around with a touch of envy.

Linda shrugged. "I think you have a wonderful family. And they're pretty interesting, too." She showed Meadow to her room to get unpacked.

It was bright and sunny and had a bathroom off the back. Meadow grinned. That was a real improvement over the outhouse at the stable.

"Have you ever slept on a real feather bed?" Linda asked.

Meadow looked at the enormous bed with a carved wooden headboard against one wall in the middle of the room.

"No, but I'll bet I can get used to it pretty fast. And I will definitely try out the shower!"

Linda laughed. "That's for later. Right now, Lupe has lunch ready for us. Let's go eat."

Lunch was served to them by their Mexican cook in the big dining room. Mrs. Bowman and Brett were already seated at the large Spanish style dining table when the girls walked in.

"Well, if it isn't my little dancing partner," Brett said.

Meadow smiled at him, then glanced toward his mother, who indicated a chair for her.

"Welcome to our home. I know you will have a good time here, but please, let me know if you need anything to make you more comfortable," she said.

"Everything is just great. Thanks for inviting me." Meadow sat in the tall upright chair.

They ate tacos that Lupe had prepared. It was Meadow's first taste of Mexican food and she knew it was going to be a favorite from then on.

After lunch, she went with Linda and Brett for a ride to the lower pasture where the cattle were being held before the drive. Brett was riding a good-looking red roan gelding and Linda was on a pretty bay mare. When Kelsey saw the herd, her ears pricked up eagerly.

"How many cowboys will it take to move the herd?" Meadow asked.

"Actually, they practically move themselves," Brett said. "They're pretty gentle cows, not like in the western movies. It will just be us and Juan, our foreman."

Meadow found out that Lupe and Juan were married and had been with the Bowmans for many years. They had a small house on the ranch, where they lived year 'round as caretakers.

"Does your mother ride?" Meadow asked.

Linda frowned a little. "Not anymore. She had a fall a few years ago and decided she's too old to ride anymore."

Meadow couldn't imagine *her* mother ever getting too old to ride.

They rode to the sorting corrals. "Tomorrow we will tag the calves and separate the steers out so we will be ready for the drive the next day," Brett said.

Meadow checked out all the different pens and chutes. "That will be fun."

They rode back around the herd, then started toward the ranch house.

On the way, she asked Linda about studying archeology. "You said you went on a dig last year. What was it like?"

Linda told her that when she had gone to the Shonto reservation, the Indians had shown them an ancient cave dwelling with some relics inside. Grave robbers had plundered most of the items, but she had been fascinated by it all and decided then and there she wanted to learn everything about that ancient society, and try to preserve what was left of it. "I want to specialize in the Athabaskan culture."

"Athabaskan?"

"Yes, the ancestors of the Shontos, Apaches, and some other local tribes. The Athabaskan tribes originated in southwestern Canada, and migrated into the American southwest sometime after 1400 AD."

Meadow was silent, thinking about the cave she had found. She knew she would share it with Linda, but had to find the right time and place.

"Didn't you say your farrier is a Shonto?" Linda asked.

"Yes, he's my dad's best friend. He lived in Oregon where we're from when he met Dad. Nueme moved back here to the Shonto reservation a couple of years ago because his folks are getting old. My dad got in touch with him when we moved here."

"That's interesting. I'd like to meet him." Linda smiled. "I'm good friends with Chief White Horse, from the local tribe near Sedona."

Out of the corner of her eye, Meadow saw that Brett had gotten that bored look again during the conversation. "I've got an idea, let's go swimming!" he said.

By then, they were back to the ranch and sitting in front of the barn.

"Okay, let's get our suits on," Linda said.

Meadow's face fell. "I didn't bring a suit."

Brett laughed. "Linda has dozens of suits of all shapes and sizes."

Linda nodded. "Maybe not *dozens*, but I'm sure we can find one that will fit you."

They tied their horses to the hitching rail and raced into the house. Linda brought Meadow to her room and started going through her huge closet. Meadow had never in her life seen such a large closet and so many clothes for one person. It was like being in a department store.

Linda saw the look on her face. "My mother is always bringing me clothes from New York." She shook her head. "I'm not really very interested in fashion, but Mother doesn't listen."

She dug around and finally found several outgrown suits for Meadow to try on. "Here, take these to your room and pick the one you like best. Keep them all, if you want."

"Gee, thanks." Meadow was a little overwhelmed by her generosity.

She tried on a couple of suits and found a red one with little white polka dots that fit her perfectly. When she looked in the full length mirror at her image, Meadow was surprised to see how well she filled it out. She hadn't seen her whole body in a mirror for a long time. Her family didn't own one and she rarely went shopping since Mom sewed most of her clothes.

Now that she was close to fourteen years old, suddenly she had curves where none had been before. She shrugged and went to show Linda her pick of the swim suits.

"That's perfect on you. The red really sets off your dark hair."

"Thanks, I love it."

Linda rooted around in the bottom of her bureau and pulled out a couple of outgrown bras. "Here, I think you could use these, too. I've always wanted a little sister to pass things on to."

Meadow felt a lump rise in her throat. "You are so nice."

They pulled on jeans and tee-shirts over their suits then joined Brett for the ride to the swimming hole.

Oak Creek meandered through the ranch and at one point cascaded down through the rocks to form a perfect swimming hole at the bottom. The rocks under this gentle waterfall were worn smooth by eons of flowing water.

After tying their horses, Brett yanked off his polo shirt and jeans. "We call this Slick Rock." He sat down on one of the slippery rocks and slid to the bottom with a big splash into the deep pool.

Linda and Meadow pulled off their outer clothes and followed him in.

The water was much colder than the hot springs swimming pool, and it took Meadow's breath away when she slid down the slippery rock and splashed into the depths. It felt refreshing after the hot ride, though.

After giving a little whine, Kelsey jumped on the rock and slid down, landing with a splash. She dogpaddled around the pool. Everyone laughed, and Meadow called, "Kelsey, go back." Her dog made it over to a low rock and climbed up, shaking herself thoroughly.

Brett and Meadow playfully splashed each other and then jumped off the high rocks surrounding the pool. After a few minutes of swimming, Linda got up on the rocks to sun herself.

"Race you across the pool," Brett said. Meadow saw the dare on his face.

"Sure, let's go!" She swam away.

Even though she had a head start, Brett easily overtook her and won the race.

Meadow tried to look unconcerned. "Let's see who the best diver is. Linda can be the judge."

"Sure, why not?"

After several dives, Linda pronounced Meadow to be the best, because she was the most graceful.

"I guess you're right, she does look pretty graceful in that suit." Brett winked at her.

Meadow felt the red creep up her cheeks, but in a good way.

The afternoon sun was starting to dip in the brilliant blue sky, turning it to purple, when they decided to head for the ranch.

Brett watched as Meadow swung up onto Foxfire. "You've got a nice mare. Is she fast?'

"Pretty fast." She guessed what was coming next.

"Race you back to the gate?" Brett seemed to know the answer already.

Linda sighed. "You two go ahead, I'm going to take my time."

"Okay, let's go!" Meadow allowed Brett to get a jump on her.

It was more than a mile back to the gate, and she was positive her Arabian could beat any Quarter horse at that distance.

Brett's horse exploded into a full run and was five lengths ahead of Meadow by the time she let Foxfire have her head.

Brett looked back and smirked at her, obviously sure that victory would be his. He was galloping at a breakneck speed, bent low over the saddle.

His horse was fast and outdistanced them for the first quarter mile, but Meadow wasn't worried, she just stuck to Foxfire's back like a burr. Up and down the hills and through the trees they galloped, jumping logs and washes.

At a half mile, Foxfire was breathing easily and still lengthening her stride, her ears pinned back in concentration. She reached the gelding's flank and then was neck and neck with him.

Brett gave her a surprised look as Foxfire pulled away, steadily gaining ground, and by the time they arrived at the ranch gate, she was ten lengths ahead and still running easily.

Meadow reined her mare in, and grinned at Brett as he came galloping up. His horse was sweating and breathing heavily from the exertion.

"Wow, she *is* fast. And not even puffing." Brett's voice was full of admiration.

Meadow stroked Foxfire on the neck. "She's an Arabian. She could have run ten more miles. She probably couldn't beat your horse at a quarter mile, but anything over that, watch out!"

"She may be fast, but I doubt she's worth a darn as a cow horse."

Meadow lifted her chin. "She's really smart and I know she'll catch on fast."

Brett held his tongue and they waited for Linda in silence, then rode on to the barn.

That evening, after another delicious meal Lupe had prepared, Meadow followed Linda out into the courtyard. Mary had gone to do some work in her office and Brett disappeared somewhere else. Meadow felt comfortable with Linda, surrounded by the perfume of the roses and the sweet tinkling of the fountain. As they talked, Meadow realized how much she'd missed not having a close girlfriend.

It seemed natural to trust the older girl with the secret of the Indian Cave. It was hard to bring it up, though. She began tentatively. "I have something really important to tell you."

"What is it?"

Her voice cracked a little and it came out in a rush. "I found a cliff dwelling when I was out looking for Foxy. It is totally full of old Indian stuff. Like they left in a hurry and never went back."

Linda's eyes grew wide. "Really? Where? On the ranch?" Meadow nodded.

"Gosh, right under my nose, and I didn't even know about it." Her eyes sparkling, she said, "When can we go see it? Maybe tomorrow . . . oh, the cattle drive. Right after that, okay?"

Meadow tried to slow her down. "Sure, but what about catching Diablo? I thought we were going to find him with Brett right after the drive."

"Didn't you say you were chasing the mustangs when you found the dwelling? Why can't we do both? The cliff dwelling must be on the way."

"Yeah, I guess that will work." Meadow didn't want to douse her enthusiasm, but she didn't think they would have time to see the cave *and* chase the mustangs.

They talked for a while longer and then it was time for bed, since they had to get up early to separate the cattle. But back in her room, Meadow found that she was too keyed up to go to sleep right away, even though the bed looked inviting.

As she opened the patio door and stood gazing out at the starry sky, Meadow realized she had mixed emotions about showing Linda and Brett the Indian cave. She was somewhat hesitant to share it with anyone since it was such a special place to her. It was almost like it was meant for her eyes only, but she knew Linda wouldn't agree with that. The aspiring archeologist believed that the artifacts should be shared and were important for understanding early Indian life.

She didn't really want to chase Diablo, either. In her mind, he was Arrow, the Sky Horse. He shouldn't be in captivity, but running free with his mares. While her rational self knew this couldn't be true, she still couldn't shake the feeling.

No use worrying about it, though. She took a deep breath, and tried to focus on the next day's cow punching. It would be fun ear tagging the youngsters and separating the steers for market. Then the following day they would drive the herd to the summer range. Oh boy, just like in all the western novels she devoured, a real cattle drive.

Eventually the calming music of the fountain and the lure of the comfortable looking bed won her over and she crawled in, sinking blissfully into the deep feather mattress. She drifted off seeing herself chasing the Sky Horse but never catching him.

Chapter 13

The Letter

Rose fretted and tidied the already neat cabin. Meadow had just left that morning for the Bowman Ranch to stay two nights, and she already missed her. Her daughter had never been away from home overnight before. Except when she was in the hospital, sick with asthma. Meadow was not the type of teen that had lots of friends that she spent the night with. She never seemed to want to leave Foxfire or Kelsey behind.

Earlier, Nueme had shown up to shoe some horses, and Shep was with him, catching up on all the news. This was the first time they'd seen their Shonto friend for a long while. The boys were both out guiding dude rides.

Rose ran her fingers through her hair, and headed for the door. Might as well go to the general store for the mail. Not that they got much, but it was something to keep her occupied.

She walked across the dirt street to the store and found Lucy manning the post office. The woman put on her best smile. "Hello, hon. Guess you were able to break away from the stable for a little while?"

Rose nodded. "It's quiet at the moment, so I thought I would pick up our mail."

Lucy turned to the pigeon holes behind her. "I guess you're in luck today." She handed a pink envelope to Rose, and held onto the white one. "Ain't you popular, all of a sudden? Two in one day. And this one looks mighty official." Lucy held it up, peering at it.

Rose held out her hand for the other letter, unsmiling. This woman rubbed her the wrong way. "It seems everyone decided to write us at once."

Lucy pursed her lips. "The official one is from a lawyer. Sure hope there's no trouble, hon."

Rose frowned, glanced at the pink one and saw that it was addressed to Monty in girlish handwriting. She absently stuffed it into her back jean pocket and turned her attention to the formal white envelope. With a sinking feeling she read the return address, "Markowitz, Dahl & Sandler, Partners in Law."Oh, no.

Lucy stared at her expectantly, no doubt hoping she'd open the letter and divulge its contents. Rose wasn't about to humor her nosiness. She thanked her quickly, leaving no room for discussion, and hurried back across the road with the letter heavy in her hand.

As she arrived at the stable, she saw that Shep was still visiting with Nueme. He was done with the shoeing and they were both resting on stumps in front of the tack room. Rose knew that Shep was trying to enlist Nueme's help in finding the Bowman's stallion. His Shonto friend was an expert tracker, and Shep figured together they could capture the stallion and claim the reward. She heard part of their conversation as she lingered near the cabin door, dreading to face the attorney's letter.

"We could sure use that money right now, and I know you could find a use for your share," Shep said.

Nueme grunted. "Could, at that."

Rose had always liked Nueme. His mild, soft-spoken manner covered a tough, resilient man. His black hair was streaked with gray now, but his large farrier forearms were as strong as ever. He and Shep had been best friends ever since she could remember, closer than most brothers.

On occasion, Nueme had told them stories about being taken from his parents as a child and put in a special Indian school. The youngsters were forbidden to speak their native languages or practice their own religion. It broke her heart to think of it. Shep didn't like the stories, though, becoming short and irritable when Nueme spoke of it. Rose knew there was something in Shep's childhood that was wrapped up with Nueme's, but he never told her about it. And she never asked. It must be too painful for him to discuss.

The letter grew heavier the longer she waited. She had procrastinated long enough. Better get it over with. Rose went into the cabin and opened the envelope with shaky hands. She scanned the letter until her eyes zoomed in on the second paragraph.

Cynthia Markowitz, the 14-year-old daughter of Benjamin and Margaret Markowitz, has sustained a substantial head injury resulting from a serious fall after being thrown from the horse Foxfire owned by Shep Shepherd, d/b/a Shepherd's Stable located at Brighten Hot Springs Resort outside of Sedona, Arizona.

The injury was caused as a direct result of the negligence of Shepherd's Stable, located at Brighten Hot Springs Resort, by allowing Miss Markowitz to ride a horse that was well beyond Miss Markowitz' known ability to control. Miss Markowitz continues to have dizzy spells which specialists say could continue indefinitely.

Naturally, we would prefer to settle this without the need for legal action against Shep Shepherd d/b/a Shepherd's Stable, and William F. Bowman owner of the Brighten Hot Springs Resort. I believe that the sum of $5,000 would be a fair amount to compensate the Markowitz family for the permanent damages sustained by Cynthia Markowitz.

The rest of the document blurred, and Rose felt faint. Five thousand dollars. It might as well be a million! Where would they get that kind of money? She was still sitting at the table, with the letter in her hand, when Shep and Nueme walked into the cabin.

"What's wrong?" Shep asked.

She handed him the letter without saying a word.

After reading it, he sighed. "I had a bad feeling about that accident. Don't worry, honey, we'll figure a way out of this mess."

Rose just looked at him. Her head felt like it was about to explode.

Shep patted her shoulder. "I invited Nueme to stay for dinner so we can discuss our strategy for catching the stallion. Okay with you?"

Rose smiled numbly at the Shonto man. "Nueme is always welcome." She went through the motions of preparing dinner as if she were a sleepwalker.

During the meal, the boys talked about the day's rides. It wasn't until afterward that Shep brought up the letter.

"Boys, we got a letter today threatening a lawsuit from that Markowitz guy. I don't want you to worry, but now you know why it's so important to keep all the rides under control. We don't want any more falls or anyone getting hurt." He handed them the document.

For once, Mike didn't make any smart remarks.

Monty took a deep breath. "What are we going to do?"

"I'll take care of it. Meanwhile, let's talk about chasing wild horses," Shep said.

Nueme and the boys all seemed relieved about the change of subject. A plan to catch the stallion was more to their taste than an impending lawsuit. Rose quietly got up to clear the dishes.

Shep pulled out a map he had sketched. "Up above Hidden Valley, where it becomes rim rock country, there's a box canyon that would be perfect if we could drive the mustangs to it." He pointed to the area he was talking about.

"I know the place." Nueme glanced from Monty to Mike. "Once I track the herd and get near enough, we can use relay riders to drive them along,"

"When are we gonna start?" Mike asked. He was always eager for action.

"I'll begin tracking at first light." Nueme stood up to leave. "When I find out where their home range is, then we'll know which way to push 'em. See you tomorrow afternoon to pack our things."

He was about to walk out the door when Rose put her hand on his arm. "Why don't you spend the night? With Meadow away, we have an extra bed. It's just a cot, though."

"That would make it easier, and I've slept in worse." Nueme sat back down at the table.

By the end of the evening, Rose was about ready to snap. Even though they hadn't talked about the letter any more, it was in the back of her mind, fraying her nerves. She crawled into bed next to Shep and felt his strong presence. He took her in his arms. "Don't worry, darlin', I'll figure a way out of this."

The next morning, after Nueme had departed and while the boys were getting the horses ready for the day, Shep and Rose discussed the lawsuit.

"Of course, we don't want to go to court if we can help it, but I'll be damned if I'll pay that so and so a plug nickel." Shep stomped around the room.

Rose had a whole new set of worries. She had tossed and turned all night with the thought of a lawsuit churning through her head. What would happen if Bill Bowman insisted that they leave? Their savings were all tied up in the stable. There would be no hope of making enough money to settle. She firmed her lips. "We can't settle. That girl caused the problem by not listening to Monty in the first place. He said she insisted on riding Foxy. What can we do, Shep? There's no way we can afford a lawyer of our own."

Shep flexed his fist. "Next week, when I go to the auction in Scottsdale, I will just stop in and see this Markowitz fella. I'm not convinced the girl was hurt that bad."

"Me either. She saw the doctor in Sedona and he said she was fine." Rose got up from the table and busied herself rinsing their coffee cups in the dishpan.

"I should have thought more about this riding stable thing before moving you all up here." The fire died from his eyes and Shep shook his head, looking at the floor. "Oh, Rose, you probably regret the day you met me."

Rose felt a pang, and quickly went to him. "Don't be silly, this is just a little setback. We'll get through it all right."

Shep's shoulders slumped. "I'm starting to think this whole Arizona thing was a big mistake."

"How can you say that? Meadow is so much better, you'd hardly know she has asthma anymore."

"What about our future, though? You know I've never worked for anyone. There will be no retirement money. Hell, we don't even own a home or any furniture."

"I have my range and sewing machine." Her attempt at humor fell flat. In all their married life, Rose had never seen Shep look so defeated.

"But I'm getting older and what will happen if I have an accident or get sick? This has made me think about what shaky ground we're on. I know you'd love to have a real home, and someplace to put down roots. I don't know if I can ever get that for you and the kids."

Rose felt like she'd just been run over by a truck. She had never heard him talk like this before. He'd always been her hero and larger than life. It scared her more than the threat of a lawsuit.

She took him in her arms as if she were cradling a baby. "We'll get through this together, as a family." Her voice was firm and steady. "We always do."

106

Chapter 14

The Cattle Drive

The day of the cattle drive, Meadow's eyes flew open at first light, anticipation coursing through her veins. It was going to be a glorious day. A brilliant, fiery sunrise lit her room as she jumped out of bed and pulled on her jeans. She rushed into the dining room to find Brett already seated and ready for breakfast.

He looked at her with a smile playing on his lips. "Good morning, Wild Woman."

"Morning." Meadow realized she had forgotten to brush her hair, again. "Uh, excuse me, I'll be back in a second."

She turned and fled to her room. Quickly running the brush through the tangled mass, she pulled it into a ponytail, and then came slinking back into the dining room.

Brett laughed. "Much better. Although I didn't really mind you appearing *au natural*. It's nice to meet a girl that's not hung up on her looks."

"Thanks . . ."

"And by the way, I wanted to tell you that you were a big help yesterday tagging calves. You're pretty tough."

"I thought it was a lot of fun. I can't wait to start on the drive."

Linda joined them and they dined heartily on *huevos rancheros* with homemade tortillas. Lupe served everyone with her usual good-natured smile.

"Where's your mom?" Meadow asked.

"Mother doesn't rise this early. She says ranch life doesn't really fit her rhythm, whatever that means." Linda rolled her eyes. "Dad's the one that really loves this place. He's crazy about everything western."

"Probably because he was raised back east," Brett said. "We totally agree with him."

Linda nodded. "If it were up us, we wouldn't live anywhere else."

"I can see why," Meadow said. "I love the ranch and all of Brighten."

They finished breakfast, then saddled their horses and joined Juan, who was already waiting for them. When they'd rounded up the fifty cows, with calves alongside them, Meadow understood why Brett had said they were easy to move. The lead cow headed up the trail without any prompting, having done this route every summer for years, and the herd fell in behind. Of course, every once in a while, one would get tired of the constant moving and break out of the pack.

A big red cow suddenly decided she didn't want to follow the others and dashed toward the trees. Meadow saw her and urged Foxfire forward to get the cow back in line. Foxfire flattened her ears and jumped in front of the cow to cut her off before she made it to the brush. The cow scooted to the side and tried to go around her, but Foxfire rolled back on her hind legs, spun and cut her off. Every turn she made, Foxfire was there first. Finally, the cow gave up and docilely followed the rest of the herd.

Meadow turned and smiled at Brett. "I guess Foxy *is* a good cow horse. She likes bossing cows around."

Brett didn't appear too happy about being proved wrong, but grudgingly admitted that Foxfire was quick to catch on. "I'm impressed that you can stick with her so well. At least you're riding a saddle today."

"I had to, so I could tie on my bedroll and supplies. I'll probably get saddle sores."

"Fat chance," Brett said.

Kelsey had proved to be a big help, too, for the cows that wanted to hide in the brush. She would dart in after them and nip their heels until they gave up and joined the herd again.

Since they had started out early morning, and made good time, they were more than halfway to the summer grazing when they stopped for lunch. Meadow was hungry and thankful that Lupe had packed several kinds of sandwiches along with various fruits for them to eat.

Juan and Brett sat off to one side, munching their food, while discussing the virtues of various cattle breeds. Linda quizzed Meadow more about the cliff dwelling. Part of her wished Linda wasn't so keen on it, but of course she would be. After all, it was on their ranch and Linda was going to study archeology. It made perfect sense, but even so, Meadow somehow felt it was a violation to take people there. But she was so happy to have been invited to their ranch and included on the drive, she answered all Linda's questions.

"Okay, amigos, enough rest. Time to get those vacas to pasture." Juan stood up and dusted off the backside of his jeans before heading to his horse.

They all mounted and the cattle moseyed down the trail. A couple more times during the drive, Meadow had to chase cows back in line and Foxfire got better and better at it. Now she watched the herd and was after the cow before Meadow even saw it break out. Linda and Juan seemed amused that Meadow wanted to do all the cutting, but Brett seemed irritated. Between Foxfire and Kelsey he hadn't had to do any cattle chasing. Meadow noticed his scowl and rode over to him and Linda. He must have complained to his sister that he wasn't getting to work any cows.

Linda gave him a withering look. "Brett, don't be such a baby. Meadow has never been on a drive before and she is our guest. Her horse has really taken to cow work."

"Juan gave me this new bullwhip and I haven't even been able to use it!"

Meadow felt the blood rush to her head. "Gosh, I'm sorry, Brett. It didn't even occur to me that I was having all the fun. You can chase them from now on."

Linda patted her arm. "Don't worry about Brett. He gets to have plenty of fun." She turned to Brett. "I'm thinking maybe we should breed some Arabian blood into our ranch horses. What do you think?"

He wrinkled his nose. "I think they look like girly horses. All prancy with their tails high in the air."

"Foxy's pretty tough for a *girly* horse." Linda wasn't being dissuaded. "I think they would make a great cross with Diablo, if we ever get him back. I'm going to talk to Dad about it when he returns."

Brett's face pinched up, like he just drank vinegar. "Yeah, whatever."

They made it to the line-camp in the late afternoon. It was a one-room cabin sitting on the edge of the summer pasture in the midst of a few pine trees. A little stream ran nearby. They hobbled their horses in the green field so they wouldn't wander too far from camp.

Meadow was worried that her mare wouldn't like the restraints on her legs, but Foxfire trusted her and didn't put up a fuss. Juan and Brett gathered wood and soon had a crackling campfire going. There were some general supplies in the cabin, but they had also brought some fresh food in Juan's cold-pack for dinner and the next morning's breakfast.

Juan cooked a dinner to rival Lupe's skills, including melt-in-your-mouth biscuits made in a Dutch oven that he buried in the campfire coals. Brett recovered his good spirits, and after dinner he disappeared into the cabin and came back with a guitar he'd stashed there.

Meadow's eyes danced. "You play the guitar?"

He shrugged. "A little."

"I love old west songs. Do you sing, too?"

"Not very well, but I'll give it a shot."

He started strumming the guitar and Meadow thought he played very well. In fact, everyone seemed to enjoy his playing and then he sang some cowboy tunes including "Little Joe the Wrangler". She loved his voice, and her eyes teared up when he sang of poor Little Joe dying on a cattle drive trying to save the herd. They all joined in singing "Home on the Range".

"It's such a beautiful night, why don't we sleep out under the stars?" Linda said.

Everyone agreed that was a great idea and put down their bedrolls around the fire.

Meadow smiled when Kelsey lay down by her, snuggling close. The moon rose as a huge disc in the sky, bathing them and the campsite in pale moonlight. She fell asleep thinking about the perfect day.

It must have been about midnight, when Meadow was roused by Kelsey growling and softly woofing. Something was bothering the horses. She could hear them hopping around with their hobbled front legs. She sat up, peering out into the pasture.

It was very nearly a full moon, and she could make out all the horses. She breathed in sharply when she saw a large whitish shape among the rest.

A dappled coat shone silver in the moonlight. It had to be Diablo. He was huge next to the other horses and was prancing majestically with an arched neck, shaking his long mane, and then pushing the mares and nipping at them. Foxfire squealed and kicked out at him. He was trying to steal the mares!

Without bothering to pull her boots on, Meadow hurried toward the horses, with Kelsey at her heels.

"Foxy," she called softly.

Foxfire tried to come to her, but was hampered by her hobbles. Diablo turned, saw Meadow and flared his nostrils. He pushed Foxfire aside, snorted and reared threateningly. Diablo started toward Meadow at a gallop, with his ears flat against his head. Meadow jumped to the side, just in time, and he galloped past her. Kelsey barked at him furiously and tried to nip him as he went by.

The stallion turned and started coming for her again. His eyes were wild, and he let out a loud shriek with his teeth bared. Her heart beat wildly with the gigantic beast charging toward her. There was nowhere to hide, her legs felt like jelly, and she couldn't possibly outrun him to the camp.

Kelsey kept up the chase, nipping at Diablo frantically, trying to herd him away from Meadow, but nothing deterred the enraged devil-like stallion bearing down on her. She gulped, standing mesmerized. Her feet were immovable, as though they were anchored to the ground, just like one of those awful dreams.

Closer and closer he came, till she could clearly see his wild eyes boring into hers.

She squeezed her lids tight, waiting, expecting the worst. Next she felt a hard shove, and she stumbled to the ground. She looked up, and Brett stood in front of her, with the bullwhip in his hands. He crouched down and cracked the whip toward the horse. Diablo veered at the last moment, and then galloped off into the night. Meadow let out a sigh of relief, not realizing she had been holding her breath.

Brett watched the horse disappear and then turned to her. "I think they named him Diablo for a reason." He offered his hand and pulled her up.

Meadow's whole body was shaking. "Thanks for coming to my rescue."

He hugged her to him. "I can't believe you went toward the horses with that stallion out there. Aren't you scared of anything?"

His arms were strong, and Meadow gradually felt herself relax.

"I nearly had a heart attack when I saw him coming for you," he said.

Brett held her so close, she could feel his heart racing and knew he'd really been worried. For some reason, this pleased her. He was still holding her when they heard Linda call out.

"Are you two all right? What happened?" She ran toward them.

Brett quickly dropped his arms and stepped away from Meadow.

Juan appeared, rubbing sleep from his eyes. "Was that the stallion? Are you okay?"

"We're fine, thanks to the bull whip you gave me," Brett said. "Good thing I had it. I think Diablo would have run Meadow down."

"Oh no!" Linda examined her. "You seem okay now."

Meadow nodded, and then found her voice. "At least, now we know Diablo's still in the area. His herd must be nearby, too."

"Yeah, we can track them from here." Brett stared off toward where Diablo had melted into the distant trees.

"No, we can't be gone another night, or Mother will worry, and we need to get some sleep." Linda sounded firm in her decision and Brett didn't argue.

After Meadow checked Foxfire over, she followed the others back to bed. She was restless for the remainder of the night, tossing and turning, still thinking about her close call. Diablo *must* be Arrow. He *must* be the Sky Horse. He'd really acted like a wild stallion, in spite of what she knew to be true about him.

She wondered if they would be able to find him and his herd of mares. She hoped not. He should be free forever. He was as wild as the range itself, and tonight he proved it.

Chapter 15

The Chase

Shep looked down into the valley where the wild horses grazed. From his perch on the rim rock, he had an unspoiled panoramic view of the herd and could see Diablo a little apart from the rest. The stallion was nibbling on the grass, but lifted his head to test the wind every couple of minutes.

The early morning air was fresh and Shep sat taking in the vista with a small smile on his face. At this moment, he was content to chase the wild ones, like he and Nueme did in their youth. It was a respite from the stable and worry about the lawsuit. And a way to make some easy money.

Nueme had told him he was happy to be back in his own people's land, Shonto country. His Indian friend knew the territory well and had easily tracked the herd to this spot. After making a mental plan, and checking the direction of the wind so as not to give Diablo any warning, Shep clambered down off the rock. Monty tossed him Shadow's reins and he mounted. Nueme and Mike sat aboard their horses nearby.

"The mustangs are in the valley, so we will need to get to our posts, and then we can start pushing them toward the box canyon."

Nueme and his boys nodded, turned their mounts, and rode to their respective waiting spots along the way. Their plan was simple. They would drive them as slowly as possible by keeping enough distance so the mustangs wouldn't spook, but keep moving forward.

If the herd outdistanced one rider, another one would pick it up from his hiding place along the way. They would move them into the canyon where they had constructed a camouflaged corral as a trap. Once they had the horses in the corral, they could rope Diablo.

Bill had told him the stallion had some training from his early days in Mexico and was broke to lead and tie. Shep figured he would remember the training and wouldn't fight the rope once it was on him. He was counting on the fact that horses have good memories.

Shep instructed Nueme to wait for the other riders to position themselves and after a couple of hours start down the slope. Nueme would ride slowly and circle around to the far end of the valley, so as not to frighten the mustangs. When he got into position, he would ride toward them at a walk, speeding up as the horses did, but staying well back. Keep them in sight but avoid panic. If they stampeded, the men would never be able to stop them.

Shep positioned himself last, at the mouth of the box canyon. He dismounted to save Shadow's strength, and after a few hours waiting, saw the herd come 'round the last bend. Further back, Monty and Mike trailed them. The boys were doing a good job. The mustangs were trotting, and some were clearly tiring, but Diablo seemed as fresh as when he started.

The mares were closing in on the canyon, when all of a sudden, Diablo skidded to a stop. He reared up on his hind legs then furiously nipped at the mares to turn them. Monty was nearest to the stallion and swung his lariat toward him. The horse ducked his head and dodged around him.

"He knows it's a trap!" Monty yelled to Mike, who was coming up from behind him. "Swing your rope around!"

Mike pulled out his lariat and swung it, whooping as he galloped toward the herd. The frightened mares turned back toward the canyon with Diablo running from side to side, still trying to guide them away. Together the boys chased them until they got to where Shep was waiting.

With the boys' horses blown out, Shep took over on his big black gelding. Shadow was fresh from his rest, and the herd, even though tired, was still spooked enough to keep going forward. He trotted behind them for the last mile inside the canyon walls, and when they slowed, Shep yelled and slapped his lariat on his saddle to get them into the corral. The lead mare finally went in and the rest followed her, including Diablo. Shep jumped from Shadow's back and put up the rails to close them in.

With a big grin on his face he whooped. "Yippee, we got 'em!" But his exuberance was short-lived.

Diablo stood stock still in the middle of the enclosure, as if assessing his options. Then the stallion started trotting around, and soon was in a full gallop. He ran 'round and 'round the corral gathering speed. Faster and faster he went, until suddenly he turned and galloped straight for the rail barrier. Instead of stopping when he got there, he gathered his mighty strength and jumped cleanly over the gate with room to spare. The big stallion raced swiftly out of sight, kicking up a dust trail as he ran.

Shep shook his head. "Well, I'll be . . ." He waited until the dust settled, then turned back to the mustangs. Nonchalantly, he put one foot up and leaned on the fence, checking them out to see which ones were likely prospects to make good ranch horses. After a while, the boys came riding in and finally Nueme arrived at the enclosure, his horse foamy with sweat.

Mike's face fell when he found out Diablo had escaped. "Now we'll never be able to catch him. He'll be too smart to trap again."

Shep wasn't concerned. "Don't worry, he won't go far without his herd." He turned back to the horses in the corral. "We have some good, young horses in here that we can break and sell. I'd wager we can get a hundred apiece or maybe a little more for them. Look, there's probably twenty good colts in there. After we catch Diablo, we'll let the older ones and the mares with foals go free again."

Monty scowled. "Oh great, a bunch of wild colts to break. I thought we were just after Diablo."

Mike punched him in the arm. "Don't be a spoilsport. You've been moping around ever since the dance, waiting for a letter from that cute blonde."

The red crept up Monty's neck, suffusing his face and he punched Mike back.

Shep stepped in. "You boys quit yer fightin'. Let's get these mustangs separated. And Mike, you can ride all the rough ones."

Mike started grinning. "Good. I need to practice for the rodeo anyway."

Monty brightened. "That's fine with me. I'll rope 'em for you."

Shep, glad they'd worked things out, climbed over the rails. "Right now we need to partition off part of the large corral, so we can move the colts."

They put up the portable fence they had built at the same time as the corral, and then it wasn't too tough separating the colts into the smaller pen. When Shep was satisfied with their handiwork, he allowed them all to rest for a few minutes, but before long he got up and tightened Shadow's girth.

"Okay, boys, let's head out after Diablo again. I'm pretty sure he's hanging out just around the next bend. We'll swing wide around him, and Monty, you lasso him after Mike and I haze him toward you. Elmer is the best rope horse we have and you're the best roper. Once we have him roped, he'll settle down." Shep was sure his plan would work.

They headed out to recapture Diablo while Nueme kept watch on the corralled mustangs.

The stallion was right where Shep knew he would be. He snorted and pawed the air, but was not as threatening without his herd to protect. Shep circled him and Mike came up on the other side. Diablo trotted forward and Monty galloped up next to him, just like he was going to rope a steer. He swung the rope neatly over his head and it settled on his shoulders. Elmer slid to a stop and pulled the rope tight.

Just as Shep had predicted, Diablo didn't fight the rope. He instantly changed from being wild and aggressive into a manageable, although high-strung horse. He remembered his early training and pranced along behind Elmer. He actually seemed glad to be taken back to his mares.

Shep smiled, watching the wild stallion trail along like any broke horse. "He's a smart one."

When they got to the corral, Diablo was hobbled to prevent another escape. The boys turned their mounts in with the mustangs, and they were content to crop grass and drink from a little stream that ran through the back of the enclosure.

Nueme had the camp set up by then, with a fire already crackling. The boys wolfed down roasted hotdogs and ask for more. Everything tastes good over a campfire.

"Gee, Dad, your plan worked great," Monty said, wiping his mouth.

"Yep, a minor hiccup when Diablo jumped out, but all in all, I'd say we all did a good day's work." Shep watched the stallion, proudly standing apart from the rest of the mustangs, gazing at the far horizon. "I've seen alotta good horseflesh in my time, but he sure wins the prize. You should've seen him take that gate. It's over six feet high, but he just flew over it, like he suddenly sprouted wings."

Nueme nodded. "That's some hoss."

"I'd like to try riding him," Mike said, his eyes gleaming in the firelight.

Shep shot him a warning look. "No, you stay off that one."

"But, he'd be better practice than these colts. If I could top him off, I could ride any bronc at the rodeo."

"I said stay off him and that's what I meant." Shep's tone didn't allow for any more discussion.

Mike tightened his jaw and sat in brooding silence.

Tired from the long ride, the conversation waned as they watched the flickering fire die down.

"Better hit the hay, boys," Nueme said. "We have another long day in the saddle tomorrow herding them ponies back to Brighten."

No one debated him as they all turned in. Shep lay for a few minutes reflecting on a satisfactory day's work. Maybe things were turning around for them. He hoped so—they needed a break.

Chapter 16

The Amulet

Meadow charged into the cabin at the stable, ready for action. Her mother was at the kitchen counter kneading bread dough. A mouth-watering, yeasty smell filled the air.

Her mother turned, wiped her hands on her apron, and hugged Meadow warmly. "I really missed you, sweetie."

"Me too, Mom. But I had a great time at the ranch and the cattle drive was so much fun. Where is everyone?"

"We decided to close the stable while everyone was away. Your father, Nueme and the boys left to capture Diablo yesterday. They spent the night up at the rim, so they could get an early start for the chase this morning."

"What do you mean? They went after Diablo already?" Meadow's buoyant mood dropped a notch. "We wanted to ride on the chase. I thought Daddy was going to wait for us."

She had just arrived back at the stable with Linda and Brett. It had only taken them half a day to return from the summer pasture, since they were no longer hampered by a cow and calf herd. They'd stopped for a quick lunch at the ranch, resting the horses, then loaded all three of them into the big stock trailer and drove to the stable.

Mom looked tired. "Your father and Nueme decided it would be better with just a few riders, so the wild ones would be easier to manage."

"It's okay, Meadow. We have other things to do, remember?" Linda said, impatiently waiting by the door with Brett hovering behind her.

"Yeah, that's right. We'll be home before dark, Mom." She glanced over at Linda and Brett. "I'll be right out, guys."

After they left, Meadow touched her mother's arm. "Is everything okay, Mom?"

"I didn't sleep well, that's all. You kids run along and have a good time." Her smile was a bit thin. "I'm enjoying the solitude today. Just catching up on the baking, and I have some thinking to do."

Meadow briefly wondered why her mother seemed so distracted, but the excitement of taking Linda and Brett to the cliff dwelling outweighed her concern, and she put it out of her mind.

Linda was anxious to see the Indian cave, and Meadow had decided it was okay for Brett to see it, too. Her shoulders became tense when she thought about them catching Arrow. But Linda's face, rapt with the anticipation of seeing a real cliff dwelling soon overshadowed everything else.

The ride was hot and dusty but they made good time up past Oak Creek through the narrow canyon to the entrance of the cave. The ladder was still in place where Meadow had left it. They'd brought flashlights, so it was easier to find their way through the long passage and into the large chamber.

"Wow." Linda sucked in her breath. "This is truly amazing. Do you know this is probably one of the most important Indian finds, ever, in this country? Just like you said, it looks like they left without taking any of their belongings."

"But why would they do that?" Meadow couldn't imagine just walking off without any of their things.

"I know that in Shonto culture, if someone dies where they live, none of them will touch or take anything from there. They probably consider this place sacred."

That's kinda creepy, Meadow thought, looking around. "Do you think someone died here?"

Brett had gone into the room with the hunting weapons. They heard him rummaging around and followed him. He had a bow in his hand. "Look at all these bows and arrows. I going to keep a set and try it out. These arrowheads are razor sharp."

Linda shook her head. "No, put it back. We don't have any right to this stuff." She turned to Meadow. "Who else knows about this?"

"Just Mike. I haven't told anyone else about it. We were going to come up here to try and find another way out, but never had enough time."

Meadow didn't mention to Linda that she had been to the dwelling a couple of times without her brother. It was like she was drawn to the place for some unknown reason. She had never told anyone about her strange dream of the Indian maiden, but every time she came to the cave, it came flooding back to her as real as ever.

Linda put a warning hand on her. "Don't tell anyone else. There are plenty of pot hunters around who would love to get hold of these relics. This is so important that I'm going to call the Arizona State University and have them send someone up to evaluate these items."

"What will happen then?"

"We will have to decide what to do with the artifacts. They should be offered back to the Shontos, if they want them. After all, this stuff really belongs to them. The main thing is, it's way too important to keep to ourselves."

Meadow was trying her best to match the enthusiasm that Linda and Brett displayed, but couldn't help but feel sad that she wouldn't have this place all to herself anymore. But it was only right that these things should go back to the Indians.

After checking out the upper chambers, Meadow led them down the steps to the shallow pool. Beyond that was a room that had what looked like carved totem poles, but on closer examination they proved to be stalagmites that had formed over thousands of years.

"I'll bet the Indians used this as a shrine. Look over here." Brett waved them over to an altar-like rock that had remnants of ashes on it.

"Burnt offerings to the gods, maybe," Linda said.

With Brett and Linda engrossed in the exploration of a storeroom filled with blankets and pottery, Meadow wandered away and found herself behind a large stalagmite formation. Kelsey was busily sniffing and pawing at one wall, as if there was something behind it. Curious, Meadow pushed on it to see what would happen and the seemingly solid wall moved a little. She shoved harder, putting all her weight against it. Slowly, she was able to open it enough to squeeze through. Her breath caught as she realized it was a hidden chamber. And it was literally filled with more relics. But these seemed different from what they found in the other rooms.

She carefully looked around, and decided it might be the Medicine Man's private sanctuary. It had many dolls, fetishes and other utensils that could be used in sacred rites. On make-shift shelves were rows of pots filled with roots and dried herbs.

While she was smelling the still-sweet essence of an aromatic herb, Meadow felt warmth on her back. She turned and was transfixed by what she saw. A shaft of light shone through from above, perfectly illuminating a cave painting. It was as though a spotlight were trained on the image of a horse with a long flowing mane. Unlike the other artwork in the dwelling, this one seemed more alive, as if the horse might jump off the rock and gallop away. Her heart fluttered like a butterfly as she gazed at it, realizing it reminded her of the silver stallion. She stood for several moments, just staring. *Arrow, the Sky Horse!*

The noise of Kelsey pawing at a colorful blanket snapped Meadow out of her meditation. She tore herself away from the image and went to see what her dog was so interested in.

"What is it, girl?" She lifted the cover up to find it concealed a large rectangular container. The Indians had used buffalo hide over a wood frame to form a chest with braided horsehair handles on the ends. Meadow pulled up the lid and inside found capes made of multi-colored feathers, ornate silver jewelry and belts, besides scary looking masks.

A real treasure chest! She kept digging and came across a beautifully beaded bag.

Meadow opened the sack and after peering inside, gasped in surprise. The bag dropped from her hands and she stared at it for a moment with her heart racing. Gingerly she picked it up again. Inside was the turquoise and crystal amulet the Indian maiden of her dream had been wearing.

She cautiously took the pendant out, and examined it more closely. The shape of a horse with a flowing mane was etched inside crystal, just like the depiction on the wall. Meadow was certain it was the same piece of jewelry the girl had placed her hand on. Concentrating on the crystal, she slowly became aware of a warm presence surrounding her, like someone was enfolding her in their arms.

Meadow felt at peace then. She didn't know why she had found the amulet, but knew she was supposed to keep it safe. As if in a trance, she put it around her neck under her blouse. Carefully, she repacked the chest and put the blanket back over it. She made her way back to the others, but she didn't mention the pendant or the secret room to them.

Brett was the one who finally broke the spell. "It's getting late. Mom will be worried."

Linda looked up from the painted shield she was inspecting. "You're right. It's hard to leave all this, though. I won't have time to make any phone calls today, but first thing tomorrow, I will find someone to help catalog these things."

Brett picked up one of the bows. "I don't see why I can't keep at least one of these."

"Maybe Chief White Horse will be okay with that, but we need to ask."

He put it back on the pile. "I guess you're right."

Meadow laid a hand over the amulet next to her heart, guilt-ridden, but not enough to give it up.

They arrived back at the stable by dusk. After rubbing down the horses, they all trooped into the cabin together. As they entered, the aroma coming from the oven reminded Meadow of just how hungry she was.

"Where did you kids go?" Mom sliced off some freshly baked bread, slathered it with butter and handed out pieces to everyone. "You were gone for a long time."

It appeared her mother wasn't terribly interested in the answer, because she turned back to peeling potatoes.

"Meadow found an Indian cliff dwelling." Linda mentioned it almost casually.

Mom swung around, the paring knife still in her hand. "What? What did you say? A cliff dwelling?"

Linda smiled and began telling her in earnest about all the many artifacts.

"Those must be worth a fortune!" Pucker marks appeared between her mother's brows. "You have to make sure they don't fall into the wrong hands."

"Yes, I know. I'm getting an expert up here as soon as possible from the University. We will have to move them to a safe place, or pot hunters may get wind of it."

"Would you two like to stay for dinner?"

"I would." Brett took another mouthful of the bread.

"We better not, though," Linda said. "You know how Mother worries. And it's getting dark."

Brett started for the door. "Yeah, thanks anyway. I'll go load the horses."

Meadow accompanied Brett outside to help with the horses, and Linda followed. After they drove away, Meadow fed Foxfire and the dude string, then returned to the cabin. With her mother working on dinner, she grabbed a pile of dirty clothes to sort for the hotel's laundry room. Meadow was going through the pockets of her mother's jeans when she felt something.

"What's this, Mom?" She held up the pink envelope.

"Oh darn, I forgot about that letter for Monty." Her mother took the letter and put it on his bed. "I think it's from that blonde girl, Cynthia."

"Monty will be happy to get a letter from her. He's in love, you know."

Her mother's face tightened. "Her father is the one that's suing us, so he better get over it."

"What?" Meadow felt her shoulders tense. No wonder her mother seemed distracted.

"That's right, you were gone. Here read this." Mom pulled the letter out of the ledger she kept for the stable.

Meadow read the letter, her tension mounting.

"Mom, what are we going to do?"

"Well, that's the real reason your father didn't want to wait to go after Diablo," her mother said. "We need that reward money. And we can sell the colts from the herd. Don't worry, honey. We'll get through this."

She went to her mother, hugging her tightly, knowing that in spite of her brave words, Mom was truly frightened.

That night for the first time, Meadow hoped Arrow would be captured. But thinking about it made her heart feel as if it weighed a million tons, and tears crept out of her eyes, slipping down to the amulet, cool against her chest.

Chapter 17

Wendell

Wendell's eyes narrowed as he watched Linda Bowman drive up in her Cadillac and park in front of the store. Before long, she burst through the door. He pasted on his automatic smile, wondering what she was so excited about.

"Good morning, Linda. To what do we owe the honor of your presence?"

Linda nodded to him and then Lucy, who was stocking the shelves. "Good morning. How is everything going in the store?"

"Just fine. No customers at the moment, but it's almost noon and most tourists like to eat hearty since they're on vacation. It always picks up later."

"Speaking of eating, why don't you two take a break and go to lunch together? I will be happy to watch the store while you're gone."

"Why thank you, Linda." Lucy walked up to her, all smiles. "We don't usually get to eat together, with someone having to mind the store all the time."

"I thought it might be a treat for you. Take your time."

Wendell raised one eyebrow, but didn't say anything. He guided Lucy through the door, pausing just outside, and then he peeked back in. He saw Linda pick up the phone.

Lucy nudged him in the ribs, and whispered, "What's she doing?"

He shushed Lucy and pulled her toward the café. He didn't speak until they were safely out of earshot. "She was using the phone."

"Why didn't she use the one at the ranch?" Her expression was even dumber than usual.

Wendell sighed. "You don't listen. I told you before. There is no phone at the ranch. The store has the only phone at Brighten."

Lucy blinked and snapped her finger. "Oh, yeah. That's why we have to take the hotel reservations and everything."

He patted her hand. "That's right." Then his face darkened. "I wonder what was so important that she didn't want us to hear."

Lucy's eyes grew round. "You think she's trying to hide something from us?"

"Don't worry about it, dear. It's probably nothing."

Lucy nodded and picked up the menu, and Wendell was sure she had already forgotten the incident. But he hadn't. There was something going on and he would find out just what it was.

Later that afternoon, Wendell was in his office concentrating on the income ledger when the phone rang insistently. He slammed down his pen and answered it with barely concealed impatience.

"Brighten Hot Springs. May I help you?"

"Yes, this is Professor Alfred Swan from ASU's Archeology department. May I speak to a Miss Bowman?"

Wendell's face relaxed and his voice became a soft purr.

"She's not here at the moment. Can I take a message for her?"

"Yes, she left urgent word for me to return her call, saying she had an important find in your area. Of course, we are very interested in looking at new sites. Please have her call me as soon as possible. My direct line is University 2445. I will anxiously await her call. Thank you."

Wendell hung up the phone, and rubbed his hands together. This was just the break he had been waiting for. He quickly dialed another number.

A secretary answered the phone. "RayCo, Unlimited. May I direct your call?"

"Paul Misner, please."

After a few seconds a voice came on. "This is Paul, what can I do for you?"

"Paul, it's Wendell. We just got a lead on finding the Indian stuff that kid Mike told you about. You have to come up with a likely ASU Archeology professor. Has to be someone that can talk the talk. You know what I mean. I need to give the Bowman girl his number. So make it quick."

Paul was quiet for a moment. "I think I know the perfect candidate. His name is George Schumer and he is a real archeologist. Got into some trouble a while back and was fired from ASU."

"Great, get on it NOW!" Wendell hung up the phone with a satisfied click. With no one to observe him, the transformation of his demeanor came quickly. He dropped the milk-toast face he usually wore and let his true nature shine through in his cold-as-steel eyes.

Wendell Halstead—at least that was his name at the present time—got up from his desk and walked the length of his office and back. He did his best thinking when he paced. This could be his big break. No one at Brighten suspected for a minute that he was somewhat of a Jekyll and Hyde character. All his life, people had been underestimating him. He knew with his unassuming looks and self-deprecating manner, he was always considered harmless.

Even his parents had misjudged him. When he left the family chicken farm in Iowa, he had taken their life savings with him. His parents had never believed in banks after the Great Depression, so it was a simple matter to rob the pie safe where they hid the money. He decided if they were that stupid, they deserved to lose their nest egg. Making him do menial chores like feeding the chickens and cleaning out the coops. Chicken slave! That's all he was to them. He robbed his parents of their whole life savings without feeling the slightest remorse. They never truly appreciated my superior intelligence anyway, he'd thought as he made off with the few thousand dollars.

Wendell never saw his parents again. From then on he made his living with petty scams, always under the radar, because no one believed a person that looked like a jolly little elf was capable of theft and larceny. He avoided violent crimes and bank jobs, not because he had any scruples about it, but because he never wanted to get caught. He was smart enough to know that the cops forget about petty crimes pretty quickly but will chase violent criminals for years.

Wendell met Lucy while in Las Vegas. He was cheating at cards and she was working as a cocktail waitress. He liked the way she would say, "What'll it be, hon?", with her throaty voice when she came to take his order. Lucy had big hair, big teeth and big boobs, all things that Wendell was attracted to. Not the brightest bulb in the pack, but he had enough intelligence for both of them.

Lucy had been a blonde when they met, but he soon found out she changed her hair color almost as often as she changed her underwear, which didn't bother him in the slightest. And she wasn't smart enough to have any scruples. A match made in heaven.

They started dating and it became apparent to Wendell that Lucy would do anything to get out of waiting tables, including hooking up with a short, bald guy. She told him what she liked best about him was that he was really smart. Well, someone needed brains in the outfit. He told her he would take care of her as long as she didn't rock the boat. The marriage seemed to work for them, but they never stayed in one place too long and had never yet pulled off a really big heist.

Wendell was salivating like Pavlov's dog thinking about the Indian artifacts. This was just the type of job he had been waiting for. A heist that could set them up for life without much danger of getting caught. He would tell Lucy just enough to ensure her silence.

He had just finished counting the till when Linda came back into the store at closing time. She walked to the back and checked her mail slot. "Did I get any phone calls?" Wendell could tell she was trying to sound casual.

"Let's see." Wendell rifled through a pile of messages. "Oh yes, here's a note. Looks like a Professor Schumer. He said to call him at home."

"Professor Schumer?"

"Yes, from ASU. He said something about Professor Swan being too busy and he was returning your call for him?"

"Oh, yes. Do you mind? This is personal."

"Of course not." Wendell smiled, walked out of the office and closed the door behind him.

The next day, Wendell headed to the stable to book a pack trip for Professor Schumer, which Linda had asked him to set up. She didn't tell him any details, except that the ASU professor would be camping out for at least a couple of weeks and would be taking two assistants with him.

Wendell could barely restrain his smirk as he hustled along on his short legs. He was dripping with sweat and puffing by the time he arrived at the round pen where he found Shep watching Mike work a mustang.

He stopped next to Shep and mopped his brow with his handkerchief. "Whew! The weather is getting pretty warm."

Shep turned and eyed him. "Yep, guess it won't cool down until monsoons start."

Wendell observed for a moment as Mike loped the horse in a circle. "You sure didn't waste any time riding those mustangs. When are you taking them to the auction?"

"Won't be long," Shep replied. "I'm taking two of them to the Frontier Days Rodeo. They don't want to give up bucking, and the rodeo contractor is always looking for good broncos."

"Sounds like you've got a plan for all of them. That's good."

"Yep."

"Listen Shep, I need to book a pack trip for a professor from ASU and his two assistants. They want to camp for a couple of weeks. Can you accommodate them?"

"You bet. Where and when do they want to go?"

"They'll be here day after tomorrow. This is Linda's deal. She said she would come over this afternoon to go over the details, but she wanted you to know as soon as possible for planning purposes. Can you have all the supplies by then?"

"Sure, I'm making a trip to Scottsdale tomorrow and I'll get everything then. They're staying a couple of weeks?"

"I guess that depends on what they find. You won't need to stay with them. Linda said just pack them in and set up the camp, then in a few days you can take new supplies up."

"So you have their supply list with you? And I'll need the money to pay for the stuff."

Wendell produced the list and money, handing both to Shep. "Here you go, they'll be here on Friday at 8 a.m., ready to head out."

"We'll have everything all set."

"Thanks, Shep." Wendell walked back to the store thinking his little scheme was working as smooth as a gravy sandwich.

Chapter 18

The Meeting

The next day, Shep loaded up Rowdy and the three other horses he was taking down to Bob Rawlins in Scottsdale. Rawlins was paying top price for Rowdy, and Shep felt he couldn't pass it up, since the man was also buying the other horses for his family.

He felt lower than a snake in a wagon rut about selling Rowdy. But what else could he do? He gripped the steering wheel with steely determination, and put the truck into first gear. It lurched and groaned as he stomped on the accelerator, pulling out of the stable.

His conversation with Rose the night before flashed through his mind.

She had a strained expression. "Won't he take another horse? You know how much Mike likes Rowdy."

Shep's voice came out gruffer than he intended. "No, he wants Rowdy. Mike will get over it." He turned away from her, not able to stand the hurt look on her face.

Then he thought of Meadow as she had watched him load Rowdy, with tears welling up in her eyes.

She had pleaded with him. "Daddy, please don't sell Rowdy."

"This is none of your affair, Meadow."

She had walked away, wiping tears with the back of her hand.

Mike's reaction was the worst, though. He watched in stony silence, then he grabbed his fishing pole, and stalked off. It would have been better if the boy had yammered and talked back, like he usually did. The silence had been unbearable.

Monty was the only one not mad at him, but all he wanted to do was moon around over that silly blonde, whose father was suing them.

Shep drove the familiar road to Scottsdale, troubled about his impending meeting with Ben Markowitz. His guts churned. All in all, this was going to be a crappy day. First he had to deliver Rowdy to a bunch of dudes, and then he had to meet with the jerk that was threatening a lawsuit. He'd probably clobber the guy. No, he thought, then I'd get arrested for assault and battery and be put in jail. That would be great for the family. A jailbird for a father.

He arrived in Scottsdale and found the Rawlins' place. It looked like about five acres, with a newly built, four-stall barn. He pulled into the driveway, and Bob Rawlins, his wife and two pre-teen daughters all met him at the barn. He could sense their excitement at the prospect of their new 'pets'.

"Now remember, Bob, Rowdy is just a youngster, so he's bound to be frisky sometimes."Shep gave the man a stern look. "I really think you should have taken one of the older horses instead of him. The other three are perfect for your family, but Rowdy is a big, strong colt and he's used to working every day. He might get hard to handle if you don't ride him much."

Rawlins patted Shep on the shoulder. "Don't worry about us." His tone oozed confidence. "Rowdy is perfect for me. And we're a very athletic family. We've ridden at stables lots of times. We'll give the horses plenty of attention and we'll learn to ride like pros in no time."

"Yes," his thin, wide-eyed wife chimed in. "We'll give them lots of treats and love and we'll get along just fine."

Shep felt like slapping some sense into them, but controlled the impulse. "Well, they aren't big dogs, you know. They're very strong animals and you have to learn how to handle them so you don't get hurt. And if you don't earn their respect you might as well hang up your spurs." He could tell they weren't listening. He tried one last time. "Anyway, you really need a trainer and all of you should have riding lessons."

But the Rawlins's were too enamored with their new acquisitions, and Shep finally gave up. "You have the resort phone number, Bob. Call me if you have any trouble. I'd be happy to switch Rowdy for another horse any time." He collected the money, and drove on to his meeting with Ben Markowitz.

The office building that housed Markowitz, Dahl, and Sandler, Partners in Law was in an upscale part of town. Like many of the structures in Scottsdale, it was wood framed and had a western facade on the front.

Shep turned in to park, feeling out of place in the lot filled with Cadillacs, Lincolns, and a couple of Mercedes. His old truck rattled to a stop near one of them and he got out with just a smidgeon of hope that he could work things out with Markowitz.

He walked into the over-stuffed waiting room, and saw that it was adorned with western oil paintings and various bronze sculptures. When he told the ginger-haired receptionist that he had an appointment with Attorney Markowitz, she told him it would be a few minutes and to have a seat. The few minutes turned into a half hour, and then forty-five minutes. Shep paced the floor and fidgeted while the redhead tapped on her typewriter. Finally, he strode over to her desk, and leaned toward her, scowling. "Is he going to see me or not?"

"Yes, sir. I will see what the holdup is." She smiled nervously, and then disappeared into Markowitz's office.

The door opened and she ushered him into the dimly lit room. The attorney sat behind his huge oak desk like a hungry coyote waiting for the opportunity to rip a jackrabbit to shreds. The hostility made the room airless, nearly suffocating. Shep sucked in a breath. Trying to negotiate with him might be fruitless, but he had to try. Instinctively, he knew this man would not give an inch and it wasn't about his daughter, it was about winning.

Shep held out his hand and Markowitz hesitated, then shook it reluctantly.

"First of all, I would like to say how sorry I am that your daughter was hurt. How is she doing?" Shep took a seat across from Markowitz. No use waiting for an invitation.

"I don't want to discuss Cynthia with you," Markowitz answered curtly. "Let's keep to the settlement issue. When will you have the money?"

"Whoa, hold your horses. I'm not convinced that your daughter was really hurt that bad. Where are the doctors' reports stating that she is permanently injured?"

"Don't worry, I'll show you the reports if we have to go to court."

Shep hardened his face. "You'll have to produce them sooner than that, if you want any money out of me."

"Why don't you sell that dangerous mare right now, and raise some of the money? Your son said she has great bloodlines and I'm sure any breeder would love to have her."

Shep looked at the other man with distaste. "I'm not selling my daughter's horse. She raised her from a weanling and it would break her heart."

"That's too bad, because if you don't come up with the settlement money by the end of August, I will sue you for everything you have."

"You're threatening me?"

"Before I get done with you, I will force you to sell *all* the horses, including Foxfire. You will have to sell the truck too, and all the saddles and tack."

"That'll be a cold day in hell!" Heat rose from within Shep's body like a volcano.

"Your precious little daughter will be out on the street, begging with the rest of you."

Something snapped in Shep, and lunging out of the chair, he reached across the desk, grabbing the lawyer by his tie.

"Don't threaten my family or you'll be sorry," he said coldly. Shep let go of his tie and Markowitz plopped back into his chair with a dazed look on his face.

Shep turned and stalked out of his office with his lip curled. What kind of a lawyer would operate like that, threatening people?

On the drive home in the twilight, Shep had a sour taste in his mouth from the incident at the attorney's office. He shouldn't have lost his temper. That wouldn't solve anything, it never had. Somehow he had to come up with more money to get the guy off his back. He began calculating how much money he still needed, just in case.

"With the amount I just received from the sale to Bob Rawlins," Shep muttered to himself, "the reward from Diablo, and the sale of the mustangs, I'll have more than half of the five thousand for the settlement. But we still have to live on something."

Where would he come up with the rest? The headache he'd had all day intensified into an all-out migraine.

Chapter 19

The Professor

Meadow lounged on Linda's bed while the older girl stuffed clothes into a suitcase without even folding them.

"Mother insists that I go on this stupid shopping mission with her to buy college outfits. It's a total waste of time. I have plenty of clothes. Too many, really. I'd much rather meet the professor and show him our find."

"I know. I wish you were coming."

"Well, he said he's Professor Swan's second in command at ASU. He must be qualified or Professor Swan wouldn't have sent him, right?" Linda sounded a little anxious.

"I'm sure you're right. Maybe Brett can come along to help keep an eye on things?"

Linda shook her head. "No, Mother's making him come, too, so we can have family time together. She must be feeling guilty about being away from us constantly at her galleries. Of course, we'll be visiting some art museums while were gone. She says we've been spending way too much time with horses and cows and need some culture. Brett's fit to be tied about it."

"I really wish you both were going to be there. We don't even know these people."

Linda put her arm around Meadow's shoulders. "Don't worry, I'm sure you'll do fine. And your father will keep any eye on things."

"That's true. Well, I'd better get back to the stable now. Have a good trip and don't buy out all the stores." After saying goodbye to her friend, Meadow retrieved Foxfire and jogged toward home.

In spite of Linda's reassurance, Meadow had left her and the Bowman Ranch feeling nervous as a barn cat that total strangers would be seeing the Indian cave.

The next day, Meadow leaned against the corral fence as her father sized up Professor Schumer and brought out Chico for him to ride. The professor was tall and angular with bushy white hair and a trimmed goatee. He wore small wire rimmed spectacles, and had a slightly bemused air about him.

The two assistants, Rick and Wally, stayed in the background not saying much. They were both dressed like clean-cut college kids on break, in jeans and open-neck shirts, and had neatly combed, short haircuts. Rick squinted through horn-rimmed glasses and looked vaguely familiar, but Meadow couldn't place where she had seen him before.

His brother, Wally, was big and beefy, and didn't appear to be overly bright. He climbed on Spot and grinned like a kid with a new toy. "We get to ride to an Indian cave? I rode a horse once at the carnival."

"That wasn't a horse, you dope. That was a little pony going around in circles." Rick looked at his brother with open disdain.

"Yeah, I guess you're right." Wally laughed without rancor, patting Spot. "But I love horses."

Her father led Brandy out for Rick and helped him mount, then swung up onto Shadow. He looped the pack horse's lead rope once around the horn and turned his head back to the dudes.

"You boys all set?" he asked.

"Yes, Mr. Shepherd, I think we are prepared for this expedition," Professor Schumer answered.

"Call me Shep and we'll get along just fine."

Meadow hopped aboard Foxfire to lead the way to the cliff dwelling. She passed the professor and other riders and checked them out as she guided Foxfire to the front of the group. They looked harmless enough. "Just follow me," she said.

They all fell in behind, with her father bringing up the rear leading the pack horse. Arriving at the cave before noon, the professor gave directions to the young men about what they would need before descending into the cave. Meadow showed the way down the ladder to the entrance of the cliff house.

"Absolutely fabulous!" Professor Schumer gazed around the cave, licking his lips. "I had no conception that it would be this complete. Most ancient sites in the Southwest have already been ransacked."

"This is amazing," her father said with a frown. "When you told me about this, I must not have been paying attention. Has Linda informed the Shonto tribe?"

Before Meadow could answer, the professor interjected, "No need to tell anyone, especially the tribe, this site is on private land. According to the antiquities act . . ."

Dad cut him off, "Never mind about that, the Shonto's should be informed. Meadow?"

She shrugged. "I'm not sure if she's had a chance to talk to them, yet."

"She needs to right away. It looks as though they left everything because someone died here. It could be sacred ground."

"Linda said something about that, but how do you know about Indian traditions?"

"Don't worry about it, just make sure she tells them as soon as possible," Dad said curtly. He abruptly turned to leave. "C'mon, Meadow, we need to get the camp set up."

She gazed after him, hurt by his tone. What was *that* all about? Dad acted as if he were mad at her about something. She was about to follow him when she saw Kelsey begin pawing at a mound of blankets. Probably a mouse.

Rick hurried over to the dog, sneering. "Stop that!" He kicked his foot at her.

Kelsey jumped back with a warning growl, her hackles raised.

"Come here, Kelsey," Meadow called, giving Rick a dirty look.

"I just didn't want her to mess anything up." He muttered under his breath, "Stupid dog."

"She's a nice dog, right, Meadow?" Wally reached down to pat Kelsey. She sniffed him tolerantly.

"We need to get to work right away." The professor started toward the blankets. "Can't waste any time."

Rick pushed up his glasses and peered around the cave. "What should we do first, Professor?"

"We need to start cataloging." The professor pulled a notebook out of the satchel he was carrying.

Meadow heard her father shout from the tunnel to hurry up.

"Okay, Daddy, I'm coming." But she lingered a moment, reluctant to leave the strangers in her cave. Just as she got out of sight of the three men, she heard Rick complain, "These damned glasses are driving me crazy."

Meadow stopped in her tracks and bit her lip, listening.

Professor Schumer answered, "Well, you need to wear them."

"Yeah, yeah, I know. Don't bug me, you old coot," Rick said. "Let's get to work, we don't have much time."

"That's true. It will be hard work to pack all of this up in a couple of weeks. We have to be very careful not to damage anything."

"Yeah, Wally, that means you. Pay attention. You know how clumsy you are," Rick said.

Meadow heard them begin moving things and hurried after her father. She caught him climbing out up the ladder. Within a short distance of the cave opening, the canyon opened up to a large, grassy mesa, where the Indians and earlier pioneers had grazed their animals. Meadow and her father made the camp for Professor Schumer and the two young men next to an old lean-to shelter.

Dad worked fiercely, slamming things around.

"What's the matter?" Meadow asked tentatively.

"There's something I don't like about them."

"Me either. And Kelsey doesn't like that Rick. Not that I blame her." Meadow paused. "Are you mad at me, Daddy?"

Her father shoved the brim of his hat up. "I wish you'd never found that place."

"Why?"

"Never mind. Forget I said anything."

His growly voice told her to not pursue the subject, but she felt a stab of pain. Why was he shutting her out?

After they finished, Meadow and her father rode back down the trail, leading the rest of the horses. She kept stealing glances at her father, wondering how to bridge the gap that had opened between them. He hadn't told her about the encounter with Cynthia's father, maybe that was bothering him. "How was your meeting yesterday?" she asked.

"It was fine."

Meadow thought it was not *fine*, but decided to change the subject. "I can't wait to see how Diablo is doing tomorrow. Will Nueme be coming?"

"Yes, Nueme wants to see the stallion, too. We have to keep an eye on him. Especially with a thousand dollars at stake."

Meadow felt a thrill of anticipation bubble up about the trip to the ranch the next day. It would be the first time to see the stallion up close, even though it would be through the bars of his new extra high corral.

They rode on in silence—her father seemed totally preoccupied.

Chapter 20

The Legend

On the drive out to the Bowman Ranch the next day, Meadow sat on the truck seat between Dad and Nueme. Her father told Nueme about the Indian Cave, and she hung on every word.

"Linda spoke to Chief White Horse about the dwelling and the artifacts," Nueme said.

That's a relief, Meadow thought. Her father was pretty adamant about letting the tribe know.

Dad looked over her head at his friend. "He doesn't have a problem with the stuff being evaluated?"

Nueme shook his head. "No, he understands how important the historical aspect of it is." His eyes became distant, as if he were somewhere other than the truck. "We've always known about the cave, but it is not a place for us to go."

"You knew about the cave!" Meadow blurted out.

"Yes, we knew someone had to find it." His dark eyes bored into hers.

Dad clamped his jaw and didn't say more, but she could see his irritation.

Nueme turned away and stared out the window.

The tension hung over them. Meadow had been around Nueme enough to know that sometimes he was just silent, but her father wasn't usually like that.

When they arrived at the ranch, the first thing she saw was the brand new, extra high corral where the magnificent stallion was enclosed. Even in that setting he looked huge.

They all watched as Diablo snorted loudly and reared on his hind legs. Like a great lion, his mane was a mantle of royalty. It floated about him when he tossed his head, shining silver in the light. He trotted over to the gate, looked back at them expectantly, then at the far horizon as if asking for his freedom. The corral was built a solid eight feet high, so even Diablo wouldn't be tempted to jump out.

A great sadness flooded through Meadow at the thought of the stallion locked up forever.

"He wants out," she said. "I think Mr. Bowman should set him free again. He wants to run on the range with the mustangs."

"He's worth too much to let him run free. The range can be a dangerous place, and Bill can't take that kind of chance with him." Her father climbed up beside her on the fence rail. "Bill will be mighty happy to see him back, and I'll be mighty happy to get that reward money."

Meadow nodded, but was glad Bill Bowman was still away on business. Even Linda and Brett had not yet returned from their shopping trip to California, and the ranch seemed very quiet without them.

Nueme leaned on the fence near Meadow and her father, a pensive expression on his face. He startled her when he spoke. "He is like Arrow, the Sky Horse, of legend."

"Arrow?" Her voice gave away her eagerness. "Please tell us, Nueme."

He turned to Dad, as though asking permission. Her father said, "I suppose she has to hear it."

Nueme nodded. "It's the right time." He spoke in his soft Indian way and Meadow was carried away to a different era, long ago.

> *At the time when day and night were still deciding who comes first, there lived a special horse that will never be seen again until he is set free from captivity. The captors wanted him all for themselves, because he was the biggest, fastest, bravest and most beautiful of all the Indian ponies. But it wasn't just for those reasons they wanted him. They knew he carried all of the deserving to the Indian Hunting Ground when it was time. He was called Arrow, the Sky Horse.*
>
> *This is what happened. The people were a happy and contented tribe with many buffalo to hunt and many horses to ride. The men spent their sunny days hunting, while the women would gather wild fruits and herbs. They lived in a cliff house*

high above the ground with everything they needed. On rainy days the people would stay in their cliff house, with the women weaving baskets and blankets, while the men would smoke their pipes and tell each other stories of the great exploits of their ancestors.

The beautiful young maiden, Meda, would go out at night and bring the Sky Horse special grains and other treats from her garden. Then she would ride on his back across the valleys and over the hills. It was said that the amulet she wore gave her special powers over the stallion, and it was true that he obeyed her every wish. And it was true that she loved Arrow and he loved the girl.

Meda was cherished by all the people because she was their Medicine Woman and had special healing powers. And she took care of the Sky Horse so that he would always carry those that passed from this life to the next, to the Indian Hunting Ground.

Coltan, the chief's son, was the strongest, bravest and most handsome warrior of their tribe, and he fell deeply in love with Meda. They planned to marry when Meda was in her full flower of womanhood, and the sun was between spring and fall. Their love shone bright as the stars in the night sky and happiness was complete for all the people.

The seasons came and went in peaceful abundance and soon it would be the wedding day of Coltan and Meda. But it was not to be.

From out of the east came a warlike clan that wanted the people's land and the many buffalo. Most of all, they coveted the Sky Horse, so that they, too, could ride upon him to the Indian Hunting Ground when it was time. The tribe made war on the people which lasted for one moon. Countless warriors were slain and the buffalo were driven away. Finally, the people had only twenty braves alive, along with their women and children.

The one thing the people still had was Arrow. He was free and chose to be with the people. When the others tried to capture him, he would run so fast that even their best ponies were left far behind. The enemies became more and more determined to have the Sky Horse.

They waited for a moonless night, and the enemy warriors watched while Meda went out for her nightly visit to Arrow. She called to him and he came to her. But then the warriors jumped out of their hiding places with many ropes and captured the Sky Horse.

He fought and reared and plunged, but they were too many and they finally subdued him. Meda tried to stop them, crying and pleading for them to take the restraints off Arrow, but they paid her no heed. She grabbed a weapon from one of the warriors and fought fiercely until a spear pierced her side and she fell to the ground. The evil ones left her lying, with her life spirit draining away, and triumphantly made off with the Sky Horse. Meda cried out for Coltan. The birds of the night heard her cry, and brought Coltan to her side.

He took his beloved Meda into his arms, and he wept, knowing she would not see the dawn awaken the sun. She whispered her last words into his ears. "One will come after me and set Arrow, the Sky Horse free." And with that, she unfastened her magic amulet, and let it slip through her fingers, as she took her last breath in Coltan's embrace. His anguish was terrible to behold and he vowed to spend the rest of his days avenging his love and looking for Arrow.

When morn broke, the people found Coltan still tenderly holding Meda, his tears bathing her face. The people were overcome with grief. They had lost their Medicine Woman and without the Sky Horse, she could not ride to the Indian Hunting Ground. Their spirits could not rest until he was set free. When they took Meda from Coltan's arms, he leaped upon his stallion and rode away without a word. The people bathed their Medicine Woman in sweet oils and herbs, wrapped her in buckskin, and put her on a funeral pyre. The magical amulet was carefully put aside, and then hidden away.

The people left their happy home that day in search of the Sky Horse, leaving behind all their belongings. It was a sacred place where Meda was slain and they knew the only pathway back was the return of Arrow. They never saw Coltan again, but heard tales of a ferocious warrior that rode at night and slew the enemies of the people.

The people wandered for many seasons searching, but never finding the Sky Horse. They never came back to their cliff home.

The old ones still tell the tale of the Sky Horse and the people still wait for Arrow to be set free.

An eerie silence settled over them all as Nueme finished his story. Even Diablo had seemed to be listening, standing quietly, with his ears pricked forward.

Meadow's eyes stung with tears and she could hardly breathe. The cave she found *had* to be the cliff house of the legend. It was an Indian girl that had come to her in the dream. Was it the spirit of Meda? And was it her amulet that she found?

She remembered clearly the words the maiden had spoken—"This is my people's place. You must . . ."All of a sudden, Meadow knew what she had to do. The amulet felt warm against her skin. She looked at Diablo gazing over the railing to the hills beyond. She climbed down from the fence to get inside the enclosure and walked toward him.

"Meadow, come back here. That horse is dangerous!" Her father barked after her.

"It's okay, Shep," Nueme said quietly as Meadow moved toward the stallion.

The stallion didn't seem upset or try to move away from her as she came close to him. He dropped his head, looking into her eyes as if searching her soul. She reached up and touched his face gently.

"Well, I'll be!" Her father's tone sounded incredulous. "I would never have believed it if I hadn't seen it with my own eyes. That horse acts like he knows you."

Meadow turned and walked back toward the others, the stallion following. He stopped short of the fence where her father and Nueme were sitting, and then snorted and danced away.

Nueme was watching quizzically, as if he knew what Meadow was thinking. Her father stared at her with a furrowed brow.

"What's the matter, Meadow? You look kinda pale."

"Daddy, I know you'll think I'm crazy, but I know I'm supposed to free Diablo. I think he's Arrow. He's the Sky Horse." She couldn't help the catch in her voice.

"What are you talking about, Meadow? You can't free Diablo. He belongs to Bill. Besides, he's not a mustang, he couldn't be Arrow. That's just a story anyway, right Nueme? It's not about a real horse."

"It is just a story." But Nueme still watched the stallion, his dark eyes inscrutable.

"Besides, he was running free when we brought him in. If he were the Sky Horse, he would have taken Meda to the Indian Hunting Ground then," her father said.

"Don't you see, Daddy? He wasn't *really* free. He still belonged to Bill Bowman and didn't have the choice. When he lived with the people, he *chose* to be with them."

"I'm not going to argue with you about some fantasy horse in a legend."

"But, Daddy . . . ."

"Meadow, I need you to promise you won't go near that horse again. Remember that he doesn't belong to us. And he's not Arrow. Just get that out of your head."

Nueme touched her father's arm. "You have to tell her sometime, Shep."

Dad shrunk back, as if he'd been burned, and strode back to the truck.

Meadow stared at Nueme. "Tell me what?"

"It's not for me to say, ask him." He followed after her father.

Oh, great. Dad had some deep, dark secret. She shivered. Maybe he'd been in *prison*, or something. If that was it, she didn't want to know. She'd love him no matter what.

She turned again toward the stallion. Her heart withered with sorrow, as she saw the splendid animal staring out to the hills beyond. She couldn't defy her father, but somehow, some way, she needed to free the Sky Horse, so he could take Meda to the Indian Hunting Ground.

Chapter 21

The Rodeo

Even though Meadow wracked her brain every day, she couldn't come up with a workable plan to free Arrow without causing a major ruckus. Not to mention the fact that her father was counting on the reward money. And he'd been awfully crabby lately, totally unlike his usual self. It must be that horrible secret weighing him down.

But always in the back of her mind was the image of the stallion, looking over the fence, waiting for his freedom.

For the next two weeks, Meadow worked steadily at the stable and before she knew it, the Fourth of July had arrived.

The day dawned clear and bright, with the early summer sun already packing a wallop. Meadow, along with her family, was happy to take a break from the stable for a day of entertainment. Her father and the boys were entering some of the events and hopefully would win some prize money.

Dad loaded Shadow and Elmer, plus the two mustangs for the rodeo stock contractor, into his truck. Monty now had his driver's license, so he practiced driving on the way to Sedona with Dad riding shotgun. Meadow rode with her mother and Mike in the Ranch Wagon.

When they arrived at the fairgrounds, Meadow saw tents and a big Ferris wheel turning. Her mood lightened.

Her parents went to meet with the stock contractor, and Monty headed for the sign-up table to enter the roping events. Meadow and Mike tied the horses to the truck and got them a bucket of water.

Mike pulled a pink paper out of his back pocket. "Look Med, I snatched this letter from under Monty's mattress. Let's see what Blondie has to say."

"You shouldn't have done that!" she protested, but looked over his shoulder when he began reading.

Dear Monty,

       I'm so sorry about what my father is doing. Please believe me that I had nothing to do with the lawsuit. I'm fine! I hardly ever get dizzy spells anymore, but Daddy is so protective. He thinks Foxy is a dangerous horse and that I shouldn't have ridden her, but I told him how I insisted with you. And I'm the one that let her run. It was really all my fault.

       Please, please write to me and say everything is okay between us. I really like you and had so much fun with you. I will try and talk to Daddy again, but he is sooo stubborn!

       I miss you.

       Your friend and more (I hope),

       Cynthia

"I knew she wasn't really hurt!" Mike looked smug.

"And she admits it was her own fault. They won't be able to sue us now, right?"

He shrugged. "I don't know. Her father is pretty sleazy. They might try faking it." He stuffed the envelope back in his jeans. "I'm going to the sign-up line now. Want to come along?"

"Sure. Then we can go see the bucking horses." She giggled. "To see which one is going to dump you."

"Ha, ha. C'mon, let's go."

She waited beside Mike while the line slowly moved ahead to the card table set up with a list and a pile of entry numbers. A rough-looking cowboy who appeared to be in charge, sat behind the table. When it was Mike's turn, the man peered at him through blood-shot eyes. Meadow thought he must have had too much fun at the festivities last night.

"So, young fella, what do ya want to sign up fer?" the man asked.

"Bronc riding."

"That all?"

"Uh…the bull riding, too."

Meadow sucked in her breath. What's he doing?

The entry man looked at Mike more closely and raised his eyebrows. "Bull ridin', huh? Are ya sixteen? You have to be sixteen to ride the bulls, ya know."

"Yes, sir. I turned sixteen on June twentieth, and Dad got me a real nice speckled pup for my birthday. I think I might have a picture of him here somewhere." Mike took out his wallet and began thumbing through it. Meadow looked on, dumbstruck.

"Never mind about yer pup, do you have a driver's license?" The entry man tapped his pencil on the table.

"No, on the day Dad was gonna take me to do my driver's test, we had an old heifer get out and had to go round her up. She was a mean old cow and gave us lots of trouble. We had to chase her for miles and . . . ."

The cowboy in line behind Mike interrupted, "Quit yer yappin' and get movin'. We don't have all day!"

"Yeah, get going!" someone else yelled.

The entry taker sighed and took Mike's money. "Okay, sign here."

Mike picked up his number. "C'mon, Meadow, let's go." When they got around the corner, he took off his cowboy hat and wiped his brow.

Meadow finally found her voice. "Mike, I can't believe you just did that! You flat lied to that guy and you're going to try and ride a bull! That's just stupid! I'm going to tell Dad." She turned to go.

Mike grabbed onto her arm, and the expression on his face stopped her.

"Don't tell Dad. It's all his fault, anyway. If he hadn't sold Rowdy, I wouldn't have to ride a bull. The prize money is $250. If I win that and the bronc riding, and with the tips I've saved, I might have enough to buy him back." He sat down on a straw bale and put his head in his hands. "He would never sell Foxy or Elmer. He just doesn't care about me."

Mike looked so miserable that her heart went out to him. After all, she would just dry up and blow away if her father sold Foxfire.

She patted his shoulder. "That's not true. He does care about you. He's just been acting kinda strange lately. But that's no reason to risk your life riding a bull."

"Don't make it worse than it is. I won't be in any danger, and I've been practicing on the steers at the Bowman ranch. I'm a good rider and it's possible I could win, but not if Dad stops me from riding."

Meadow wasn't convinced. "These bulls are a lot harder to ride than a steer, and they're mean, too."

"Let's go look at the bulls. You'll see they're not so bad."

She reluctantly followed him over to the holding pens. As they got close, the smell of ripe dung permeated the air, and one lonely calf bawled in the background.

A cowboy idly leaned on the corral fence, looking over the bulls. He had short bandy legs, a chaw of tobacco in his cheek and a dusty black hat pulled low on his forehead.

He waited until they were next to the fence, then spat tobacco on the ground. "See that big ole black, over in the corner?"

It was hard to miss the one he meant—an enormous black bull, with his large horns and small mean eyes staring back at them. Patches of dried manure peppered his side. He stuck out his long tongue and licked a fly off his nose.

"Yeah, what about him?" Mike asked.

"That's Tornado. He's about the orneriest bull ever born. He's a twister and nobody has stuck with 'im yet." The cowboy seemed to know all about him. "If ya draw 'im and ride 'im, you'll win the money for shore."

Mike looked the smaller man over. "You must have drawn him before."

The cowboy grinned. "Nope, I'm too smart to ride 'em. I'm Smiley the Clown." He stuck out his hand, shaking with each of them in turn.

"Glad to meet you. I'm Mike Shepherd, and this is my sister, Meadow. So you've fought Tornado before?"

"Yep, and he's pure evil. He would just as soon gore you with those big ole horns as look at ya."

Meadow swallowed and elbowed Mike in the ribs.

"Don't worry, Med. I probably won't draw him, anyway."

Meadow sat on a bale of hay watching her eldest brother practice his roping. Monty had entered the calf roping and he was partnering with Dad in the team roping. He coiled his rope, and then swung it over the plastic steer head stuck on another bale.

She looked up as Brett appeared from the direction of the grandstand.

"Hi, Meadow." He sat next to her.

"Hi, Brett, I didn't know you were coming to the rodeo. Did Linda come, too?"

"Yeah, she's around somewhere. She's with the love of her life, Dave," he said, his voice dripping with sarcasm.

"Oh." She didn't know how to respond to that. She thought Dave was pretty cool.

"It's a good thing Mother isn't here. She definitely wouldn't like Linda hanging out with a deputy sheriff."

"Are you entered in any events?" Meadow asked, to change the subject.

"No, Mother doesn't approve of me participating in such a lowbrow sport. It's okay for me to watch, but she doesn't want me rubbing elbows with the riffraff."

Now she knew what was really bothering him. It wasn't Linda and Dave at all. Brett was mad that he couldn't get in on the fun by entering the rodeo.

"Are you in anything?" he asked.

"No, I wanted to get in the ranch pony race, but you have to be fourteen. Did you bring your horse? We could ride in the grand entry together. They don't care who rides in that."

"No, I didn't bring him."

"That's okay, you can borrow Shadow, and I will ride Elmer. C'mon, it'll be fun." She tugged at him playfully.

"Okay." Brett smiled at last.

Monty looped his rope over his arm and made his way over to them. "How it's going, Brett?"

"Hey Monty, guess who I saw when I was coming over here . . . ."

"Who?'

"Cynthia and her family. They were walking around the exhibits."

Monty reddened, and quickly turned away. "I'd better go. I've still got to get my saddle out." He hurried away towards the truck.

"I think he really likes her," Brett said.

"I hope not. Let's get the horses. It's almost time for the grand entry."

They rode side by side into the arena, then waved to the crowd and lined up with the other riders during the national anthem. Brett was grinning, sitting tall in the saddle, finally having fun, and Meadow felt good that it was her suggestion.

They rode out together and she handed Elmer over to Monty so he could put his saddle on for the roping.

"Let's watch him rope from near the calf chutes." Meadow found her way over to the pens and climbed up the rail fence. Brett followed her and they had a good view of the arena from their perch.

Monty rode up and got positioned in the roping box. He glanced up into the stands as he waited for the calf to be released. Meadow thought he looked more nervous than usual. Must be because he knew Cynthia was up there, somewhere, looking at him.

"Next up, Monty Shepherd from Brighten Hot Springs," the announcer blared.

The calf jumped out, and Elmer charged past the lowered barrier. In no time Monty was in perfect position for the throw. He swung the loop and let go. The rope sailed smoothly over the calf's head and Elmer slid to a stop, pulling the noose tight. The calf was jerked off his feet, but then jumped up and tried to run.

Monty was off his horse in one swift motion and Elmer backed up to keep the rope tight. Her brother heaved the calf to the ground, quickly tied its legs together, and threw up both hands, showing he was finished. After climbing back up on Elmer, Monty waited for the arena cowboy to untie the calf.

"The time on that run is nine seconds flat. Good job, Monty!" the announcer boomed out.

"Yaaay, Monty!" a familiar girl's voice screamed out amid the scattered applause.

Meadow looked in time to see Cynthia jumping up and down, then leave her spot and race over to join Monty.

Cynthia caught up with him just outside of the arena, near Meadow and Brett. "Oh, Monty! You were wonderful!"

"Well, it was a pretty good run, thanks to Elmer." He grinned and patted his horse.

"You're sure to win," Cynthia said.

"No, there were a couple of times better than mine, but I'm happy we caught the calf."

"Well, I think you're the best." Then her voice became whiny. "But why didn't you write to me?"

Monty shifted in the saddle. "Your dad is suing us, remember?"

Her eyes filled with tears. "I can't help that. He's so stubborn. You can see that I'm fine. Maybe a little dizzy sometimes, but nothing serious. It was all my fault." She began to sob in earnest.

Meadow looked on in disbelief as Monty jumped off of Elmer and took her in his arms.

"Please don't cry, Cynthia, it's not your fault."

Monty was still trying to console her and didn't notice Ben Markowitz come hurrying over, shoving his way past people. "Take your hands off my daughter!"

Monty dropped his arms and stepped back, as Cynthia turned to her father and screamed at him, "Why don't you just leave us alone? He hasn't done anything wrong. It's you, you and your stupid lawsuit! I hate you! All you think about is money! Just leave me alone!"

She was crying hysterically by now and ran off into the crowd that had formed. Ben Markowitz looked at Monty with an ugly glower.

"Now see what you've done. She's upset, and it's all because of that fall. She never acted like this before she hit her head. You tell your father that he'd better have that money before the end of August or I'm taking everything you have!"

Meadow saw her parents making their way through the throng, but Markowitz was too wrought up to notice. Dad had his dangerous look. "You lay off the boy!"

Her father was about to raise his clenched fist when Mom put a restraining hand on his arm. Dad leaned down into Markowitz's face. "Anything you need to say, you say it to me, not my kids!"

The attorney quickly backed up, with his face draining of all color. "I'll see you in court!" he managed to bleat out.

"Shep, please." Mom pulled at his arm.

Dad appeared to be having a hard time containing himself, but he finally lowered his arm.

Linda and Dave turned up, pushing their way through the people. Dave wasn't wearing his deputy uniform, but he seemed as if he were on the alert for trouble. "Hi, Shep, how's it going? Everything all right?"

"Yeah, I'm just going to get Shadow warmed up for the team roping. Let's go, Monty."

Dad spun around and headed toward the horse corrals with Monty. Meadow and Brett trailed along behind Mom, who was walking next to Linda and Dave.

Mom turned to Linda. "How's the dig going?" She knew that Linda and Meadow had been spending every spare minute at the cliff dwelling.

"Pretty good, I guess. But that Professor Schumer won't let me help with anything and his two assistants don't seem very knowledgeable."

Dave smiled. "Not everyone studies as hard as you do."

"You're right about that. I just can't get enough of it."

Meadow still thought there was something fishy about the three men working at the cliff dwelling. It seemed strange that Rick appeared to be in charge instead of the professor.

"When is your father going to be back from his trip?" Mom asked.

"He had to extend it for a couple of weeks, so about the middle of August. Now Mother has gone to New York for an opening of a new store. Brett and I are on our own out at the ranch. We'll probably get into all sorts of trouble."

Mom laughed. "I doubt that very much."

"Don't worry," Dave said, "I'll keep a close eye on Linda."

"I'll bet you will."

They all found a seat in the grandstand to watch Mike take second place in the saddle bronc riding. Meadow and Brett came down to meet him at the gate afterward.

"Wow, great ride, Mike!" Brett slapped him on the back.

Mike grinned. "Thanks, I guess you owe me lunch. Remember our bet? I said I would be in the top three."

"You got me there."

The three of them walked around for a while checking out the food booths before deciding on hotdogs. Brett treated Meadow as well as Mike, ordering a hot dog for each of them, which included bags of potato chips and soda pops.

Once they were settled down, Mike seemed tense and was barely eating his food. The mustard seeped out of his bun and dripped onto the picnic table in a little golden pool.

Meadow herself felt a knot in the pit of her stomach. Her brother must be even worse off.

Brett looked back and forth between them. "What's wrong with you guys? You're not worried about the bull riding, are you?"

She gave him an accusing glare. "You were in on this, too! Don't you know how dangerous it is?"

Mike absently mopped the mustard with his napkin. "Brett, tell her. We've been practicing out at the ranch on the roping steers. Some of them buck pretty hard."

"That's right, Meadow. Mike's a darn good rider. He'll do okay."

"I know he's a good rider, but bulls are different. They try to kill you when they buck you off. I think you should quit while you're ahead."

"I can't back out now. I'm all signed up and paid. I'm going to find out who I've drawn to ride right now." He stood. "And don't tell Mom and Dad."

He walked away, leaving his hotdog half-eaten.

"Brett, I have a bad feeling about this." Her stomach felt like she'd been cinched too tight.

"Mike knows what he is doing. Come on, let's go up to the grandstand, the team roping is about to begin." He took her hand and pulled her to her feet.

After they made their way up to the stands, they joined Mom, sitting near Linda and Dave. Meadow forgot her worry about Mike for a while, as she proudly watched Monty and Dad take top honors in the team roping. Next on the agenda was the crowning of the new Rodeo Queen. Meadow and Brett decided to walk around the carnival, since neither one of them wanted to watch that. The bull riding was last on the agenda and there was plenty of time to check out the carnival.

As they walked, the pleasant aroma of popcorn and cotton candy wafted by their noses, and they could hear the drone of the loudspeaker in the background.

A sleazy looking carnie tried his best to lure them in to the sharp-shooting booth with his sing-song chant.

"Come on young fella, wouldn't you like to win a prize for the little lady? Look how easy it is, only three bull's-eyes and you win any prize here—even the big bears. Three shots for only twenty-five cents."

Brett decided to try his luck and plunked down a quarter. The rifles were set up all in a row, with targets on the far side of the booth. He chose a rifle and took aim. His first three shots hit to the left of center.

He frowned, and checked the sight. "I think the gun is a little off." He plunked down another quarter.

This time he adjusted for the error in the gun-sight. Three shots hit smack in the middle of the target.

Brett mimicked the carnie's speech pattern. "Okay, little lady, which bear do you want? Just pick one, any one you want." He gestured to the stuffed animals with flourish.

Meadow giggled and pointed. "That white one on the end with the red bow."

The carnie sort of sneered as he retrieved the white bear and handed it to Meadow. She beamed. Brett won it just for her. She carried the bear, and they wandered up the fairway, chatting like old friends.

"You going to the rodeo dance tonight?" Brett asked.

"Sure, it should be fun." She sneaked a glance at him. "You and Mike will probably be surrounded by girls, just like the last time."

Brett gave her a teasing look. "Don't worry, I'll save some dances for you—now that I know you can dance."

She couldn't help but feel a little thrill shoot through her. It was sorta flustering, though. Boys her own age always gave her a lot of attention, but boys her own age were boring and immature. Brett was definitely not boring. Maybe a little conceited, but really good looking. They were getting along so well, she decided it was the right time to bring up the subject of the stallion. Maybe she could enlist his support.

"What's your father planning to do with Diablo?"

"He will just use him for breeding, I think. That horse hasn't been acting right since you brought him back to the ranch. He acts kinda, well, I know it sounds crazy, but kinda sad."

Meadow plunged right in. "That's because he should be free on the range. You can't keep a horse like him in a stable. Maybe your Dad could breed his mares during the breeding season and then let Diablo go free the rest of the year." She gave him a sidelong peek to see his reaction.

Brett shook his head. "I don't think Dad would agree to that. What if he gets hurt while he's out there?"

"Diablo won't get hurt. I'm positive of that. He's meant to be free." As she said it, she could feel the warmth of the amulet under her shirt.

"There's something you're not telling me, isn't there?" Brett looked at her quizzically.

The heat crept up her face, but she wasn't ready to tell him her secret. She thought he might think she had imagined the whole dream, and she was afraid he wouldn't believe the legend of the Sky Horse.

As they were talking, the boom of the announcer's voice interrupted them, saying that the bull riding was about to begin. They hurried back to the grandstand.

Meadow sat in the stands with Brett, with the new stuffed bear on the seat beside her, petting it occasionally. They watched as rider after rider tried to stay atop the wild bulls that jumped, bucked and snorted. Eventually most of them ended up in the arena dirt, and then they had to evade a mad bull on foot.

Smiley the Clown, sporting an orange wig, striped shirt, and baggy trousers, did his job, diverting the bulls' attention away from the cowboys by carefully choreographed moves designed to entertain the crowd. Only one rider so far had actually made it the full eight seconds that qualified the ride to win money.

Her queasiness returned tenfold, and she wasn't sure whether it was from the hotdog or from nervousness. She hadn't told her parents that Mike was riding, not having the heart to spoil his plan. Glancing over at her father and mother, she saw that they were enjoying being spectators for a change. They looked more relaxed than they had in a while. Thank goodness Dad was feeling better. Probably because he and Monty had won the team roping with the purse of one hundred dollars, and he'd just sold the two mustangs for a total of three hundred to the stock contractor.

Dad and Mom were sharing a bag of popcorn, and every once in a while her father would throw a kernel into the air and try to catch it in his mouth. Mom laughed at him whether or not he was successful. Dave and Linda sat holding hands, while Monty was down at the corrals tending to the horses. Meadow knew Monty felt bad about the scene with Markowitz, and most likely didn't feel like socializing right now. She tightened her lips. Cynthia's father was such a jerk.

Then the announcer came blaring back on.

"Next up we have a young cowboy, just sixteen years old, and he's got his work cut out for him. Please welcome Mike Shepherd riding Tornado! Or should I say, *trying* to ride Tornado. That bull has never been ridden yet!"

"What the hell!" Dad jumped to his feet and sent popcorn flying everywhere. He shoved his way down from the stands toward the announcer's booth. It was slow going having to wend his way through the mass of people crowding near the arena fence. Mom sat as if frozen to her seat, face ashen.

"He's only fourteen, why did they let him enter?" Mom's voice was stricken.

Meadow felt worse than ever, and Brett didn't look too good either. She went down to the bucking chute to be near Mike, and climbed up the fence nearby. Tornado was bashing his horns against the side planks. Bellowing loudly, the bull crashed against the restraining walls again.

"Ready, son?" The lanky cowboy asked, nodding his head toward the chute.

Mike looked pale and scared. She saw him take a gulp of air, jam his hat down on his head, and then put his leg over the bull's writhing back.

Tornado bellowed his displeasure and reared up on his hind legs trying to climb out of the chute. Mike tried to sit firmly, but it wasn't easy on the thrashing bull. He wrapped the rigging rope tightly around his left hand. He raised his other hand and nodded to the gate keeper.

Meadow saw Smiley waiting near a barrel in the arena, his large red nose shining in the sunlight. He bobbed his head toward Mike and gave him a thumbs up, but from her perspective, Smiley the clown wasn't smiling.

The gate swung open, and Tornado burst out with a gigantic leap. He landed on stiff front legs turning to the left at the same time. He twisted and bucked, his hind legs going up vertical. Meadow saw Mike's head snap back, but he was still on top.

Tornado let loose with another enormous buck and twisted back the other direction. The bull put her in mind of a powder keg that had just blown up. She thought the roping steers Mike had practiced on must seem like children's ponies compared to this heaving, bucking mass of pure muscle.

Tornado twisted and turned, first in one direction and then the other. Wouldn't this ever be over? One more tremendous buck with a twist and Mike was wrenched loose from his back and slid off to the side, but his hand was entangled in the rigging.

Meadow screamed when she saw Mike fall and she started to scramble down the fence into the arena. A strong hand grabbed her arm, and held her back. She looked up to see that Brett had joined her.

"Are you nuts? You can't go in there with that bull!"

"But Mike is caught in the rigging!"

"You can't do anything. The outriders will get him loose."

Meadow felt the bile rise in her throat as Tornado kept bucking and twisting with Mike hanging off his side, flopping like a ragdoll. The outriders galloped up next to him, and soon had the rigging loosened. Mike's hand came free and he fell heavily to the ground.

The mad bull turned, pawed the ground and came charging back toward Mike. He was semi-conscious, moving sluggishly. Tornado was coming fast, and at the last minute, Smiley jumped between Mike and the furious bull.

The clown distracted Tornado and ran back toward the fence with the bull in hot pursuit. Just as Smiley reached the barrier, the enraged bull caught him on his horns. With a great toss of his head the bull threw Smiley up into the grandstand. Spectators shrieked as he landed in their midst with blood gushing from the wound in his back.

Meadow saw her father vault the fence and sprint over to Mike, who was still unable to get off the ground. The bull noticed the two figures still in his territory and started another charge towards them. Dad quickly scooped Mike in his arms and raced toward the fence.

Tornado was coming fast and was nearly on them when two outriders closed in on the bull and flung their lariats over his horns. Tornado was jerked to a stop just as he was about to reach Dad, with a limp Mike in his arms. The announcer piped up and his matter-of-fact voice grated on her nerves.

"Well, folks, we've had a little excitement here at the rodeo today. Don't worry, the ambulance is standing by, and I'm sure our young cowboy will be fine. Let's give a round of applause to our brave clown, Smiley, Mike Shepherd and his father, Shep."

The ambulance entered into the arena and the attendants placed Mike and Smiley onto gurneys and loaded them in. Dad climbed in with them.

Meadow found her mother and Monty and they all rushed to the Ranch Wagon. The ride to the hospital seemed endless, and Meadow sat in an agony of regret for not having warned her parents. From the back seat of the car, she could see her mother gripping the steering wheel grimly, deathly quiet, with Monty next to her. The flashing red beacon ahead of them reflected grotesquely on their faces and the eerie moan of the siren seemed to go on and on.

She momentarily blocked the horror of what was happening, and thought back to the fun she had been having until everything had gone so terribly wrong. Her mind flashed on the white bear Brett had won for her. Wonder what happened to it, she thought numbly. She even forgot to worry about Arrow or the Indian cave for a few hours. It was amazing how quickly a person's life could change.

Chapter 22

The Medicine Chest

Rick frowned impatiently as Professor Schumer neatly stacked another crate onto the pile he had ready to go. It was late afternoon on the day of the rodeo.

"Hurry up, you old fart! The stack doesn't have to be perfect, you know. We're just taking them up top and restacking them for the plane." Rick took a swig from his canteen and wiped his mouth with the back of his hand.

The professor stood up and regarded Rick coldly. "I really don't see what my occasional flatulence has to do with this project. We have to be careful of these artifacts. Do you want something to get damaged?"

"I'm just tired of the whole damned thing. "I thought we'd be done by now. It just ain't American working on the Fourth of July. And you're slow as a slug packing everything."

"And it's obvious to me what an uneducated ignoramus you are." The professor turned back to another pot and started wrapping it carefully.

Rick balled up his fist, then unclenched his hand slowly, rethinking his idea of decking the guy. He'd better back off a little. Professor Schumer wasn't as frail as he appeared, having the energy and stamina of someone half his age. Rick couldn't push him around the way he did Wally. He'd bide his time and an opportunity would present itself. He looked around the chamber with a critical eye. At least now it was mostly devoid of all the relics that they could pack. Too bad they couldn't carve off the wall paintings and take them.

It had been two long weeks since they'd started this job. Way too long for his taste. Every day packing and carrying this crap up to the mesa. They'd rigged up a pulley system to help transport the crates up the steep incline, but it was still a lot of work. It'd better be worth it in the end.

And not only the work, but every night listening to the professor drone on about how he got fired from ASU because he just couldn't keep his hands off the goods. The school had apparently noticed that priceless pieces kept disappearing on his watch. Not having any real evidence against him, the university hadn't pressed charges, but they were making it impossible for him to get another teaching post.

When Rick asked why he kept stealing if he liked teaching so much, the professor whined about low teacher pay. What a load of horse crap that was! Rick happened to know professors got paid well, not to mention the whole summer off with pay.

But it was a good thing they'd had the shady professor with them. He knew everything there was to know about Indian artifacts and he told Rick this huge find was unique. And he had the contacts to buy the stuff. The authorities had been cracking down on illegal artifact sales in the last few years, so they had to be extra cautious in how these were disposed of.

Professor Schumer suddenly looked up from the pot he was wrapping. "Something has been bothering me since we started this project. Now I know what we're missing."

Rick let his crate slide to the ground. "What?"

"We haven't found any of the Medicine Man's sacred articles. They would be worth a fortune by themselves."

"Why is that?"

"Because the sacred items are passed down through a line of Shamans or Medicine Men, as the Indians call them. It is very rare to come upon them, but I thought in this dwelling, they might have been left behind since they seem to have taken nothing at all with them." The professor rubbed his head. "A collector would pay a premium for such ancient artifacts."

Rick looked around the chamber with renewed interest. "Where would they be kept?"

"They usually kept them in a special room, sort of a Medicine Man's laboratory, if you will."

"We been through this place a hundred times. There ain't no other rooms."

They were interrupted by Wally coming out of the passage, puffing like a locomotive. Good thing he's strong, Rick thought, otherwise he'd be totally useless. He's strong as an ox, but not quite as smart.

"Okay, boys." Professor Schumer had finished with the crate. "This one is ready to take up top for the plane. I have finished cataloging everything now. I think we have most of the really valuable items packed."

"Yeah, we need to get outa here before the rodeo is over and they get suspicious about where these things have gone," Rick said. "But we need a little rest, first. We've been going at it non-stop since early morning."

The professor huffed. "All right, but not too long. If that girl, Linda, checks up at ASU's archeology center down in Phoenix, I want to be long gone. She and Meadow have been bona fide pests hanging around and watching everything we do. This rodeo is a genuine break for us."

"Yeah, we'll have everything gone before they get back. It's a good thing Linda isn't a trained archeologist yet. She sure noses around a lot. She must go home at night and study this crap. I'm having a hard time answering her snoopy questions all the time." Rick plopped down next to the professor.

"I'm well aware of what a trial she has been, coming every day and taking all those pictures with her Brownie. And that Meadow is just a kid, but watches us like a hawk. You would think she had a vested interest in all of this."

"Yeah, she's a royal pain in the ass, too. I don't think they will suspect anything for a while, but it's a good thing Wendell let us know they'd all be at the rodeo," Rick said. "We got a lotto work done in a short time."

"You're not kidding about the work." Wally mopped his sweaty neck. "Do you think it's gonna be worth it for a bunch of old Indian things?"

"Don't be an idiot, Wally. We're going be set up for life when we finish this little deal." Rick wrinkled his brow. He hoped.

"I'd sure like to be set up with Linda for life." Wally put on a wistful look.

Rick's laugh had a nasty edge. "Fat chance you'd have with a girl like her." He tossed Wally their canteens. "Here, go fill these up at the water hole."

"Okay." Wally lumbered toward the steps to the lower chamber.

Rick watched his brother go, knowing it would take a few minutes to get down the winding passageway to the underground pool, which the professor said must have been the early cave inhabitant's water supply. "What time will Paul be here with the plane?"

"Before dusk. That's why it's imperative to have it all ready."

"Good, then we can get outa here. I'm thoroughly sick of this place." Rick leaned back.

They didn't speak for a few minutes, waiting for Wally. After a while, Rick looked toward the lower steps. "I wonder where that dolt is, he's been gone a long time."

Just as he was about to go look for him, Wally came hurrying back up the steps, out of breath. "I found another room, Rick." His eyes were wide. "A secret room!"

"What? Are you crazy? Where?" Rick eyed his brother with narrowed eyes.

"Well, I was following the passage and then I kinda took a wrong turn, I guess, 'cuz I ended up at this dead end . . . ."

"Yeah, yeah, then what?"

"Well, I was mixed up, so I stopped and leaned on the wall trying to figure out where I was . . . ."

Rick interrupted. "Get to the point, you dope!"

"Well, like I said, I was leaning on this wall and it sorta opened behind me and I fell into this secret room. It has more stuff in it!" Wally grinned like the Cheshire Cat.

The professor rubbed his hands together. "Probably the Medicine Man's cache."

"Can you find it again, you big oaf?" Rick asked.

Wally nodded and they followed him back down the inner steps. After making a couple of wrong turns they found the secret chamber. The professor focused in on the pile of blankets and triumphantly uncovered the chest buried there.

"This is fantastic! I hoped it would be here somewhere." He carefully opened the lid and revealed the treasure. "No doubt about it, this stuff is worth ten times more than all the rest put together."

The soft sheen of silver jewelry with turquoise and other precious stones made Rick lick his lips. Packed alongside the silver were dolls, fetishes and masks used in the religious and healing ceremonies, as well as small pots and jars with powders and potions in them. The professor kept digging until he came to a small beaded bag. He frowned when he found it empty.

"This bag was made for a special piece. I wonder what happened to it."

"Well, it's gone now, so I guess we'll never know," Rick said. "Come on, let's get this stuff outta here."

The professor nodded. "Yes, we'll put the Medicine Chest in a crate of its own for special handling."

Rick and Wally carried the chest to the upper chamber and the professor started to put it in a crate. He wasn't quite finished when they heard the whir of an airplane engine in the distance.

"At last, Paul is here," the professor said. "Rick, you and Wally go start loading the plane while I finish this crate."

"You need to supervise how the crates are put on the plane. I can finish this, it's almost done anyway," Rick said.

"Yes, that will be better, I suppose." The professor got up then looked back just before he left. "Be very careful with that, Rick."

Rick nodded, and knelt down in front of the crate containing the Medicine Chest while the professor and Wally went up top to begin loading the plane. After making sure they were gone, he took the chest out, refilling the crate with a blanket and a few rocks. He shoved the chest back down the steps, pushing and pulling, till he finally managed to get it back in the secret room. He closed the door and heaved a sigh of relief. As he hurried back to the top he almost laughed out loud at his good fortune. It was just the lapse in judgment he had been waiting for. The old coot was pretty careful, but he goofed this time. He smacked his lips as if he'd just eaten a juicy steak.

Rick arrived at the mesa in time to see the plane still circling, looking for the landing spot. Professor Schumer waved it over to the place they had decided was the most level.

The Piper Super Cub bounced down the field and came to an abrupt halt in a swirl of dust. Paul Misner stepped out of the rented plane with a glower on his sharp face.

Wonder what's wrong with him? Rick snorted. Oh well, there's always something wrong with that weanie. For a guy with a good job, he sure has a lot of problems.

The professor hurried over to him. "Hello, Paul, you're late. We want to get this load gone before those nosey girls get back from the rodeo."

"You won't have to worry about them for a while. I heard from Wendell that the Shepherd boy got hurt at the rodeo."

The professor raised his eyebrows. "What happened?"

"Tried to ride a bull, the damn fool. They don't know for sure if he's going to make it," Paul answered.

"Is that the boy that saved you from the river?" Wally asked.

Rick smiled wickedly. Leave it to Wally to bring up a sore subject.

Paul shifted uncomfortably. "Yeah, that's the one. Lots of brawn, but low on brains."

Rick laughed outright. "That's for sure, if he was smart, he would a let you drowned."

"Just . . . just shut your mouth and load the plane." Paul's face was suffused in red.

Rick shrugged and ambled toward the boxes that were stacked neatly under the lean-to, feeling pleased with himself.

"Come on, everyone. We all need to help with this. It will be dark soon." The professor walked briskly over to help carry crates.

They finished loading in record time, and before long before the plane was taxiing down the makeshift dirt runway. It took off and disappeared into the sunset with its cargo stowed precariously in every square inch of available space.

Chapter 23

The Operation

Meadow and her family gathered around the young, fresh-faced doctor. The hallway smelled of antiseptic and they heard little beeps emitting from unidentifiable machines out of unknown places. It made the whole experience surreal to her, listening in despair to the doctor's words directed at her parents.

"Your son has internal bleeding and his arm was practically torn from its socket. He may also have a concussion." Dr. Ames paused, then went on. "We need to operate immediately. The nurse is getting the consent forms for your signatures."

Meadow studied the doctor's face. He didn't look any older than Monty. And he's going to operate on Mike?

"Will he be all right after the operation?" Her ashen-faced mother had grabbed on to her as if she were a life jacket, her nails biting into Meadow's arm.

The young doctor gave Mom a sympathetic smile meant to boost her morale.

"He's young and strong. If anyone could make it through, it would be your son."

"You mean he might *die*?" Dad could barely choke out the word.

"I won't lie to you. This is a very serious situation. If he makes it through the operation and the rest of the night, then his chances are pretty good, if infection doesn't set in. We also have to worry about his brain swelling from the concussion."

Meadow felt her stomach heave, but forced herself to stand stoically, trying to be strong for her mother. She watched as her parents signed the consent forms, and saw Dr. Ames disappear through the double doors marked Operating Rooms.

Linda, Dave, and Brett were seated in the waiting room when they got back from the conference with the doctor. Her father told them what the doctor had to say, and then Dave stood up. "This is going to be a long night. Let's go to the cafeteria and get some coffee."

"Okay." Dad's voice was low and deflated.

He grabbed onto her mother's arm and guided her through the door. The rest of them followed silently. They were the only ones in the cafeteria, and it was quiet as a tomb.

Her parents sat with Linda and Dave sipping coffee. Meadow was with Monty and Brett a few tables away. Her soda waited in front of her.

She poked at the bubbles rising to the top with her straw. "I can't believe I just let him sign up to ride without telling anyone. I might have stopped this whole mess."

"Don't blame yourself, Med," Monty said. "You know what a hardhead Mike is. He would have found a way to ride if he was determined."

"He came out and practiced at the ranch and he was good." Brett put his head in his hands. "Too bad he drew the worst bull on the circuit. If he hadn't gotten hung up, this wouldn't have happened."

"He's gonna be fine. You'll see, he'll be fine." Monty sounded like he was trying to convince himself as much as any of them.

Dad finally came over to their table.

"Monty, I need you and Meadow to go back to the stable and take care of the horses. Linda will take you back to the rodeo grounds to get the truck and to pick up Elmer and Shadow. Your mother and I will be here all night, but we'll get word to you if there's any change."

"Okay, Dad."

Two hours later they arrived back at the stable, with Elmer and Shadow in the back of the truck. Meadow helped Monty unload and do the chores. She was glad to have a mindless activity to occupy her. Kelsey stuck close to her heels, as if she knew something was amiss. When she threw Foxfire her flake of hay, instead of digging in as usual, her mare came and stood close to Meadow, nuzzling her, also sensing a problem.

Brett and Linda offered to come and keep them company at the stable that evening, but Monty told them they didn't really feel like talking.

Meadow heated up some leftover stew for dinner, served some to Monty and forced herself to eat few bites. For once she didn't have to be asked to clean up the dishes. In fact, she began cleaning and straightening with a zeal unlike her usual aversion to housework. Monty watched her flurry of energy with a frown.

"Calm down, Med," he told her. "Mike will be okay. You know he's strong as a horse."

"I know."

"Remember when you were in the hospital? Sick with asthma? Mike and I were really worried when Mom and Dad spent the night there with you."

"You were worried? About me?"

"Of course about you, dopey. But everything turned out okay that time and it will this time, too."

She went over and hugged her big brother, feeling better. But the night was long, and she didn't sleep much. She figured Monty probably didn't either.

Early the next morning, Brett came over to tell them that their father had just called. When Meadow saw him hurrying over, she thought the news had to be positive, until she saw his face.

"Your dad said they were staying at the hospital longer because there were some complications. He said for you to keep the stable open, and they would try to get back later in the day." Brett looked tired, too. "I'm so sorry the news isn't better."

She turned to her brother. "Oh, Monty, what are we going to do?" Her tiny ray of hope had just sputtered out.

"We'll do just what Dad told us to do." Monty rose abruptly and headed out to tack up the horses.

Brett stayed with them and helped saddle the horses and take care of customers. Business was steady all morning, and time went by fast, with them all taking turns guiding the dude rides.

At noon, Linda showed up with hamburgers for everyone.

"Has there been any more news?" Meadow waited without breathing.

Linda shook her head. "No, I haven't heard a word."

Meadow couldn't eat, and Monty barely touched his food either. After lunch, Linda left to work at the resort office, since Wendell and Lucy had taken the day off. Brett stayed at the stable to help. He tried to talk to her, to take her mind off Mike, but she felt like a sleepwalker and could not respond.

Finally, she turned from him. "Please stop, Brett. I don't want to talk right now." She saw the hurt on his face, but what did it matter? Nothing mattered right now, except Mike.

As the day went on, and they didn't hear from her parents, the feeling of a cold hand gripping her heart intensified. A sob would sometimes catch in her throat, but she would not let herself break down in front of the customers. The stable kept them busy, and she reminded herself the money they were making was for Mike's operation. She spent as much time as she could with Foxfire and Kelsey who were the only ones she wanted to be with.

Meadow felt like she would burst if she held in her emotions any longer. After she and Monty fed the horses, she had to get away and be alone. She wandered aimlessly and found herself at Mike's favorite fishing hole, where she collapsed on the bank, sobbing. She had never in her life felt so helpless. Mike just had to get better. But what if he dies? Oh no, that's too terrible to think about. Then she cried some more.

After an hour or more had passed, she continued to lie at the creek with tears dried on her face, unable to face Monty. Kelsey snuggled next to her as if trying to impart strength from close contact.

It was just getting dark when she got back to the cabin, the Ranch Wagon now parked next to it. Meadow rushed up to the door and yanked it open. Her mother sat at the table with Monty. She looked haggard, her blue eyes shadowed with fatigue.

Meadow cautiously crept into the room, afraid to ask about Mike.

"Where's Daddy?"

"He wouldn't leave Mike, even though the doctor told us both to go home and get some rest. Your father made me leave without him." Her voice broke. "Mike has gone into a coma."

Meadow's lip started trembling and her mother gathered her in her arms. "Try not to worry, honey."

But the words sounded hollow. How could any of them not worry?

That night, Meadow again lay awake, her mind imagining the worst. At last, she fell into an exhausted, fitful sleep. She had a disturbingly real dream about Meda, the Indian maiden.

Meda was in a tiny jail cell and her face was worn and old. She beckoned for Meadow to come toward her. As Meadow drew near, Meda spoke: "You must free Arrow so I can be free."

In her dream, Meadow let the stallion go free and then he magically flew up to the heavens with Meda on his back and she was young and beautiful again.

She awoke with a start from the vivid dream, knowing exactly what she had to do. Dawn had not yet broken over the horizon, but she tiptoed out of bed and into the darkness. As usual, Kelsey met her at the door.

"Stay here."

Kelsey sat with a little whine. Her father always said Kelsey had decided Meadow was her special charge she needed to protect. And it did seem that way since Kelsey tried to accompany her everywhere.

Foxfire greeted her with a soft nicker as she opened the corral. Meadow quickly bridled her and swung onto her back. She turned Foxfire toward the Bowman Ranch and let her have her head. The mare responded eagerly with her fast, floating gallop. She seemed to sense the importance of their quest and knew exactly where they were going. It was so dark, Meadow couldn't see her hand in front of her face, but she trusted Foxfire to find the way and buried her face in her mane and let her run.

The sun finally began to give the early morning a bit of light, as it climbed slowly from the horizon, still partially hidden behind the mountains to the east.

Meadow could now see some of the trail. In a short while they had covered the distance to the ranch and Foxfire galloped through the Bowmans' gate. They slowed to a trot, and made their way to the barn. When Diablo saw them he nickered a greeting. She hurriedly put Foxfire in a stall, and then went to the stallion's corral.

"Easy, boy, remember me?" She spoke softly to him as she entered.

He pranced over to her and snorted with his eyes ablaze. She touched the amulet, and then took a step forward. At once she felt the warm presence surround her. Diablo's eyes softened and he dropped his head for her to pet him.

"I knew you were the Sky Horse," she whispered, stroking his sleek neck. "I've come to set you free."

She quickly walked to the gate, with the stallion following. Swinging it wide open, she watched him trot through, then break into a gallop. He stopped short of the ranch's outer gate and turned back, facing her. She saw him rear up on his hind legs, and paw the air as if to say thank you, and then he turned and galloped out of sight.

Meadow again reached for the pendant, and it still felt alive and warm in her hand. A weight lifted off her heart, and she was suddenly totally at peace, for she knew without a doubt Mike would not die. Arrow had other business to attend to. After getting Foxfire, Meadow left without anyone knowing they were even there.

Chapter 24

The Heist

Meadow quietly opened the hospital room door and peeked in. It had been a week since the accident, and the doctor said Mike would likely be discharged in another few days if he continued to progress so well.

Mike was half sitting, propped up with pillows, but he was facing toward the window, so she couldn't tell if he was awake. His left arm was in a cast all the way to his shoulder and was held up by a sling attached to a hook hanging over the bed. The stark white walls of the room were unadorned, as though to maximize the institutional feel of the place. A few magazines lay piled on the bedside tray along with a plastic container of water with a bent straw sticking out of it.

"Are you awake?" she asked softly.

The rest of her family was at the stable working, now that Mike was out of danger. Her parents had agreed to let her accompany Linda into town. Only family members were allowed in his room, so Linda dropped her off and went to do some errands.

When he turned his head toward her, his face lit up. "Meadow, am I glad to see you! It's just plain boring lying here all day with nothing to do."

She smiled. "You must be feeling a lot better if you're bored."

"Yeah, I'm ready to get out of here right now."

To prove it, he unhooked his arm, swung his legs over the side of the bed, and tried to get up. He made it part way before falling back to the bed. "Ohhh, I guess I'm not as strong as I thought."

"You need to take it slow." Meadow fluffed his pillows behind him again. "You gave us all a good scare, you know, being in a coma for two days."

"I know, and I had the strangest dream while I was unconscious. It seemed very real to me."

"What was it about?"

His eyes became strange and unfocused, almost like when he was unconscious. "I was in this beautiful land that had all sorts of flowers, trees and streams with waterfalls . . . and lots of animals of all kinds. It was paradise. No cars or anything like that. It was all Indians that lived there, and this beautiful Indian girl was my tour guide."

She swallowed. "An Indian girl?"

"Yeah, and she would just take my hand and we would fly—no, float—through the air to the next village. Everyone I saw was young and happy and they would wave as we went by."

"Then what happened?"

"She asked me if I wanted to stay forever . . . in that place, I mean. I said even though it was wonderful, I didn't want to leave my family to live there. And she nodded and said, 'Go back, it's not your time.' As soon as she said that, the vision disappeared and I woke up." Mike sat staring into space for a moment, then shook his head. "Isn't that weird?"

Goose bumps had broken out on Meadow's skin. "I don't think it's weird, but I do think there are a lot of things we don't understand."

Mike grabbed her hand. "Don't tell anybody about it, okay?"

"I won't."

"I don't even know why I told you, it sounds pretty corny when I say it out loud. It must have been that knock on my head. What's been happening at Brighten since I've been gone?"

Meadow shifted and looked at the floor. "For one thing, I'm in deep trouble."

"How come?"

"I let Diablo go free."

"What? Why'd you do a dumb thing like that?"

She looked out the window. "I just felt like he had to be free, to make everything right again."

"Do you know how hard it was to capture him?"

"Bill Bowman will be home next weekend, and Dad is making me tell him why I did it." She stood and walked around the room. "Dad's really mad at me because he won't get the reward now. I don't know what to do."

Mike's face was puzzled. "But why *did* you do it, when you knew it would cause problems? You must have a reason."

She shrugged. How could she tell anyone about the amulet or her *own* dreams? They'd think she'd lost her marbles.

Mike shook his head. "You *are* in deep trouble. And I thought I was the only one that did really dumb stuff. You know how much we needed that money."

"I know," she whispered.

After saying goodbye to Mike, Meadow waited in front of the hospital for Linda. It was not long before her distinctive powder-blue Cadillac pulled up. The car was a graduation present from Linda's parents, and Meadow was pretty sure it was a one of a kind in the little back-water of Sedona. The Cadillac was the fanciest car Meadow had ever ridden in and she was fascinated by the automatic windows. Who knew you could push a button and have windows go up or down? The big tail fins looked sort of dumb, though.

As she climbed into the passenger side, Linda asked after her brother. "Is he in good spirits? Knowing Mike, he must be getting pretty antsy by now."

"So true, but he's holding up pretty well. Did you get everything done?"

"Yes, except I was trying to call Professor Schumer. His phone just rang and rang."

"Why don't you just call from Brighten?"

Linda glanced over at her. "Wendell and Lucy are back from their little vacation, and I didn't want them overhearing, just in case."

"What do you mean? You don't trust them?"

"I just want to be careful. I had Dave do a background check on Wendell Halstead. He doesn't seem to have a police record, but he also doesn't seem to have any background at all. It's like he came from Mars or something."

Meadow screwed up her face. "I never have liked Wendell and Lucy. And I always thought there was something fishy about that professor and his assistants. Have you talked to Professor Schumer at all since they moved the stuff?"

Linda's brow wrinkled. "I've only talked to him once since the artifacts were taken to ASU storage. Right after the rodeo. At that time, he said the transport went just fine. But I've tried several times since then with no answer. I'm getting worried."

"Why don't we try calling the university direct?" Meadow asked. "Maybe we could get a hold of the other guy. What was his name?"

"Professor Swan. Good idea. There's a phone booth at this drugstore." She swung the big car into a parking space.

Linda left the phone booth door open, so Meadow could hear, and put a few coins in the slot. She dialed the main telephone number at ASU. Linda asked for Professor Swan, and after a short wait, she finally got through to him. She motioned for Meadow to come close and listen in.

Professor Swan spoke. "No one ever called me back regarding the find, Miss Bowman. We have no artifacts from your area in our storage facility."

"But a Professor Schumer contacted me, cataloged everything, and put them in ASU storage," Linda told him. "Is he available?"

"I'm sorry. Professor Schumer was let go a few months ago."

Linda's face lost all its color. "Oh, no. For what?"

"I am not at liberty to divulge that information. Suffice it to say, he will not be working with antiquities again."

"Do you know where he is now? Does he have any friends he might stay in contact with at the school?"

"He kept to himself while here. I'm sorry, Miss Bowman. I haven't any more information," Professor Swan said.

"I'm afraid he might have just stolen all the relics from the cliff dwelling on our ranch. Please, you must know something!" Linda was pleading now.

"If he stole the items, you must contact the authorities," Professor Swan said. "I'm sorry I can't be of more help."

Linda hung up the phone and turned to Meadow. "Did you hear all that?"

"Yeah, now what do we do?"

It only took a moment for Linda to decide. "Let's go see Dave. He's on duty today."

They walked into the small, austere room that served as the sheriff's office, and Dave looked up from his desk. His rugged face broke into a smile when he saw Linda.

"Hello, ladies, you're the best looking visitors I've had all day."

"Hi, Dave." Linda smiled and he took her hand.

Meadow could feel the electricity flow between the two of them. Linda retrieved her hand and got to the point.

"It turns out that Professor Schumer is a crook. I just finished talking to Professor Swan from ASU. He was the one that was supposed to catalog the artifacts, and he never got that message. He said Schumer was fired a while back. Someone set us up with a ringer."

"What do you think happened?" Dave asked.

"I think the only ones that could have intercepted the call were Wendell or Lucy. It had to be them. Now everything is missing."

"It may be Wendell and Lucy behind it, but we have no real evidence," he said.

"That's true, but I'm going to watch them like a hawk from now on. I'm just glad I kept a list of the artifacts and got pictures of everything in there." Linda paced the floor.

"Take it easy, Linda. We'll get to the bottom of this. Did Professor Swan say if he knew Schumer very well?"

"He just said that Schumer was kind of a lone wolf."

"That doesn't surprise me, criminals don't usually have a lot of close friends. I'll make some phone calls to the Phoenix police." Dave took her hand again to stop her restless laps around the office. "I have some friends on the force down there."

While Linda and Dave were talking, Meadow stood uncomfortably in the background, feeling as if she were invisible. To get out of the way, she edged over to the wall near some metal file cabinets, and read the wanted posters.

She browsed the faces, idly going from one to another. Then she stopped and went back for a second look at one that looked vaguely familiar. Where had she seen him before? As she studied the poster more closely, it suddenly dawned on her. It was the black jacketed hoodlum who had accosted Linda at the dance. His name was listed as Melvin Richard Downard.

"Wanted for Murder" it said under his picture. She peered at the fine print that read he was wanted for a double homicide of a young couple. Horrified, she took a step back.

"Look at this poster." She beckoned Linda and Dave to come over. "Do you recognize this guy?"

She wanted to be sure she hadn't just imagined that he was the same person.

"That's the guy that grabbed me and you punched him!" Linda stared at the mug shot. "Look, Dave!"

"That's him all right, those posters just came in the other day and Sheriff Lodge put them up. I hadn't even had a chance to check them out. Man, I should've known he was a major criminal. I'll keep a sharp lookout for him, he could still be hanging around here."

"I hope he's long gone!" Meadow could still picture him leering at Linda.

After they returned to the car, Meadow didn't feel much like going home. It hadn't been very much fun at the stable lately, ever since she'd let Diablo loose.

Linda seemed to pick up on her mood. "I know what we should do. Let's go up to the reservation and tell Chief White Horse what happened. I want him to know about it right away so he can keep a watch out for the stolen stuff. Do you have time?"

"That's a great idea. I didn't tell anyone how long we'd be gone, so it's okay to get home later today."

The reservation was not too far outside of town, and Meadow drank in the peaceful beauty of the majestic red rocks as the luxury car purred down the road. The miles flew by, and before long they turned off the main highway onto a dusty dirt track.

They drove for another mile or so and the rocks opened up to a grassy plain. A large flock of sheep grazed, intermingled with a few goats. A couple of children were tending them. Meadow was surprised to see some small modern looking houses that were all similar as they drove into the village. "Nueme lives in a tepee. I thought the village would be like in the movies with tepees everywhere."

Linda smiled. "Not many live that way anymore. These houses were built by the government. The Indians have a hard time making it on what they get from the feds, so the housing is provided if they want it. See the large tepee in the center over there? That's where they have tribal council meetings."

As they drove on through the town, a yellow dog barked at them halfheartedly, then flopped down under a juniper. The town looked quite poor, although there were late model pickup trucks parked in front of houses here and there. Meadow saw some women working at a loom, weaving a rug with bright red, grey and black geometric designs. One woman had a plump baby strapped to a board on her back.

Linda drove down the main street to the end, and pulled into the driveway of the only house with a decorative wooden fence. It was larger than the others and even had some landscaping around the front. Cheerful hollyhocks brightened the yard and various earthen pots sat on the porch.

"This is Chief White Horse's house." Linda parked, they got out of the car, and went through the gate. Once they reached the porch, a large man opened the front door and welcomed them with a friendly smile.

"Linda, it's good to see you. Come in." He stood back and held the door for them.

"This is my friend, Meadow. Meadow, Chief White Horse," Linda said as they entered the house.

"It's good to know you, Meadow. You can call me Joe. That's what my friends call me."

She took the hand he offered. Wow, a real Indian chief considered her a friend! She had hoped he would be in traditional garb with a big headdress, but he had on jeans and cowboy shirt, although he wore his silver hair long down his back with one feather in it.

The house was sparsley furnished, the simple decorations were Shonto weavings on the floors and a painted shield hung over the fireplace. Linda had told her on the way out that Joe's wife had died a few years back.

Only one photograph sat on a sideboard, featuring a pretty auburn-haired woman holding the hand of a young boy. Meadow briefly wondered what had happened to the boy, and then went to look at the shield, which had a hunting scene on it. It was similar to the one they'd found in the cave.

Joe caught her studying it. "That was handed down to me by my great, great grandfather."

She turned to him. "It's beautiful. It looks just like the one we found in the dwelling."

Linda sat down on the couch, her face anxious. "The artifacts are why we wanted to come up and talk to you, Joe. They're missing."

His smile faded. "Oh, what happened?" He sat down next to her.

Linda briefly outlined the day's findings. "So we wanted to alert you and the tribal police in case you hear of any of the things turning up. I'm so sorry, Joe, I wanted to restore the relics to your tribe after everything was cataloged and photographed." She pulled an envelope out of her purse. "Here are copies of the prints."

"Does Sheriff Lodge know about this?" he asked.

"He does by now," Linda said. "We stopped in and told Deputy Redland before we came up here."

"That's good. They're both fine men and have worked with us before. I have a few contacts in the Phoenix area, as well. Believe it or not, I'm a graduate of ASU, myself. We may be able to track down the artifacts." Then he smiled again. "If the Great Spirit agrees." He stood and went toward the kitchen. "Now let's have some refreshments."

Meadow had sat and listened intently to their conversation, but squirmed a little when he mentioned the Great Spirit. The amulet hung warm under her shirt. It really belonged to the tribe. But she didn't want to give it up, so stayed quiet.

The chief rattled around in the kitchen and soon brought out some tea, pinion nuts and fresh peaches on a platter. It looked good and Meadow was hungry because they hadn't thought to stop for lunch. She bit into a juicy, sweet peach and ate a handful of nuts. She tasted the tea and found it delicious with a slight mint flavor.

"What kind of tea is this?"

"It's made from an herb found here. It's called Green thread," the chief said.

"Very good." Linda seemed to be enjoying the light meal as well.

"Colt was here earlier, taking a short break."

Linda shifted in her seat, looking uneasy. "Uh . . . is he still in Flagstaff?"

"Yes, taking the summer session. He wants to get done with college fast."

"Oh . . . he certainly will. . .didn't he start when he was sixteen?"

"Yes, he's a smart boy." Joe's chest puffed out a little.

"Colt?" Meadow hadn't heard this name before.

Linda turned to her. "Oh, sorry, Meadow. Colt is Joe's son. He's studying business in Flagstaff."

"Is he the boy in the picture?" Meadow eyed the photo.

"Yes, with his mother. As you may have noticed, she was not an Indian. Irish through and through."

"She's pretty," Meadow said.

"I met her when we were both at university. She was studying anthropology." Joe got a faraway look. "Smartest, kindest woman I have ever known, although once in a while that Irish temper would flare."

Outside the house they heard a truck approaching, then a door slam. Joe got up and looked out the window.

"This must be the day for visitors. It's my good friend, Nueme."

He opened the door and invited him in to share in the food.

Nueme nodded to the girls. "Hello Linda, Meadow."

"Help yourself, Nueme," the Chief said.

"No, thanks, I've already eaten. I'll have some tea, though." Nueme took a seat across from the girls. "I just came from the stable, Meadow."

"Oh." What now?

"The girls were just telling me that the artifacts have been stolen," the Chief said.

"Huh. Doesn't surprise me. Shep told me there was something funny about the whole thing." Nueme's face darkened. "But it will be bad luck for the thieves."

"Why?" Meadow wanted to touch the pendant, but she forced herself to keep her hands in her lap.

"Those artifacts were special, and the Spirits of the Dead will not like it."

Chief White Horse nodded gravely.

Nueme sipped his tea and then, seeming to remember something, turned to Meadow. "Your father told me you let Bill Bowman's stallion loose."

Meadow looked down and stared at her feet.

"Shep thinks there must be a connection to the legend I told you. Since you think Diablo is Arrow."

"Yes." Her voice was barely audible and she couldn't bring herself to look at Nueme.

"Is there more to it than just that?" Nueme pressed. "Has something happened to you?"

Tears sprang up, and Meadow wished she could melt into the floor. But she knew there was no escape. She had to tell the truth.

"I had a dream about an Indian girl, and she told me to let the stallion go free. In two different dreams." She finally met Nueme's eyes. "When you told me the legend, it all made sense."

"What else?" Somehow he knew there was more.

"And, I found this." She pulled the amulet from under her shirt. "In my dreams, the girl was wearing this. I found a medicine chest and it was inside, in a bag."

Chief White Horse sucked his breath in sharply, and then he leaned forward and examined the pendant without touching it.

After a minute, he sat back and nodded. "That's the amulet of Meda the medicine woman, our prophetess. It has deep spiritual significance."

Meadow pulled it off over her head. "Here, take it." She held it out to the chief.

He quickly drew back. "No, I must not touch it. The prophetess was killed and I must not touch it. I will call a tribal council to determine what is to be done with it. You keep it safe for now."

The relief that flooded in was overwhelming. Meadow gulped and blinked back tears. The others talked for a few more minutes, but she didn't hear a word. Linda finished her tea and rose to leave. Meadow followed her out to the car, and before she knew it, they were on the road to Brighten.

Linda looked over at her. "So you found a secret room with Meda's medicine chest in it."

"I'm sorry I didn't tell you. I just couldn't. Are you mad at me?"

"No, I'm not mad. Maybe the thieves didn't find it. It might still be there."

"It was the last time I looked."

"That's good. We'll leave it right there for now. And you let Diablo loose after you found the amulet?"

Meadow shifted in her seat. "Yes, but only after Nueme told me the legend. Then I knew Diablo was Arrow, the Sky Horse."

"I figured there had to be some good reason you let him go." Linda leaned over and squeezed her hand. "When Dad gets home I'm going to make sure he knows all the details. I just hope he sees it the way we do. He's a businessman first and foremost."

Meadow nodded. "I'm just glad you're not angry. Everyone else is. And I'm pretty worried about the meeting with your father."

"It'll be okay. I think you'll be able to bring him around."

Despite her encouraging words, Linda's expression was grim, and Meadow knew it would be no easy task to convince Bill Bowman that Arrow should run free.

Chapter 25

Bill Bowman

After a long canter up the trail, Meadow arrived in Hidden Valley. All during the ride, she'd been practicing her speech to Bill Bowman explaining her actions. He'd been home a couple of days now, but her dread of the meeting with him had made her procrastinate. The explanation had been whirling around in her mind for days.

She sat back slightly and Foxfire slowed to a walk and then stopped. As she scanned the valley, she sighted the wild horses off to her left near the tree line. The stallion was grazing a little ways from the herd. He raised his head and after flaring his nostrils, he trumpeted a welcome. Foxfire answered with a soft nicker. The stallion came roaring across the valley and circled around, inviting them to come over to the herd.

"Easy, Arrow." Meadow laughed at his antics, as he danced around them.

Every once in a while he would jump and kick out for no particular reason. He was just showing off for Foxfire and wouldn't hurt them. Since she'd let him loose, Meadow had been to the valley many times and each time he'd put on a big show, as boys often do for girls. When she touched him, he always settled down. Meadow figured he would never leave the valley. He lived here because he chose to. He came to her because he wanted to.

She slipped off Foxfire and signaled for Arrow to come nearer. He dropped his head and walked to her. Meadow put his face between her hands and looked deep into his great dark eyes. She sighed, and for that brief moment, she was completely happy.

Clouds started gathering, with the sky turning dark, and a clap of thunder broke their peaceful reverie. She gave Arrow a final pat on his neck and swinging up onto Foxfire, turned back to the trail. It was monsoon season, and every afternoon they'd been getting heavy downpours.

Meadow heard the brush crackle, and then saw a horse and rider coming out of the trees, approaching them. A thrill shot through her. It was Brett. He came abreast of her on his roan, Calypso. She hadn't spoken to him much since Mike's accident. He often came to help out with the dude rides at the stable, but they would each go on different trails, so they never got a chance to say more than a quick hello.

"Hi, Meadow, what are you doing up here?" He looked especially good that day, with his cowboy hat shoved back on his head and strands of sandy hair curling out from under it.

"I came to see the wild herd."

"What do you mean, you came to see them? I thought I could see you touching Diablo, but I wasn't sure from where I was across the valley."

Before she could answer, thunder cracked again and huge raindrops began splattering on them.

Brett turned Calypso to the upper trail. "C'mon, let's go to the cliff dwelling for shelter, we're too far from home." He galloped away, with Meadow close behind. They tied their horses to the brush, and made their way down the ladder and along the passage.

As Meadow looked around the cave, she was again struck by how desolate the place seemed without all the Indian furnishings. It made her sad to think those villains had all those beautiful things.

"Much better out of the rain." Brett sat down cross legged in the main room. "Sit here." He patted the floor next to him. "I've missed talking to you."

"Me too." She sat down across from him.

Brett offered a warm smile. "We've sure had a lot of fun together. I think you're about the bravest girl I've ever known."

She felt her face flush. "We have had fun." Her mind flashed to the bear he won for her. What happened to it?

Brett abruptly quit smiling. "Now, tell me about the stallion." His voice had an edge.

She was confused with his sudden change of tone. "You mean about me going to see him?"

"Yeah, Linda told me that you think he's some kind of magical horse, or something."

"It sounds like you've already made up your mind that I'm crazy . . . or delusional."

"Well, you have to admit, it does sound pretty wacky."

Her face tightened. "I don't have to admit anything. And I think you're being pretty mean about the whole thing. I know what happened, and I don't have to answer to you or anyone else." She stood up. It seemed no one was on her side, except maybe Linda and Nueme.

Brett snapped back. "All I know is that you let my dad's valuable stallion loose, for no good reason that I can think of, just when your parents could really use the reward money, too. That seems pretty selfish to me." His voice escalated as he talked.

"You don't know everything, and I think you should just shut up!"

"I thought you were mature for your age, but apparently you're still just a dumb kid, just like I first thought."

Stung by his words, Meadow turned and fled through the tunnel, only stopping when she reached the ladder.

"C'mon, Kelsey." Meadow helped her midway up the ladder, and then was about to follow, when she felt Brett's hand on her arm.

"Meadow wait, it's still raining outside!"

"I don't care, I just want to get away from you!" She yanked her arm away and climbed out into the storm.

The wind had come up and the downpour was steady. Already the water was rushing down the canyon in a constant stream, making the trail slick. Meadow jumped up on Foxfire and they headed down the path, slipping and sliding all the way. She was soon soaked through. She could feel her temper cooling as her body chilled down.

The worst part about it was that Brett was right. Diablo was Bill Bowman's horse, and she had no right to let him go in spite of the dream. And Dad could definitely use the reward money. She firmed her chin. It was time to confront Bill Bowman. She needed to set things right with him. But how?

As she rode, Linda's words kept revolving in her head. She'd said her father was first and foremost a businessman. A plan gradually took root, and Meadow knew what she had to do, even though it was the hardest decision she'd ever made.

Linda opened the door to the ranch house with surprise reflected on her face. Meadow thought she must look like something the cat had dragged in, as she stood shivering and dripping on the wide veranda, her long hair hanging in wet ringlets.

"I have to talk to your father," she said.

Linda put an arm around her, and escorted her into the house. "You're soaking wet. Come to my room, I'll find something dry to put on." She led the way and pointed to the bathroom. "Get in the shower and warm up. I will lay out some clothes for you."

While Meadow was showering, she heard Linda rummaging through her closet. When she emerged she saw the older girl had put some outgrown jeans and a pullover top on her bed. Linda was nowhere in sight and must have gone to tell her father that Meadow was there to speak to him.

She took her time dressing and, finally, gathering her courage, made her way through the house to Bill's office. She was about to knock on the heavy carved door when she realized it was slightly ajar. Linda was inside, speaking to her father. Meadow stood rooted to the spot, unable to stop listening.

"So you see, Dad, Meadow has a pretty good case for letting Diablo run with the mustangs."

"Let me get this straight. You want me to believe in some Indian legend that Diablo is really, what'd you call him . . . a Sky Horse or Arrow or something? And that Meadow has control over him somehow? Linda, be serious. She's a little girl with a big imagination, that's all."

"But, Dad . . . ."

"You know things have really gone to hell since I've been gone and the Shepherd family showed up. Mike got hurt, the Indian artifacts were stolen, not to mention a lawsuit on our hands. Now to top it off, Meadow let Diablo loose. Damn it, I have a lot of money tied up in that horse."

"But Dad, the stable's making money and I really like Meadow and her family."

"They seemed to be a nice family when we first met them, now I'm not so sure. Everything has really gotten out of hand since they got here."

"What do you mean?"

"Just yesterday I met with Wendell to go over the books. He said Shep was unhappy with the stable arrangement. What is he unhappy about? They're not even being charged for the cabin and stables, or being asked for a cut of the profits. It doesn't make any sense. Wendell also insinuated that Shep had something to do with the artifacts being stolen, since he is in deep financial trouble. How could I be so wrong about a person?"

Linda's voice rose a notch. "I think you're wrong about Wendell, not Shep. Shep didn't have anything to do with it, but Wendell might have. We need to keep any eye on him."

"Now *you're* imagining things, Linda." He sighed heavily. "Just send Meadow in. I want to get this over with."

Meadow hastily retreated to the den to wait.

"Did you hear any of that?" Linda looked worried.

Meadow nodded numbly.

Linda hugged her. "Oh, sweetie, don't worry. We'll get all this straightened out. We both know your father is not to blame for any of it. My dad is stubborn, but he's fair. The truth will come out. Now go in and make your case. I know you can do it."

When Meadow entered through the open door, Bill Bowman sat behind his huge desk, with his head in his hands. She thought he knew she was there, but he didn't speak. She felt very small standing in the center of the room—as if she had walked into a court of law and he was the judge, about to pronounce her guilty and sentence her to a life of hard labor.

The seconds ticked by without him saying anything, and she looked around the room. There was an assortment of books lining one wall. It must be heavenly to have so many to choose from. She kept glancing around and her eyes finally rested on a western painting. It featured a lone cowboy perched atop a boney-looking horse in what looked like Monument Valley.

"Do you like my latest acquisition? It's an original Maynard Dixon."

She jumped a little at the sound of his voice. "Yes, sir. It's—nice." Her voice came out sort of squeaky. Meadow suddenly felt that most of her resolve must have gone down the shower drain.

"Nice? I guess that's one way to put it. Sit down on that chair." He pointed to a straight-backed wooden chair opposite the desk. "Well, young lady, I think you have some explaining to do. I want to hear your version of the story. Don't leave anything out."

Meadow took a deep breath. Okay, here goes. She started slowly, but gained momentum as she talked. She spoke of the cave, her dreams and the legend. The only part she omitted was about the amulet. That still seemed too private.

"So you see, I *had* to let Diablo go free." Her eyes pleaded for him to understand.

"It sounds pretty convincing the way you tell it." Mr. Bowman furrowed his brow. "But that doesn't solve the problem of my need for a breeding stallion. Diablo is a very valuable horse. I can't just let him roam around on the range."

"But I know he will be all right."

"Let me tell you a little about his history. He has superior Spanish breeding and was raised on a large Estancia near Mexico City. He was destined to be their new herd sire."

Meadow sat silently, listening intently.

"It's common practice in Mexico for them to halter break the yearlings, and then turn them out until they are three years old. Then they round them up and train them to ride."

"So Diablo was broke to saddle?"

"Well no, not exactly. You see, when they rounded up Diablo, he was unridable. Not one vaquero on the ranch could stay on him."

Not surprising, Meadow thought.

"Then, that night, he jumped out of the corral and disappeared for two years. When I arrived to look at stallions they had just found him again, and brought him in to the rancho, but he was as unmanageable as ever."

"Then what happened?" She was picturing Diablo on a Mexican rancho, refusing to be dominated.

"When I saw Diablo, somehow I knew he had to come to my ranch." His eyes had a faraway look. "As though something came over me, and I knew I was meant to own him."

Meadow fingered the outline of the pendant under her pullover.

"Of course, the *Patron* didn't see it that way. He wanted to keep Diablo for his ranch, so it took a lot of persuasion in the form of American dollars to change his mind about selling him." Bill shook his head a little, as if he still didn't understand exactly how it all happened.

Meadow, however, understood perfectly. "He *is* meant to be here. And I have a proposition for you." She purposefully tried to sound like her father—a good negotiator.

For the first time that day, Mr. Bowman's lips curved up the tiniest bit.

"Okay, let's hear it."

"Diablo lives in Hidden Valley now, with the wild mustangs. He won't leave. He lives there because he wants to. I go and see him all the time and he comes right to me. I can bring him in to the ranch anytime you want, and you can use him for breeding."

"I don't know . . . why are you certain you can bring him in?"

"I know he will agree to come if he's not confined. You could use the back pasture for breeding. But you have to let him come and go freely."

"What about this year's loss of breeding time? Now it's too late in the season to breed my mares, thanks to you letting him go." He frowned again.

"I've thought about that, too." She swallowed, then plunged ahead. "To compensate you for your loss, I will give you

Foxy. She's already in foal to Diablo and she's a wonderful ranch horse."

Meadow managed to say all words she had rehearsed in mind, but the last part came out with a little gulp.

"Foxy? You'll give me Foxy?" His face registered complete surprise. "My kids have told me all about your wonder horse. Are you sure?"

"Yes." She breathed deeply again. "But you still have to give Daddy the reward for Diablo."

Bill sat quietly considering what she said with a thoughtful look.

Meadow took a tissue from the desk and wiped her nose. "She's got great bloodlines and I have her registration papers. The cross with Diablo will make really good ranch horses."

"I need time to think all of this over. I'll let you know what I decide later this week." He dismissed her and ushered her out of his study.

She made her way to the living room and sank into an overstuffed chair, feeling drained. Linda joined her, bringing in some hot cocoa on a tray.

"Here, I think you could use some sustenance." Linda handed her a cup.

"Thanks."

"Dad can be pretty intense. He used to doing huge business deals, but he's not used to dealing with an articulate teenager." Linda smiled apologetically.

"You were listening?" Meadow gratefully sipped on the cocoa, slowly feeling its warming effect.

"I couldn't help it with the door open."

"I'm glad you heard."

They were interrupted by Brett bursting into the room, dripping wet, much as Meadow had been earlier. "What are you doing here? I rode all the way to the stable looking for you. I thought something terrible had happened when you weren't there!"

"Brett, take it easy," Linda said. "She came here to talk to Father. Have some cocoa and warm up."

"No, thanks. And Meadow, you'd better get home right away, before they send out a search party." He turned on his heel and slammed his way out of the room.

Meadow watched him go. "Wow, I guess he's still mad at me."

"Why?"

"We went to the cave to get out of the rain, then he said some mean stuff to me about letting Diablo loose and I told him to shut up."

Linda gave a little chuckle.

"What's so funny?"

"Brett's not used to girls talking back to him, that's all. They're usually so enamored with him, he's gotten conceited. I think it's good to take him down a few pegs."

Meadow stared at the floor. "But he was right about Diablo. I shouldn't have let him go."

"Well, it's all water under the bridge, now. And it's really between you and Father. Brett doesn't need to stick his nose in," Linda said pointedly. "Did you get things straightened out? I was making cocoa and didn't hear what he decided."

"I'm not sure. He said he'd let me know." Meadow looked out the window. "The rain has let up. I'd better be going."

"I could drive you home. Foxy can stay in the stable."

"No, I'll be okay." She wanted as much time as possible with her mare, in case Linda's father decided to take her up on the offer.

Meadow retrieved Foxfire and started towards home, this time riding slowly, her heart weighed down with the enormity of it all. She told herself the most important thing was to keep Arrow free, and make peace with Dad. Maybe he'd forgive her if she got him the reward money. Things had not been right between them ever since she found the cliff dwelling.

But she didn't know how she would survive without Foxfire.

Chapter 26
Thick as Thieves

Flashing neon signs declared *Vacancy* and *Air-Cooled* at the Red Rock Motor Court in Sedona, Arizona. The motel was old and somewhat worse for wear, but Rick couldn't care less about that. He sat in the draft of the noisy window swamp cooler, along with Wally, Professor Schumer, and Paul, listening to Wendell rant.

"How could you forget that chest, the most valuable part of this heist?" Wendell spat out, looking at his gang in disgust.

"I know we had it out, ready to be moved. I can't understand how we overlooked it." Professor Schumer had a puzzled expression. He squinted at Rick. "Remember, you finished packing it."

"Yeah, then I rushed up to help load . . . and sent my brother back to get it. You brought it up for us, right, Wally?" Rick stared holes in his brother.

Wally nodded. "That's right, Rick."

"Well, we've gone through every crate and it's not there," Wendell barked. "It must still be in the cave dwelling."

"It's no problem. We can just go back and get it. Paul can fly us in, and me and Wally can go get the chest." Rick used a placating tone, as if the rest of them were idiots.

Wendell looked at him sharply, his eyes cold as a gun barrel. "It's *not* so simple. By now they know someone has absconded with the goods. We'll have to be careful."

Rick offered Wendell what he hoped was an earnest look. "We'll make sure no one sees us, won't we, boys? If it looks like they're watching the cave, or anything, we'll just fly by."

Wendell snorted, irritation still showing on his face. "Okay, I guess we have no choice. Paul, go ahead and arrange for the plane tomorrow, then pick up Rick and Wally. We need to move fast on this."

Paul, silently cowering in the corner, nodded his head.

"What about fencing the other items, Professor?" Wendell asked.

"You know I have to take it slow. It would be preferable to sell everything to one buyer. We'll get more as a collection, instead of breaking it up. I may have identified that party, however. I'm meeting with him tomorrow."

"Good, keep me updated. You can phone me at Brighten during the day. We need to unload this stuff pretty soon. The last thing we want is for anyone to start sniffing around."

"You'll be the first to know," the professor said.

"Okay, everyone get going, you all know what you have to do." Wendell abruptly ended the meeting. He rose from the table and quickly exited, with the professor and Paul following suit. Rick watched them get into their vehicles and drive away.

"Well, that worked like a charm, if I do say so myself." Rick lit up a cigarette and lay back on the lumpy single bed.

Wally closed the door, and slumped down at the table with a big dumb look. "I don't know about double crossing them, Rick. It seems pretty risky to me."

"*Everything* seems pretty risky to you. That's because you've got no brains, you big tub o' lard." Rick took a puff and inhaled deeply. "I have it all worked out, and that's all you need to know."

Wally put on a hurt expression, and his lip quivered. After glancing over at him, Rick softened his tone, knowing he had gone too far.

"Haven't I always taken care of you ever since we were little?"

His brother, hanging his head, just nodded.

"When Mom had all sorts of disgusting men over at all hours of the night, who protected you then?"

Wally remained silent, his eyes still glued to the floor.

"Who always had all the good ideas? Haven't things always worked out the way I said they would?"

He nodded again.

"So don't worry, big guy." He patted his brother on the shoulder.

Wally sniffed. "Okay, Rick. Whatever you say."

Rick chuckled to himself, knowing he could always manipulate his younger brother. He'd been doing it all their lives. Wally wasn't a deep thinker, but Rick had to be careful how much he told him. For some unknown reason, Wally had scruples about right and wrong.

His brother didn't know about the couple that was in the wrong place at the wrong time. He would never know about them if Rick had anything to do with it. Wally just wouldn't understand how he *had* to kill them. How that stupid kid had tried to fight for his wallet, and Rick *had* to stab him. Then his stupid girlfriend had started that stupid endless screaming and he *had* to shut her up. The whole episode was very simple, but he knew Wally just wouldn't understand.

Rick had planned on double crossing the rest of the gang from the start. He just needed to bide his time for the right opportunity and it came when he switched the dummy crate for the one with the Medicine Chest in it. Wally didn't know the difference when he went to retrieve it. The less his brother knew, the better. Then Rick simply hid the dummy crate under a juniper instead of loading it on the plane. In the flurry of activity that day, no one had been the wiser.

Until that little toad Wendell had checked the Professor's list of artifacts, and went digging around, no one knew it was missing. That Wendell was a real pain in the ass, but Rick figured they'd be gone with the chest before the little toad knew what hit him.

Rick really hoped that the goofy professor knew what he was talking about. He said the chest contained the real treasure. He and Wally would be set up for life. Although, sometimes he wished he could just be rid of his brother. He was a real millstone around his neck. Not bright enough to be much help, and not mean enough to do any damage. No one would miss him, that's for sure.

Chapter 27

Searching for Clues

Meadow stood next to Foxfire with a brush and curry comb in her hands. She systematically curried with one hand and then brushed with the other until the mare's coat gleamed like a new copper penny. Foxfire had her head down, with one hind foot cocked, enjoying the attention.

She still hadn't heard back from Bill Bowman, and worry constantly nagged at her. Mike had just gotten out of the hospital and was sitting on the porch of the cabin watching her groom Foxfire. His arm was still in a cast, but a shorter one that only went from his wrist to midway between his elbow and shoulder. The doctor said he thought Mike would regain full use of his arm in a few months.

"You're gonna brush all her hair off if you keep that up," Mike called down to her.

She ignored his comment and kept on brushing.

"What's bugging you, anyway? You've been acting funny ever since I got home."

She shrugged. "Oh, nothing."

She hadn't told anyone about her proposal to Bill Bowman. She finally turned and smiled at her brother. "Everything's good now that you're home. I'm just worried about finding the artifacts."

It wasn't a total lie. She *was* concerned about the missing artifacts. The clip-clop of hooves made her turn toward the trail.

Brett Bowman rode into the stable yard leading a group of dudes. He helped them dismount and tie up their horses, before telling them goodbye. Mike yelled down to him from the porch. "Hi, Brett!"

"Hey, Mike, are you done loafing around and sleeping all day in that hospital? I've been doing your job since you've been gone and I'm getting pretty darn tired of it."

"Well, it's about time you did some work, you lazy bum," Mike retorted, grinning.

Brett laughed and headed for the cabin, giving a sidelong glance at Meadow. She studiously avoided looking at him. He sighed as he climbed up on the porch and sat down next to Mike. They chatted while Meadow continued her grooming.

Pretty soon she heard the groan of her father's truck pulling into the stable yard.

Her father stepped out. "Doesn't anyone care that I'm home?"

"I'm glad you're home, Daddy." Meadow ran toward him.

Foxfire suddenly lifted her head and whinnied to the horse in the back of the truck. Dad had been on a trading trip, so a new horse wasn't unusual, but Foxfire greeting a new horse *was* unusual. Meadow peered between the rails and saw a familiar buckskin face looking out. "Rowdy!"

Mike and Brett stopped in mid conversation, and looked over to see the gelding bobbing his head up and down, apparently anxious to get out and see his old friends.

"Rowdy." Mike voice reflected disbelief, as he climbed from the porch.

Dad was grinning from ear to ear, while he unhooked the gate, put the ramp down, and unloaded Rowdy into the stable yard.

"Mike, I guess you got your favorite horse back. That numbskull that bought him did nothing but feed him carrots for a month, and then tried to ride."

"Uh oh, what happened?" Mike asked.

"Rowdy kicked up his heels and bumped him right off. So I just traded ole Chico for him. Of course, I had to charge them a hundred dollars boot, cuz Chico is well-broke and gentle as a dog. I told them they can let him stand for a year and it won't make any difference."

Mike didn't say another word, just stood with his face buried in Rowdy's black mane. The buckskin turned his head and butted him affectionately.

"This is the best day I've had in a long time," Mike finally said, turning to them.

Her father was still grinning, and Meadow got a lump in her throat, seeing her brother and his gelding together again. Brett hadn't moved off the porch. She guessed he didn't want to interrupt the family moment.

Meadow heard another horse approaching, and Nueme arrived on his appaloosa. He rode to the fence and dismounted, tying Appy next to Foxfire.

"Hello, Nueme. Did you find out anything interesting up on the mesa?" her father asked.

"Uh huh, a small plane has made at least a couple of trips back and forth."

"There's probably no use watching the cave entrance now. I doubt if they'll be back to the scene of the crime," her father gazed up at the dark clouds, "and it looks like it's getting ready to pour."

"The Tribal police have the word out to the Phoenix force to watch for unusual activity, like any artifacts surfacing. Problems, it's a big city."

Her father nodded. "Yes it is. We need a lucky break."

As Shep and Nueme continued talking, Meadow tried to listen in. She wanted to be in on any new developments in the case.

"Hey, Meadow, come on up here." Brett hadn't moved from the porch.

Meadow reluctantly tore herself away from her father and Nueme and walked up the steps. "What?"

"Why don't you sit down? Don't you think it's about time we buried the hatchet?"

Meadow perched on the edge of one of the old wooden chairs next to him, ready to flee at any given moment.

"I'm sorry I lost my temper the other day. Dad told me about your offer to give him Foxy. I think that's amazing." Brett flashed his gorgeous smile. "But then, you never cease to amaze me."

"I guess I lost my temper, too," Meadow said. "Has your Dad decided to take her? I haven't heard from him."

"Dad hasn't told me either, but he is wondering how you plan on bringing Diablo in for the breeding season. I'm wondering that, too." He fixed her with his slate blue eyes.

Meadow squirmed a little under the scrutiny.

"Diablo does what I ask him to. We . . . we have an . . . an agreement." It sounded lame, even to her, but he was making her nervous. She wondered why she always sounded so dopey when she talked to Brett. She hadn't been nearly so tongue-tied when she had talked to his father.

"What do you mean? A wild stallion will just follow you?" He frowned. "Are you trying to tell me it's magic or something?"

Anger welled up in her. "Why don't you ever believe me?" She didn't know why it bothered her so much that Brett didn't understand. And she didn't know how to explain it to him. She got up to walk away, but he grabbed her arm.

"Wait," he said, "Don't go."

She jerked her arm out of his grasp, and walked away without answering. Meadow didn't know where she was headed, but found herself on the boardwalk near the store. Might as well get the mail, since she was there. Her encounter with Brett had upset her more than she cared to admit. She grimaced. He was just a stupid boy. Who cares what he thinks?

Kelsey had followed along, and Meadow told her to stay outside when she went into the store. Patterned after an old time general mercantile, it had the feel of a bygone era with a potbellied stove in the middle. Mostly it was filled with foodstuffs for camping, but she always checked out the touristy knickknacks in one corner.

Meadow wandered down the souvenir aisle browsing the newest acquisitions. There were some fascinating little ceramic animals. All the figures were somewhat Disney-like with mothers and baby animals. She picked up the deer family to examine them and thought it must be Bambi with his mother and sister. Did Bambi have a sister?

As she was studying them, Meadow became aware of a voice in the background. She peeked around the shelf and saw Wendell pacing back and forth and talking on the phone. He seemed to be giving orders to someone on the other end. "He got the plane from a different place? Good, so they're on their way now?"

He listened for a moment. "I don't care if it *is* difficult, get on it and make the deal! Tell him we'll have it later today, and then he can examine it."

He slammed down the receiver with a bang. He walked over to the open door and noticed Kelsey. He turned as if to go back into his office. Meadow waited until she thought it was safe to exit, and then she crept toward the door. She was almost there when she heard a voice, making her jump.

"Hold on a minute, Missy. What can I help you with?"

"Uh, I just came to get the mail." She actually had forgotten all about the mail after what she'd just overheard.

Wendell walked over to their pigeon hole and pulled out an envelope. "Well, here it is. It looks like it's just an advertisement." He handed her the letter. "I didn't see you come in. How long have you been in the store?"

"I just walked in. You were on the phone . . ." she answered before she realized her mistake.

Wendell's eyes turned cold, but a smile quickly followed.

"Oh, yes, a guest wanted to know if we could book them an airplane. He was a little rude when I told him no. Nothing to worry about."

"Guests do have the strangest requests sometimes. Well, 'bye. I have to get back to the stable."

"Goodbye."

She thought she could feel his eyes boring into her back as she hurried away.

Meadow didn't trust the guy. They didn't have any real proof involving him, but just now he'd been talking about renting a plane. Nueme said the thieves used a plane to get in and out. Would they be coming back to the cliff dwelling? But why would they, if the artifacts were all gone? Her heart gave a little thump.

Maybe they found the secret chamber! No one knew about that except her.

"Come on, Kelsey." She sprinted back to the stable.

By the time she got back, everyone had disappeared. She'd hoped someone would be around to go with her, but probably more customers had shown up. And Mike would be lying down by now. The doctor said he still needed a lot of rest and must lie down every afternoon. Rowdy happily munched hay in the corral next to the cabin.

Foxfire was still tied to the hitching rail, waiting patiently. Not bothering to go get a bridle, and using the lead rope for a rein, she swung on and galloped off toward the cliff dwelling.

Chapter 28

Rick and Wally

Large drops of rain were just starting to sprinkle down when Meadow arrived at the cave entrance. She was still thinking about the overheard phone call and her confrontation with Wendell. He must be involved somehow, but if so, why was he still around?

A flash of lightning eerily illuminated the opening and almost simultaneously, a loud crack of thunder made her flinch as she dismounted.

She'd take a quick look and get back home before the downpour. She dropped the rope to ground tie Foxfire. By now Kelsey was proficient at climbing down the ladder and preceded Meadow into the cave. Loose pebbles and shale cascaded down the steep passage as she made her way through, then up the steps to the main room.

She looked around to see if there were any crates left behind that she hadn't noticed when she was there with Brett. It was just as barren as she remembered, but they hadn't gone down to the secret room.

It was the perfect hiding place, but did the thieves find it? She started down the steps past the pond. Making her way through the maze of tunnels, she finally arrived at the hidden doorway. Cautiously, she pushed against the rock until it opened.

Meadow peered around in the dim light, looking for anything out of order. The blanket that had been covering the chest was thrown to one side. Her heart sank. They found the chest. Some rubble looked like it had been disturbed, and she began moving aside the debris. The crate with the chest in it was underneath, where it had been concealed by someone.

With a huge tug, she pulled open the top of the crate, and saw all the shaman's tools, masks and jewelry still intact in the chest. She was intent on the artifacts when she heard Kelsey growl behind her. Before she could turn, a hand came out of nowhere and violently shoved her aside. She fell face first to the ground with Kelsey standing protectively next to her, snarling.

As she gingerly turned over, Meadow saw the outlines of three figures backlit in the entrance of the room. She couldn't see their faces, but recognized Rick's voice.

"Well, little girl, what do you think you're doing with those things?" His tone was nasty. "And you'd better keep that stinkin' dog back."

"Don't hurt her." Wally put his hand on Rick's sleeve.

Rick shrugged him off. "Shut up, you dope."

The third man spoke. "What'll we do with her?" It was Paul Misner, sounding nervous.

Rick bent over her, and Meadow got a good look at his face. He had taken off the horn-rimmed glasses now that he wasn't trying to cover up his identity.

She gulped. It was the same man who was on the wanted poster in Sheriff Dave's office. The murderer. Rick had some kind of club in his hand, and she cringed as far back from him as possible. She held onto Kelsey, afraid that Rick would hurt her.

Kelsey growled another warning, as Rick reached down and grabbed the pendant that had come out from under Meadow's shirt in the tussle. He ripped the ornament off her neck and backed up a few steps to examine it.

"It looks like you've already taken a nice piece of jewelry for yourself. I think this will fetch a tidy sum." He tucked the amulet in his pants pocket.

"What are we going to do with her?" Paul asked again.

"Don't worry, I'm going to take care of this little busybody. She won't interfere with anyone ever again."

"Just like you killed that couple?" Meadow blurted out.

"What does she mean?" Paul's voice rose an octave.

"Shut up, you little brat." Rick raised the club menacingly at Meadow and took a step toward her.

As he approached, Kelsey, with a deep snarl, lunged out of her grasp and leaped for Rick, knocking him off balance. She clamped her powerful jaws down on the offending arm, ripping his shirtsleeve and drawing blood.

Rick curled his lip and swung the club toward the dog, but Kelsey dodged the blow and attacked his other arm. Rick backed up trying to get a swing at the dog, but she was too fast for him. She darted in and out, biting his legs. She was gradually driving Rick back, with him swinging viciously whenever he got a chance.

Meadow let out a little whimper of fear for her dog and Kelsey looked toward her at the sound. In that split second, Rick saw his chance and brought the club brutally down on her head with a loud whack. Kelsey fell to the ground and lay still.

"You've killed her!" Meadow screamed.

"You're next." Rick had an evil smile, and raised the club, coming toward her.

"Wait a minute, I didn't sign on for murder!" Paul yelped shrilly.

"Rick, you can't mean that, you already killed her dog." Wally started toward Rick. "You can't hurt her. What did she ever do to you? Did you really kill someone, like she said?" He sniffed and wiped his sleeve across his face.

"You big dummy. Do you want to give everything up for some stupid brat? Use your head for once in your life."

"No, Rick. You can't hurt her. It's wrong. I won't let you." Wally swallowed hard and held out his hand as he took a step towards his brother. "Give me the club."

"Wally, listen to reason." Rick changed his tone and stepped back. "Don't you want to be rich?"

"Not if it means hurting someone." Wally was still advancing toward Rick with his hand out.

"Okay, you imbecile. You asked for it!" Rick raised the club and hurled it toward his brother.

The club struck Wally with a glancing blow to the shoulder. He stumbled, but he righted himself and kept advancing. Rick saw that his brother was not deterred and pulled a switchblade knife out of his belt, opening it with a sharp click. He brandished it threateningly at his brother. "Easy, Wally, don't make me hurt you."

Wally kept coming, and Rick stabbed at him, catching him in the side. Wally grunted and slumped down. Rick looked shaken and went toward his brother. Wally suddenly righted himself and grabbed Rick around both arms and they fell to the ground, wrestling to get a hold on each other.

Meadow watched the fight with grim fascination, her muscles tense, waiting for a chance to escape. When the men fell to the ground, she seized the opportunity to dart around Paul. He grabbed her as she passed, but she wiggled out of his grasp. He yelled to Rick. "She got away!"

Rick shouted in the background, "Stop her, you idiot!"

Her eyes streamed as she thought of Kelsey, lying lifeless back there. She skirted past the pool, and held her breath when she heard footsteps coming from behind. Blinded by her tears, she forced her legs forward, until she felt the steps. She was partway up, when she stumbled and slid back. A viselike grip clamped onto her ankle.

She was jerked back off the steps, and fell with a thud on the stone floor below. The wind was completely knocked out of her, and she gasped for breath for what seemed an eternity. She looked up to see Rick standing above her with a cruel grimace. He raised his hand and she saw the glint of the knife edge coming for her throat. He hesitated for a moment as if savoring her terror while Wally's blood dribbled off the blade onto her neck. She gathered all her strength and shoved his arm, then swiftly rolled to one side. She felt a sharp pain as the blade whizzed by her ear, nicking it.

Rick came for her again and she scrambled frantically to get away. He was too fast, and before she could escape, he grabbed her from behind and held her in his iron grip. She could feel the buttons of his shirt dig into her back and the sour odor of his sweat made her want to gag.

Meadow reacted without thinking and reached around, scratching like a wild thing, her fingernails making a rasping sound on his day's growth of beard. Four angry welts appeared and a trickle of blood dripped down his face in response to her desperate attempt to flee.

"You're quite the little hellion, aren't you? Too bad you won't live long enough to grow up." Rick seemed pleased that she was fighting for her life, like a cat toying with its helpless prey.

He brought the blade up to her throat, and Meadow knew the end was near. Her heart thudded painfully in her chest, and her breath came in short bursts. She closed her eyes, expecting the worst.

A familiar warm feeling began to surround her. And then, Rick's hand opened, as though against his will, and the knife clattered onto the rock surface below. His grip loosened and Meadow scuttled away, hiding behind a large stalagmite, not sure what had just happened.

"What the hell was that?" Rick demanded of Paul, who had come up next to him. "Did you see anything? Something came over me. It was weird, it . . . it made me drop my knife."

From behind the mineral formation, Meadow watched as Rick bent down and cautiously retrieved the knife as if it might bite his hand.

"No, I didn't see anything. You're imagining things. Let's get out of here while we can." Paul was puffing from the exertion of dragging the chest out of the room.

"Well, something was here. I think it was a ghost or something." Rick warily looked around. "Yeah, let's get out of here, quick. Where's Wally?"

"He's in pretty bad shape, losing blood. I don't think he can make it out."

"That's fine with me. He deserved what he got." Rick grabbed one side of the crate.

"What about the girl?"

"She'll die down in this hole along with Wally."

Paul swallowed, but picked up the other side of the crate, and they started up the steps with their treasure.

Meadow shook like an Aspen, and stayed hidden for what seemed like hours, but was probably no more than a few minutes. She wanted to make darn sure they were gone. She sat with her eyes closed, trying to recover from her fright.

Her eyes flew open and she flinched when she felt something wet on her cheek. She gasped when she saw Kelsey's black muzzle and her brown eyes looking into her own. Meadow didn't dare speak, but hugged her dog to her breast, her eyes brimming over again. Kelsey winced when Meadow gently felt the lump on her head.

Kelsey's hackles were down, so she thought Rick and Paul must be gone. Just to be sure, she slowly crept out from her hiding place, checked in every direction, and then tiptoed back to the secret room to find Wally. He was still lying on the ground, and his eyes were open, but clouded with pain. His side was seeping blood.

"Can you take off your shirt? I want to look at that wound."

"Yeah, it hurts," he said.

He seemed bewildered at the turn of events, but shrugged out of his shirt. Meadow examined him. The wound didn't look too deep, but he was losing a lot of blood.

"I'm going to wind your shirt around you to stop the bleeding, so sit up." She tore pieces from the shirt and balled them up to put tightly against the jagged gash then wrapped the rest around his middle and tied it.

"Do you think you can walk?" she asked.

"I'll try." He struggled to stand, but fell back weakly. "Sorry. I can't get up."

"Don't worry, Wally. I'm going for help. You just rest here and I'll be back before you know it. Here's your canteen, try to drink some water. And don't move too much."

Meadow raced out of the room and up the steps, heading for the entrance. She figured Rick and Paul would be gone by now, and she could run Foxfire all the way to the stable to get help.

When she reached the main room, she saw rain pouring down in buckets outside the cliff dwelling. She hurried in the dark through the passageway, feeling her way. Instead of getting lighter toward the opening, it remained dark. It took a moment to realize why. The ladder was gone and the cave opening was covered over. Her legs turned to jelly and she sank onto the stone floor.

Chapter 29

Waters from Above

The wind gusted and then rain came down in sheets as Rick pulled up the ladder leading down to the cave below. He glowered at Paul, standing by and doing nothing, like the helpless sissy he was. "Make yourself useful and go get some of those lean-to boards to cover this hole up."

While he was gone, Rick collected brush to pile on top. When they were finished covering the cave entrance, Rick looked over their handiwork with satisfaction. "Now they can't get out and probably no one will be able to find the opening for days. They'll both be dead by then, and won't be able to accuse us of anything."

"You're crazy. They can accuse us of locking them in and causing them to die."

He wielded his knife in front of Paul's nose. "Don't ever call me crazy again!"

"Okay, okay. Whatever you say," Paul said, backing away.

"That's better." He slid the knife back into its sheath. "Let's get out of here."

"Wait, there's the girl's horse." Paul squinted through the rain at Foxfire still standing where Meadow had left her.

Rick picked up a brushy branch and waved it at the mare. "Get out of here. Git!" He shouted and vigorously waved the stick at her.

Foxfire snorted and bolted out of sight.

"Okay, let's get to the plane." Rick grabbed one handle of the crate.

Paul lifted the other side, and they started toward the upper mesa. As they were nearing the aircraft, a large ghostly form appeared out of the pouring rain. The huge stallion stood directly in front of the Piper with his ears laid back. He reared at them on his hind legs.

"Oh my god, I'm not going near it!" Paul stopped dead in his tracks, dropped the crate, and backed up.

"It's just a horse, you wuss." Rick let go of his side, standing his ground.

He still had the brushy branch and started waving it toward Diablo. The stallion shook his head and reared again.

"He's is not acting normal, but I'm not scared of any stupid horse." Rick started forward, holding the branch in front of him. "I'll get rid of him."

"Well, I'm not going anywhere near him." Paul inched backwards.

Rick continued on, waving the stick and made it about midway to the plane. The horse suddenly leapt forward and charged with his teeth bared. Rick dropped the branch and darted back toward Paul who was cowering behind a bush. The stallion thundered past Rick, hitting him with his shoulder and knocking him to the ground. He circled back toward the aircraft, as if standing guard.

Rick groaned and rubbed his shoulder, slowly regaining his feet. "That horse is nuts! He must have eaten some Loco Weed, or something."

"Now what'll we do?" Paul asked.

"If we can't get to the plane, we need to walk down to Brighten. Wendell can get us out from there."

"That's a long hike, and it's still raining." Paul's voice was whiny.

Rick glared at him. "We have no choice, unless you want to take on that giant, nutty horse, or stay here all night with no provisions. Besides, the rain has let up."

Paul muttered under his breath, but followed Rick to the crate. They picked it up between them and started down the path. They stopped when Foxfire came out of the brush and stood in their way. As they approached her, she laid back her ears, and pawed the ground.

"Another nutty horse!" Rick picked up a rock and flung it furiously at Foxfire, yelling at her. "Get out of here." Foxfire sidestepped the rock and galloped around them toward Diablo.

"Now what?" Rick watched the mare and stallion meet and sniff noses briefly, and then Foxfire turned and galloped back past them, down the trail towards Brighten. "Good riddance."

Half carrying, half dragging the crate with the medicine chest in it, Rick chafed at their slow progress. Rivulets of rainwater had washed out sections of sand, and loosened rocks, making the footing treacherous.

Paul slipped and fell. "I wish I had hiking boots."

"Well, you don't, so let's go."

Paul clambered up, covered in mud, and they continued to slog along the trail. As they came to a steep section, both feet slid out from under him and he went sprawling for the second time. He lay there groaning. "I can't go any farther. My feet hurt, and now I've sprained my ankle, I think."

Rick couldn't believe what a useless piece of crap this guy was. "You big baby, I wouldn't give a rip if you sat there and croaked, but I need your help carrying this. So get up and move, or else I'll make sure you never move again."

Paul looked at him dully, seemingly beyond fear. "You shouldn't have scared the girl's horse away. Then you could have ridden it to get help from Wendell." He sounded sullen, but he got up once more, and picked up his end of the crate.

They plodded on, with Paul limping. When they finally reached Oak Creek, it was swollen with rainwater and overflowing its banks. Uprooted brush and trees rushed by with the swiftly moving stream.

Paul took one look and stopped. "We can't cross that. I'm not getting swept away again."

"Don't worry. It's just a little creek. This is nowhere near as deep as the Brighten River. We can make it." Rick was trying his nice act on Paul. He would get rid of him when he didn't need him anymore. "The crate will float, so it shouldn't be a problem. Come on."

Rick started in, pulling Paul with him, still hanging onto his end of the crate. Paul's eyes flitted back and forth over the swirling water. "Steady, Paul, just float it across."

Paul winced. "Damn! My ankle is aching and there's an undertow. Let's go back."

"No, we're almost halfway now. Don't let go."

The crate bobbed between them, but was increasingly difficult to hold on to, with the swift current threatening to yank it out of their hands. Rick was concentrating on keeping his grip when he heard a roaring sound. He looked up and the last thing he saw was a huge wall of water bearing down on them.

Chapter 30

Trapped

Meadow stared up at the covered opening and trembled. How were they going to get out? If she didn't get help soon, Wally might die. *She* might die if someone didn't find them. She hadn't told anyone where she was going, and hadn't taken the time to write a note. That was dumb.

She took a deep breath and squared her shoulders. She'd better do something, even if it turned out wrong. Those creeps wouldn't get away with this. And Wally needed help.

There had to be another entrance to the cliff dwelling. Although she'd looked for it a couple of times without success, Meadow had always been convinced there must be another way in and out. The Indians had to have another entrance if something prevented them from using the main one. "Come on, Kelsey, let's find a way out."

Kelsey gave a little whine, and then started back the way they'd come, as if she understood the words.

They made it up to the central room and Meadow peered over the edge. The sun had come out and the wet rocks glistened. You'd have to be a trained rock climber with special gear to scale down that cliff face. It was a sheer drop to the canyon floor with nothing to hang on to. They went down the steps to the lower chamber and Kelsey led the way past the pond and through to another passageway. They explored several routes that seemed promising but became dead ends. The main passages all eventually ended up back where she'd started.

As time went on, worry about Wally plagued her. She went to look in on him. He was asleep or passed out, she wasn't sure which. She saw that his wound had stopped bleeding, but there was a big pool of blood next to his side. His breathing seemed to be labored. Ripping a piece of her shirttail, she went to the pond, and wet it for Wally's brow. When he felt the coolness, he blinked once, then nothing. She held the canteen up to his lips, but the liquid just dribbled down his chin.

Tired and frustrated, she came out of the room and sank down next to the pool, gazing at its stillness, totally at a loss as to what to do next. Meadow sat staring at the water, almost in a stupor. It seemed they were in an impossible situation. No way out and no one knew where they were.

Still looking at the pool, she gradually became aware of a faint light on the far side, creating a subtle shimmer in the water. It must have been there all along, but she'd never noticed it before. She made her way over to look more closely, and saw a slight rippling above the light spot.

That's strange. What can be causing the ripple and where is that light coming from? She stepped into the cold pool. It was much deeper than the other end. Diving under the water, she found an opening where the light was filtering through. When she swam back up to the surface, Kelsey was swimming back and forth, apparently looking for her.

Meadow got out of the water and Kelsey followed her out, shaking herself vigorously. She took Kelsey's face between her hands and looked into her eyes.

"You have to listen. You can't come with me. Stay here with Wally. Stay." She made her voice as firm as she could, afraid Kelsey would try and follow her under water.

Kelsey cocked her head then sat down, but her eyes seemed worried.

Meadow prepared by taking several deep breaths, then she dived down toward the opening and swam through it. A light shone at the other end, and she aimed for it. The swim was longer than she'd anticipated and her lungs felt like they were about to burst.

Keep swimming, don't breathe in, keep going, too far to go back. She tried to swallow some of the air left in her mouth, now feeling light headed. The light was closer and getting brighter, but she could no longer feel herself swimming. Her arms and legs were leaden and her brain seemed to be shutting down. *Need rest. Give in and rest. Just rest. . . .*

Meadow closed her eyes but could still see the light and now felt like she was floating toward it in a dream. She saw Meda riding on the back of Arrow, and he was flying through the air, up toward the sun, his silver mane floating in the breeze. Then there was nothing but darkness.

Chapter 31

The Search

The sun was low in the sky as Shep watched Foxfire gallop into the stable yard, blowing hard, as if from a long run. She skidded to a stop, then trotted to the tack room, letting out a shrill whinny.

Shep, along with Nueme, Brett, and Monty, was sitting on the stumps set up as chairs, resting against the rustic boards. Shep jumped to his feet and caught Foxfire's rope.

"Easy, girl." He patted her neck to calm her, but Foxfire was agitated, and kept stamping and looking back the way she had come. "How did she get loose? Meadow was grooming her when we left. Where is she anyway?"

"I haven't seen her since before noon," Brett said.

Shep frowned. "That's when we got the big rush of people and we all took out rides." He tied Foxfire to the hitching rail. "Maybe she's down at the cabin."

He found Rose slicing tomatoes, and Mike sitting at the table. "Have you seen Meadow? Foxy got untied somehow and was galloping around."

Rose dropped the tomato and turned. "I haven't seen her."

Shep looked at Mike. "Did she tell you where she was going?"

"No, the last I saw her, she was going over to the store. That was earlier, before I lay down."

"I doubt she's still over there, but I'll go check with Wendell." Shep strode across the street and stepped into the store. It wasn't closing time yet, but no one was manning the counter. Strange, they must have closed early. He knew they lived in an apartment in the rear of the store, so he walked back and knocked. The door was not latched and it creaked open.

He poked his head in. "Wendell . . . Lucy . . . anyone home?"

Still no answer. After entering, he was surprised to see the place in total disarray. It looked like they had vacated in a big hurry, with the dresser drawer half open, clothes strewn about and dirty dishes in the sink. Just as he was about to leave, Bill walked in.

"Shep, what are you doing here?"

"I came to ask Wendell and Lucy if they'd seen Meadow. They weren't in the store, so I came back here. It looks like they left in a hurry."

Bill scanned the room. "Yes, I can see that." He turned back to Shep. "Is Meadow missing?"

"She left before noon today and Foxy is acting peculiar. It's probably nothing to worry about. She might be out picking berries or something."

"That's probably right. I'm sure she's around somewhere." Bill walked around the disheveled room. "Wonder where Wendell and Lucy are? This seems suspicious, especially since I saw a plane circling the mesa earlier. I came here to phone the sheriff about it."

Shep tightened his jaw. "A plane? How long ago?"

Bill saw his reaction. "Around two o'clock or so. But I'm sure it was nothing. Probably just some tourists looking at the red rocks."

"Probably." Shep headed for the door. "It's getting late. If Meadow's still not back, I'm going to ride out and look for her."

She wasn't back when he returned to the cabin, and Shep had a bad feeling, as if a rat was gnawing on his guts. He saw that Rose was fretting nervously like she couldn't decide whether to stand or sit. "I'll go find her. She can't be far."

He took down his hunting rifle from the cabin wall and placed it in the scabbard. He was about to walk out with it, when he went back and got his Colt .45 and stuck it into his belt. "Just in case it gets dark and we run into some wild animals," he told Rose.

He headed to the tack room with Rose and Mike close behind. Nueme, Monty, and Brett were still sitting outside. "Let's saddle up, Monty. Meadow must be out on the trail somewhere.

Foxy's still stomping around and whinnying. She must have ridden her with the halter and something happened."

"Maybe she's up at Hidden Valley. I know she goes up there to see the stallion," Brett said.

Shep caught his breath. "What? That stallion is dangerous!" He fixed the scabbard onto the saddle and put the pistol into one of the saddle bags.

Brett and Nueme started toward their horses without being asked.

"I'm going, too," Rose said. She had dug out some flashlights.

"Good idea. You ride Foxy, she must know where Meadow is."

Mike watched his mother saddle up. "I want to go."

"You can't ride with a cast on. It might reinjure your arm."

"But, Mom—"

"No buts. Besides, someone needs to be here in case she shows, to tell her where we are. You can go let Bill know that Brett is coming with us."

Mike nodded, obviously unhappy about the decision.

The riders headed out, with Rose and Foxfire in the lead. The mare was anxious and pulling on the bit, so Rose let her break into an easy canter. By the time they reached Oak Creek, the water had receded, but they could see where it had overflowed. The stream was still running swiftly, and the banks were slippery, but the horses were able to make their way and ford the still turbulent creek.

"You don't think Meadow was caught in a flash flood?" Brett's face was tense.

"I don't think so, judging from how Foxy wants to cross and go on up the trail," Shep answered.

They reached the other side and Nueme told them to hold up. "Look at these tracks," he said. "Two people walked down the trail since the rain stopped. They were carrying something heavy. But they didn't come out the other side."

Rose's eyes grew huge. "Do you think Meadow was one of them?"

"No, these are men's footprints, wearing street shoes."

"Oh, no." Rose turned to Shep, her face crumpled. "You think those thieves came back, and Meadow ran into them?"

"Let's go search the Indian dwelling first." Shep urged his horse forward.

The group arrived at the cave entrance in record time with Foxfire leading the way. She went directly to the brush pile that Rick had made and stopped.

"This looks different from the last time I was here," Rose said. "Are you sure this is the right place? I don't see the cave entrance."

"It looks to me like someone deliberately covered it over." Shep stepped off Shadow and started pulling the brush away.

Monty and Brett dismounted to help with removing the debris, while Nueme rode on to the mesa, looking for more tracks.

Shep found the ladder intact underneath the pile and put it down the cave entrance. By the time they were finished removing the rubble, Nueme had returned.

"The plane is up on the Mesa," he said. "For some reason the men didn't go back to it. They walked out. And there are horse tracks all around the plane."

"The mustangs must be up on the Mesa," Brett said.

"Just one horse. A big one." Nueme had a strange look on his weathered face.

"Well, let's get to cliff dwelling before we lose all the daylight." Shep started down the ladder.

Nueme stayed above to watch the horses, while the rest of them followed Shep's lead.

"Meadow . . . Meadow, are you in here?" Shep called loudly.

The silence was deafening as they continued on their hunt. Reaching the main chamber, they were suddenly greeted by a black dog bounding up from the lower level, wiggling with happiness at seeing the family.

"Kelsey! Where's Meadow?" Shep cautiously followed Kelsey down the steps, afraid of what he might find.

She ran to the edge of the pool and whined. Shep glanced at the water, then at Kelsey. She whined again, and then led them to the inner room, where she went to Wally and licked his face. He groaned and his eyes fluttered.

"Look, it's Wally. He's hurt!" Rose went to his side and carefully unwrapped his shirt. "Oh, no, it looks like a knife wound."

Shep's face grew even tighter. "You boys check out the rest of the cave, but stay together. Make sure there's no one else lurking in the shadows. Meadow isn't in here because Kelsey would be with her."

The boys went out, and Shep propped Wally up and started questioning him.

"Wally, can you hear me? Where's Meadow?" He gave Wally a little shake.

"Rick . . . don't know . . ." Wally's voice faded and his eyes rolled back in his head.

"What's he talking about? He must be delirious," Rose said. "He's weak from loss of blood."

Shep checked his pulse. "I don't think he has the strength to walk out. And we're not going to get any information out of him."

"We need to get him to a doctor," Rose said.

Monty and Brett appeared back in the doorway.

"We looked everywhere, they've all gone," Brett said. "They must have taken Meadow."

"Oh, no! What can we do?" Rose grabbed Shep's arm.

"Don't worry, honey. We'll find her. Remember, Nueme said her footprints weren't with the others at the creek, so either they never saw her, or she escaped somehow." Shep wasn't feeling all that sure, but he needed to be strong for the others. "Right now, we have to get Wally out of here for medical attention."

"Brett and I can carry him out," Monty said, and Brett nodded.

"We can make a travois out of the wood up top to carry him down the trail. Elmer will pull it with no problem." Shep said, heading out of the room.

They roped some planks together and hitched the makeshift travois behind Elmer. After Wally was secured on it, Shep took Rose aside. "You and the boys need to take Wally down the mountain. Nueme and I will keep going."

Rose started to argue. "The boys can take Wally. Monty knows how to drive now and he can get him to the doctor. I want to go with you."

Shep put both hands on her shoulders. "No Rose, Foxy shouldn't have to keep going. She's already made two fast trips up here today. Nueme and I will find Meadow." He didn't tell her the real reason, that he wanted her safe with the boys, just in case things got ugly with the thieves. He could see on her face that she knew the Foxfire story was only an excuse, but she gave in to please him. She hugged him tightly before she mounted up.

Her chin quivered. "Find her for me."

"I will, darlin'."

He watched her and the boys ride away, his mouth set in a grim line. He pulled the Colt .45 out of his saddlebag. "Here, Nueme. I know you're a good shot."

Nueme took the pistol. "Just hope we don't need to use it."

"Me, too. Let's ride."

They rode on to the mesa top, where the plane stood out like a wart on someone's nose. Shep stopped in front of it. "You go east and I'll head west. If you find her, signal with one shot. I'll do the same. Either way, meet back here in a couple of hours."

After the earlier rain, it was a balmy summer evening, and Shep wished it was a pleasure ride instead of a desperate search. He kept pushing away the thought that Meadow might have met up with the pot hunters.

Hours later, when he met up with Nueme the second time, the temperature had begun to drop. The moon had risen in the east, casting long shadows, with its glow helping them to search. But it seemed hopeless. There was no sign of Meadow.

By then, it was close to midnight and a band tightened around Shep's heart. "We haven't come across a single sign of any activity, except right here at the lean-to and at the entrance to the cave."He knew his voice sounded defeated.

Before Nueme could answer, they heard horses approaching from the south. A light shone through the brush preceding the riders, and then Shep could make out Deputy Dave Redland. Behind him rode Bill, Linda, and Brett.

Dave reined in next to Shep. "When Bill called about the plane, he told me you were up here looking for Meadow. Any clues so far?"

Shep sighed. "No, we've covered this whole area. And we're mighty glad to have reinforcements. Did Rose get Wally to the hospital all right?"

"Yes, she took Mike with her and left Monty to tend the horses. Since you hadn't shown up, we thought you could use some help. We fanned out on the way up here and searched the entire trail." Dave's expression told him they'd come up empty.

"Well, let's rest for a few minutes," Bill said."You two look like you could use some food." He dismounted and pulled out supplies from his saddle bags. Dave and Brett went to gather firewood, while Linda lit a lantern that had been left at the old lean-to site.

Before long, a fire was going with coffee perking.

"You thought of everything." Shep had never tasted better coffee.

He didn't have much appetite for the sandwich that Linda handed him, but forced it down. He had to keep his strength up. He had to keep going until they found her. He couldn't remember if he'd had lunch that day. Didn't matter. All that mattered was they find his girl.

"We've thoroughly covered the area up to this point, and you two have searched the mesa," Bill said. "She couldn't have vanished into thin air."

"Not even any tracks, other than the two men walking out," Nueme said.

Kelsey sidled up to Shep and whined. He petted her absently. "I was hoping Kelsey would catch her scent. You know that wherever Meadow goes, Kelsey's not far behind, but she hasn't found any scent of her. It's like she sprouted wings and flew out of here."

"She's up here somewhere," Dave said. "You're sure she wasn't still in the cliff dwelling somewhere? From what Linda told me, it's pretty big."

Shep nodded. "I'm sure. Kelsey would have been with her, or at least taken us to her."

He put his head in his hands. Something was nagging at the back of his mind, something about the pool . . . then suddenly the fog lifted and he looked at Kelsey. "The pond . . ."

"What about the pond?" Brett asked.

"Kelsey knows. She tried to tell us when we first got there . . . what if the men . . ."

Shep's voice broke and he couldn't finish the sentence. It was too terrible to contemplate. His beautiful daughter at the bottom of that pool.

Linda had been sitting quietly listening, but now she sucked in her breath sharply, and hastily wiped away a tear.

"No, no, I don't believe that . . . She got away." Brett shook his head and walked away from the campfire.

"I'm sure she's fine, Shep." Nueme put his hand on his shoulder. "You know no one pushes Meadow around—she's a tough kid, especially when she's mad."

Shep clenched his jaw so hard it hurt. "I hope you're right, otherwise I'll hunt down every one of those bastards." He stood up, strode over to Shadow and prepared to ride back to the Indian cave.

Chapter 32

Riding the Wind

Little by little Meadow's eyelids slid open, and she smelled the moist sweet scent of grass. The sun warmed her body, but her face was shadowed by something. She squinted up, and saw a silhouette in front of her, with a soft nose that nuzzled her gently.

Her eyes adjusted to the light, but it was hard to tell if she was awake or dreaming. Somehow she knew it was Arrow above her, and she was not afraid. A short distance away, she heard a restful burbling sound. Meadow turned her head and realized that she was lying in lush grass, next to a pool of water. The private glen had trees and bushes all around, and it felt as if she were in a secure nook, safe from the danger lurking outside.

She looked around, still not certain whether she was in her world, or the next—like the one Mike had described to her. Meadow sat up abruptly in confusion, and the stallion stepped back with his eyes growing large and his nostrils flaring.

"Easy, Arrow." She put her hand out to him.

His look softened, and he dropped his head to her again.

Still in a dreamlike trance, Meadow got up and went to his side and grabbing his silvery mane, swung up to his back. He was bigger and taller than Foxfire, but it was as if she had springs in her feet and she landed square on top of him. Arrow knew what to do and started off without any urging.

Riding him was like flying. In fact, she wasn't sure that they *weren't* flying. She couldn't feel or hear his hoof beats. She looked down, and the ground seemed very far away. Arrow sailed along and she clung to his back, holding onto his shimmering thick mane with both hands, letting him find the way. He seemed to know where they were going, so she just hung on.

Before long they were flying above Oak Creek, in between the steeply etched canyon walls. She could see the ravages of the floodwater that had come down, sweeping away everything in its path. They rode on along the creek past uprooted trees and brush.

The stallion seemed to be searching for something. He flew down, landing right in the creek bed. Meadow held on and remained astride him, as they walked around boulders and over logs, splashing along in knee-deep water, following the stream. Before long they rounded a corner, and she sucked in her breath sharply.

A man lay face down on a sandy bar, not moving. Arrow came to a stop on the bank nearby. She slipped off his back and gingerly made her way over to the body. Drawing near, she saw the contorted face of the man who had almost killed her. His eyes were partially open, staring at nothing. Flies swarmed around, lit, then buzzed away.

A bitter taste arose in her throat, and she started to back up. But wait . . . there was something glinting in the sun, sticking out from under him. She took a step closer, and peered down to get a better look. As if by its own volition, her hand reached down to touch it. It was a chain . . . . She pulled on the very end to avoid touching Rick's lifeless form. The chain seemed to be stuck, so she tugged harder, and it finally came sliding out from underneath him.

It was the amulet.

Holding it in her hand, she walked into the water and rinsed it off, and then dried it carefully with her shirt. It glistened in the sunlight, as she brought it up close to her cheek, then next to her heart, feeling its familiar warmth.

Chapter 33

The Rescue

Shep rode in heavy silence toward the cave entrance, dread mounting with each step. Even the footfalls of the horses seemed muffled and subdued as the others followed, their faces reflecting fear of what the pool might hold.

The eerie stillness was broken by a trumpeting whinny in the distance.

Shep's head swiveled in time to see Nueme, bringing up the rear, swing around to look back to where the Piper sat, high on the mesa. Next to the plane, the big gray stallion, shining like a ghost horse in the moonlight, pawed the ground. He whinnied again, and galloped toward them.

"Arrow." Nueme's voice showed no surprise.

The stallion came near, and then veered off, turning west. He looked back over his shoulder at them as he trotted away. Kelsey gave an excited bark and ran after him.

"Kelsey, come back here!" Irritation boiled up in Shep. This was all he needed right now. "What do you suppose she's doing, chasing after that horse? She knows better than that!"

"We must follow her." Nueme said it mildly, as if it should be obvious. He shined his light where he'd seen Kelsey disappear, and then urged his horse forward.

Shep hesitated for only for a moment before spurring Shadow after Nueme. Anything was preferable to searching the cave pond. His pulse quickened when he saw how excited Kelsey was acting. Maybe she'd finally caught Meadow's scent. He squeezed his legs again and his horse shot past Nueme's appaloosa. He heard everyone else break into a trot behind them. They rode, hugging the cliff line where it jutted up sharply next to them, using flashlights to pick their way through the thick brush.

A couple of times Shep thought they'd lost Kelsey, but then he would see her circling back looking for the riders. After making sure they were following, she dashed off again in a great hurry. Once in a while Shep caught a glimpse of a thick silver tail. A glimmer of hope grew inside him.

After awhile Kelsey disappeared through what appeared to be a solid wall of rock. As he drew near, Shep realized the trees and brush camouflaged an opening large enough for a horse to narrowly pass. He rode through and flashed his light around. The other side opened into a glen with large oak trees. Kelsey raced through the grass, yipping, towards an indentation in the cliff wall on the far side of the small basin. The stallion was nowhere to be seen.

Shep put Shadow into a gallop, chasing after Kelsey. He found Meadow next to a bubbling spring lying deathly still, her face like wax. Kelsey was whining and licking her, but she didn't move. Shep felt the huge weight of fear descend on his chest as he jumped off his horse and lifted her limp body. "Meadow," he managed to choke out.

The others arrived altogether, making a circle around them.

"Is she all right?" Linda asked.

"Meadow, Meadow wake up." Shep's eyes leaked like a drippy faucet as he tried to rouse her.

She blinked once, and her lids started to rise, but her eyes were unfocused, as if her mind was somewhere else, far away. Meadow seemed to be making an enormous effort to concentrate on his voice, so he kept talking, pleading with her to come back to him. Her eyes finally rested on his face.

"Daddy?" she moaned. He leaned closer but could barely hear her. "Daddy, you're here."

"Meadow." He hugged her fiercely. The strain of the long night had taken its toll. He never wanted to let her go.

"I'm all right, Daddy," she whispered.

He looked intently into her face. "Don't ever scare me like that again, okay?"

"Okay," she said with a weak smile.

Now everyone was off their horses, and gathered next to them.

"It's dark out. What time is it?" She looked around in confusion. "Just a minute ago, I was riding Arrow and it was light out. How long was I lying here?"

"You were riding Arrow? You mean Diablo?" Brett asked.

"Yes, he took me down Oak Creek to where Rick and Paul were swept away . . . ." her voice trailed away as if she just remembered something unpleasant.

"What do you mean, did you see them?" asked Dave.

She nodded. "Yes, Rick's dead. But the other man is alive. I can tell you where he is." She sat up. "Is Wally okay?"

"We got him out and he's at the hospital by now," Linda said.

Shep stepped in, his voice firm. "No more questions. We've got to get you home and into bed, sweetheart."

Brett spoke up. "Since Mike let me borrow Rowdy, he's the freshest horse here. She can ride with me."

Meadow gave a weak smile. "He must really like you. Mike never lets anyone borrow Rowdy."

Shep raised his eyebrows, looking from Brett to Meadow. He shook his head a little. "That's fine, let's get going." He boosted Meadow up behind Brett and they started off with her sitting straight up, holding onto the cantle. He reined Shadow back to allow Brett to lead, so he could keep an eye on Meadow. But as they rode, the gentle swaying of Rowdy's hips lulled his exhausted girl into drowsiness. He saw her lean against Brett's back, and her eyes drooped.

Meadow was still asleep when they arrived home in the wee hours. Shep gently lifted her off Rowdy, and carried her into the cabin. Rose fought back tears as she tucked her into bed, and he sat for a long time just watching her sleep.

Chapter 34

Another Letter

Meadow slept till past nine the next morning, then sat bolt upright as the memories came flooding back. Her mother turned and smiled at her from stirring oatmeal on the stove.

"So the sleeping beauty finally awakes." Her mother walked over to give her a hug. "Don't ever go chasing after thieves all by yourself again."

"Sorry, Mom." She *did* feel bad for making them worry, but she knew she would do the same thing again. How could she let those awful men just get away? Her mother would never understand. She looked around. "I'm so glad to be back home. Where is everyone?"

"They're searching for the robbers. No one got much sleep last night, but Dave thought they'd better try and find them before they get away. They left again just after dawn."

"But I *told* them that Rick is dead, and Paul is lost. I know where they are. Why didn't they ask me?"

"Honey, you've had a lot of excitement. After Wally got fixed up, he told us about Rick attacking you. That's a horrible thing to have to go through."

"I'm okay, Mom." Wally didn't know everything that happened, but she wasn't about to tell her mother about the knife to her throat. She shivered.

"I think you might have been delirious last night, and that you just dreamed it about riding the wild stallion and finding Rick's body," her mother said gently.

Now that her mother put it all into words, even Meadow wasn't so sure it happened. It had seemed real, but it was also dreamlike. Then she remembered the amulet. She ran to where her dirty jeans were piled with the other laundry items, and grabbing them, felt around in the pockets. It was there! With it gripped in her hand, she hurried back to her mother.

"I wasn't dreaming the whole thing." Meadow held up the pendant. "Rick tore this off me and put it in his pocket. See, the clasp is broken. I found it again under his . . . uh . . . body."

"That's beautiful!" Mom said, examining the piece of jewelry. "Is it one of the Indian relics?"

"Yes . . . uh . . . Chief White Horse told me to keep it safe." She didn't feel like explaining everything. It was way too complicated.

"Oh?"

Meadow was grateful her mother didn't press the issue. But then Mom went on, searching for a plausible explanation. "Well, maybe Rick dropped it in the cave before he left, and you just don't remember."

She sighed. Mom obviously doubted the story about Arrow and the amulet. It *did* sound far-fetched. The only way anyone was going to believe her was to prove it to them somehow.

Her mother wouldn't allow her to ride out after the search party, saying that she needed help at the stable that day. Monty had also stayed behind to wrangle the dudes, but Mike still wasn't able to ride, so he walked across the road to help Linda with the store. Wendell and Lucy were gone, so Linda got stuck minding the store and post office, until a replacement could be hired. It was high season and all the facilities needed to be open for their guests staying at the resort.

By dinnertime, the search party hadn't returned and her mother kept a plate warm for Dad while she served Meadow and her brothers. Mike regaled them all with stories about happy, souvenir-collecting tourists that came into the store that day. He said it'd been fun telling the dudes tall tales about wild horses and Indians. Linda told him the sales of knickknacks were way up for the day and that she wanted to hire him on full time. Meadow smiled, listening to him yammer. He was a born salesman.

Then Mike produced a bombshell. He pulled out a letter for Monty. This time it was a baby blue envelope. Everyone knew it had to be from Cynthia.

He waved the letter in front of his brother's nose. "Hey, Monty, I've got a letter from your girlfriend."

Monty scowled and snatched it out of his hand. He opened it and quickly scanned the words. His scowl turned into a grin, and Mike grabbed the letter back and started reading out loud, imitating Cynthia's annoying voice.

Dear Monty,

> *I miss you so much. It's been terrible not hearing from you since the rodeo.*

> *I hope Mike is doing okay. I heard that he got out of the hospital.*

> *How have you been? I hope you haven't met any other girls that you like. My summer has been so boring since we were up there. I haven't even been taking riding lessons, it's been so hot. I've had some pool parties for my friends, but nothing else.*

"Mike, give that to me!" Monty lunged at his brother, but Mike leaped across the room, cast held high, and climbed to the loft, where he kept reading.

> *My brother, Ralph, is such a bore. He doesn't even come out of the house to swim. I think he is embarrassed because he's so fat. Oh, I don't want to be mean, but he is such a bore.*

> *You've probably been wondering how my health has been, well, I've been fine, not even any headaches or dizzy spells anymore. I told Daddy I was fine.*

Monty started to go up after him, but in the end just sat down and shot daggers in Mike's direction. When Mike got to the next part, he dropped the mimic, and started coming down the ladder.

> *Well, I think he finally believes me. He's dropping the lawsuit!! Isn't that wonderful!!*

> *I'm not sure why, but just after Mr. Bowman's lawyer came to see him, he decided that I was okay. He told us that he decided not to pursue any action against your family. I'm so happy!! Now we can see each other when you move back to Scottsdale for the winter. Even Daddy said it was okay. His attitude has certainly improved towards you and your family.*

*Let me know when you are moving down and we can
meet somewhere, okay?*
   I hope you can write to me soon, I really miss you.
   Your Good Friend, (and more soon!)
   Cynthia

Mike plopped down at the table with a stunned look on his face.

Mom's puckered brow cleared, then she beamed. "So Bill's attorney fixed our problem! Whoopee!" She jumped up and grabbed Monty, dancing around the room with him.

Meadow pulled Mike up, and they danced along with them. They were all still laughing and dancing when Dad came in.

"Seems like I got home just in time for a party. What's the happy occasion?"

Mom showed him the letter from Cynthia. He nodded when he read it. "I knew Bill had called his lawyer. He told me today he got it all straightened out. He's also giving us back all the money we're due that Wendell pocketed."

"Oh, Shep, that's wonderful! What a relief!" Mom pulled out a hankie and dabbed at her eyes.

"Did you find Paul and Rick?" Mike asked.

"Just Paul. He was downstream from the crossing—dazed and wandering in circles. Not really hurt, though. No trace of Rick."

"What do you think happened to him?" Mom asked.

"He must have gotten away with the Indian chest." Dad shook his head sadly.

"No, I told you—he's dead." Meadow got the heebie-jeebies thinking about him face down in the sand with all those nasty flies.

"Why didn't they find the body, then?" Monty asked, with a superior air.

"I don't know." She felt all eyes upon her. No one believed her.

"Maybe a mountain lion ate him," Mike said. "Would serve him right."

That evening after dinner, they all sat on the porch enjoying the summer twilight, with the threat of an impending lawsuit no longer hanging over their heads.

Meadow was just starting to think everything was going to be all right, when the peaceful family scene was interrupted by the sound of a pickup towing a horse trailer. It pulled up and stopped in front of the cabin. Her heart trembled when Bill Bowman stepped out of the truck and tipped his hat to them.

"Good evening, folks," he said, "I've come to collect my new Arabian mare."

She sucked in her breath sharply and looked to her father, eyes pleading.

Her father had a stony expression. "That was the agreement you made. Go and fetch Foxy."

Knowing that this day might come didn't help. Meadow felt breathless, as though she'd just been kicked in the stomach by a cranky mule. With a clenched jaw, she left the porch to get Foxfire, determined not to make a scene.

Her mare followed trustingly, not knowing she was being betrayed, and given away like an old shirt. Meadow handed the lead rope to Bill Bowman without a word. She couldn't face saying goodbye, so turned and walked away in silence. She could hear Foxfire trying to follow and when Bill restrained her, she let out a questioning nicker.

Hearing that last nicker made Meadow want to crawl into a hole and never come out.

Chapter 35

Without Foxfire

Meadow rode Rex through the Lazy B Ranch gate, leading Foxfire back to her new home on the Bowman's property. This was the second time in as many weeks her mare had run away from the ranch, returning to the stable. She tied Rex to the hitching rail, and brought her mare to the barn.

"Foxy, you live here now." She firmed her resolve and put on a stoic mask as she ushered her horse into the extra high corral that had been built for Diablo.

Foxfire didn't believe her, though, and worked on unlatching the gate. Meadow swallowed the lump in her throat and refused to let tears betray her.

"That mare misses you." Juan poked his head out of a nearby stall that he was cleaning. "Two times now she has gotten away from me and runs right back to you."

"I know."

Juan shook his head. "What was the boss thinking, taking her from you?"

"I made a deal with him. He wants her for a brood mare."

Juan shook his head again and went back to raking.

She was still watching Foxfire and worrying that she was losing weight when Linda came out of the house and walked over to her. "Hi, Meadow. Wait up, and I'll ride back to the resort with you. I have to open the store."

"Okay."

Juan saddled Linda's horse for her, then looped the reins across one of the wooden rails. He disappeared back into one of the stalls.

Linda touched her arm. "I'm so sorry, Meadow. Dad thinks taking Foxy was the right thing to do, but I totally disagree with him."

"Don't blame him, it was my idea."

"Well, since Wendell and Lucy took off, Dad's been angry at the world. He's been going through the account books and has found quite a few discrepancies."

"Like what?"

"There are problems with the hotel and cabin accounts, and who knows how much he skimmed from the store and the bar. Dave and the Sheriff are on the case, but so far there's no clue where he and Lucy disappeared to."

"Well, I hope they find him soon, I think he was behind everything."

"You could be right," Linda said. "By the way, a reporter from the Phoenix Gazette contacted Dave about the case. Dave told him it was really because of you that the rest of the gang was caught and the artifacts were located."

"Me? What did I do?" It still made Meadow sick to her stomach to think about her confrontation with Rick, and she'd tried to put it out of her mind.

"If you hadn't gone after the crooks that day, I'm sure they would have gotten away. Remember, Foxy led us all back to the cliff dwelling the very day the robbers came back. If you hadn't gone there, Dave wouldn't have known where they were or caught up with them. So you're really a hero."

"Oh." She didn't feel much like a hero.

"Anyway, that reporter may want to talk to you about it before he writes his article."

"I don't want to talk to any reporter."

Linda squeezed her hand. "Don't worry, sweetie, you won't have to. I'll take care of it."

After that, Meadow had seen little of Linda. The older girl was busy helping her father run the resort. Brett told everyone he preferred to help out at the stable, but he would grudgingly work in the store if he had to. Bill Bowman had been interviewing prospective managers for the last two weeks, and had narrowed it down to several candidates.

As she worked steadily at the stable, Meadow tried not to think about Foxfire, but every morning there was a sharp pain when she looked out the window at the empty corral. Dad didn't put another horse in that particular spot, and Mom said she was proud of Meadow for not making a fuss about missing Foxfire. She didn't make a fuss because she felt dead inside. It wasn't just her mare, there was the problem with Dad. Ever since the incident at the cliff dwelling, Dad had been acting strange. Cool and withdrawn.

Meadow didn't feel like riding for fun anymore. She mindlessly worked, guiding the dude rides, and then went for long solitary walks with Kelsey as her only companion. When she was out of sight of the stable the tears would come, and Kelsey would whine and lick her hand.

Lonely and depressed, she tried her best not to let it show. After all, she reasoned, losing Foxfire was her own fault. She didn't regret letting Diablo go free. She was pretty sure it was the right decision, but she was starting to doubt that she rode him and saw Rick's body, which had never been found. Nobody else believed she had ridden the wild horse. What if it had all been another one of her vivid dreams? She just wasn't sure anymore.

She hadn't been to Hidden Valley since Bill Bowman had taken Foxfire. And now she doubted the rapport she had with Diablo. Would he even come to her without Foxfire?

The summer passed, one day much like another, and nothing mattered to her, not even eating. Her mother tried to tempt her with all her favorite foods, but she just pushed it around on her plate, taking a bite once in a while to make Mom happy.

One night, when Meadow and the boys were already in bed, her parents sat out on the porch and talked right outside her open window. She was wide awake and heard every word.

"That article in the Gazette about Meadow foiling the cave robber's plot was really something," Mom said. "Too bad it didn't seem to cheer her up."

"She's pining away for her mare, but she'll just have to get over it. Don't worry, darlin', she'll come around pretty soon. Meadow is made of stern stuff, and this is just a lesson in growing up. Kids need to learn that life doesn't always go the way they would like. She'll figure it out and be stronger for it."

"But Shep, she's not even fourteen. Young for such a hard lesson."

"Hell, I was her age when I left home to make my way in the world. She'll be okay."

"Are *you* okay, Shep? You never told me why you left. It's been bottled up inside you for long enough. Tell me the story; maybe I can help. You haven't been yourself this summer."

"Nothing to tell," Dad said, tersely. His chair scraped and the porched floor creaked as he left.

Meadow sniffed, knowing that somehow it was all her fault. Mom and Dad never fought, until now. She had to find out her father's dark secret and put it right.

Chapter 36

Time to Plot

Wendell Halstead sat idly tapping his fingers on the table in his Las Vegas hotel room, waiting for Lucy to finish up in the bathroom. She'd been in there for hours, doing god knows what. Probably dying her hair again, he thought, curling his lip. Couldn't she just pick a color and stick with it for cripes sake? It didn't used to bother him, but lately she'd been getting on his nerves.

He paced the room, and then spotted a newspaper on the nightstand. Lucy must have bought it earlier when she went out for coffee. He picked it up and saw that it was the Phoenix Gazette. What a ditz! We're not even in Arizona right now. Oh well, better than nothing.

He plunked himself back down and started thumbing through it, casually scanning the headlines. On page three something jumped out at him, and he stopped to slowly reread it.

INDIAN POT HUNTERS FOILED BY 13-YEAR-OLD GIRL!
Artifacts Recovered; One Thief still at Large

Wendell glared at it for a moment, and as he read on, his frown deepened.

He swore under his breath before yelling through the still-closed bathroom door. "Did you see this, Lucy?"

"What?" She poked her head out with a towel wound around her hair.

"This story about the artifacts. It says here that girl, Meadow, bravely faced the crooks and ultimately brought down the whole gang."

"Except for us, of course," Lucy added with her toothy grin.

Wendell got up and started pacing again, his face burning as if he'd been slapped hard.

"That little bitch! I'll bring HER down before this is all over!"

"Let it go, Wendell." Lucy turned back to the mirror and taking off the towel, revealed platinum blonde locks.

"Never! I'll never let it go. To think some little punk teenager ruined my brilliant scheme and made us wanted criminals!"

"But we did pretty well with the resort scam. Isn't that good enough?" Lucy started combing through her hair, preening in front of the mirror.

"No! We could have had a fortune, and she interfered. And now the cops are on to us."

"They haven't the slightest idea where we are," Lucy managed to get in.

"Well, it's the last time she'll ruin any of my plans. I'll see to that! Besides, they never found the medicine chest—says so right here. I'll bet that little brat knows where it is, too."

Lucy shrugged. "You could be right." She screwed her mouth up, like she always did when something new occurred to her.

"You bet I'm right and I'm going to prove it!"

Lucy let out a sigh and went back to her hair.

"We'll have to lay low for a while, and it will take a little time for me to get a plan together, but little Miss Meadow hasn't seen the last of us." Wendell narrowed his eyes to cold slits, what Lucy called his snake look.

He sat back down at the table and took out a pen and paper. Coming up with a good scheme was always easier when he wrote it out. His smile was more like a sneer as he marked number one, two and three on his list.

1. Terrorize the girl.
2. Locate Indian chest.
3. Eliminate Meadow.

For the first time in several weeks, he had a purpose, and it felt good.

Chapter 37

Colt

The stable was slow on Monday, and with little to occupy her, Meadow wandered off with no particular destination in mind. The fog that threatened to engulf her didn't seem to be getting any better.

Kelsey stayed close, as they wound through the forest paths without paying attention to the direction. The only thing that seemed to ease her pain somewhat was to explore the woods, pretending she still shared the experience with Foxfire.

At least she still had Kelsey. She shuddered as she thought back to when Rick had almost killed her precious dog. Meadow stopped for a moment to hug Kelsey.

"We still have each other, don't we girl?"

Kelsey whined and nuzzled against her.

"I think you miss Foxy, too."

She reached into her pocket and gave Kelsey one of the oatmeal cookies she'd grabbed on her way out, and then they kept going, meandering farther into the woods.

Before long, she found herself crossing the Brighten River on the upper log bridge. As she looked down into the depths, she briefly wondered what it would feel like to be pulled along by the river's swift current. Meadow continued on like a sleepwalker, finally realizing that she'd reached the gorge with its splashing stream.

"Wow, how'd we get this far, Kelsey? We must have been walking for hours."

Kelsey made her way down from the overlook and began lapping from the creek. Meadow realized she was thirsty, too, and went to retrieve the tin cup. She dipped it into the icy water. The sweet taste immediately refreshed her.

She swung around when Kelsey let out a low woof, and looked up at the bluff above them. Meadow thought at first it was another of her visions.

There stood a dark horse, a thin rope around his nose, with no saddle or bridle. He was untied, but waited without moving for his master, who sat leaning against a fallen log.

He was a young man, shirtless, but wore fringed buckskin pants. His straight black hair hung to his shoulders, and was held in place by a beaded red headband that stretched across his forehead. A stream of sunlight perfectly outlined him against the mossy backdrop and highlighted his striking bronze skin and aquiline profile. He seemed lost in some private meditation.

Transfixed by the beauty of the scene, Meadow wondered if this could be another one of her imaginings. She climbed up on the bluff, and he slowly turned his gaze on her. His eyes were an unusual dark green, like the moss-covered stones in the gorge, and seemed to hold a wisdom that belied his youth. He didn't seem surprised to see her.

"You must be Meadow. I was waiting for you."

She was amazed to hear him speak perfect English. From the way he looked she had expected him to speak in his native tongue at the very least.

"How do you know who I am?" she asked, her heart beating faster.

"You're famous up on the res," he answered.

"The res?"

"The Shonto Nation, commonly known as the reservation. You're famous there."

"Famous for doing dumb stuff, you mean." She looked away from him.

"Not at all. You're the one that Meda entrusted with the amulet. And you freed the Sky Horse. You must be someone special." His words felt like a balm to her, soothing her soul.

"Do I know you?" she finally asked, thinking there was something vaguely familiar about him.

"I'm Colt. Chief White Horse's son." His sudden smile lit up his face.

Meadow couldn't help but smile back, even though she hadn't felt much like smiling lately. She remembered the picture of the small boy with his mother at the Chief's house.

"Were you riding up near the cliff dwelling a while back? I thought I saw an Indian riding away when I was up there one time. But then, I just wasn't sure."

"That was me. I often go riding alone when I'm home from college. It's a nice change from campus life. Right now I'm on a break from summer school."

"Were you watching me that day? Did you know about the cliff dwelling?"

"Yes, to both questions. I've been riding these mountains since I was a child. I wanted to see who had *discovered* the dwelling."

Meadow listened silently, as Colt went on.

"I knew the designated one would find it. The Shonto won't go in because death visited those walls."

"But you've been in it?"

"Yes, I'm an exception. I'm what some call a half-breed, so no rules apply to me. I don't belong in my world *or* yours." He paused for a moment. "But it was right that you found it." He smiled again.

His warm smile felt like a gift to her. She was drawn to him——not just to his astonishing good looks, but she could sense his pureness of heart.

"And you were destined to let Arrow go free," Colt added in a low voice. His statement was so simple, and yet she felt a huge weight lift off her. Maybe things would work out after all.

"Meadow, you must always believe in yourself, even when others don't understand. You must trust your instincts."

"But everything is so wrong, right now. No one believes me and my father . . . ."

"He will tell you everything when the time is right. You are a daughter of destiny, a descendant of the Sun God and Earth Mother."

His words were cryptic, but the understanding dawned on Meadow. She frowned. "You mean *I* descended from Native Americans? And that would mean Dad is part . . . ."

Colt smiled again. "All will be clear in time."

Meadow managed to return his smile, and she began to relax, to almost feel *good*. The fact that none of it made sense at the moment didn't seem to matter.

"Come, sit by me and take in the splendor of our surroundings." Colt patted the ground next to him.

She sat by his side, and was transformed by the breathtaking sight of the waterfall cascading down the emerald green gorge to the pool below. As before, when she had been in this place, it felt mystical to her. She felt completely at peace for the first time since she'd found the cliff dwelling.

Kelsey had found a comfortable spot directly in front of them. They all sat companionably for a time without speaking, enjoying the feeling of being at one with nature.

The sun was getting low in the sky, but she hadn't noticed until Colt broke their silent reverie. "It time to go home now," he said.

"Yes, I had better get going before my folks start to worry."

"I'll give you a ride home on Smoke." Colt nodded to his waiting horse.

Meadow saw now that Colt's horse was not really black, as she had first thought, but a dark, smoky grulla color.

"What a beautiful stallion."

"Yes, Smoke is from the wild mustang herd. He tried to take over the herd, but Arrow won that fight and made him an outcast. I felt like we were kindred spirits, so I caught and tamed him."

"Have you been up to Hidden Valley lately? Did you see the herd?" Her voice was tinged with longing.

"Yes, just yesterday. Arrow doesn't like me getting too close though, especially on Smoke."

"I haven't been up there since . . . ."

"Since your mare was taken away." Colt finished her sentence, then jumped up on Smoke's bare back effortlessly.

"Come," He held out his hand.

Meadow gave him hers, and he pulled her up as if she weighed less than a feather.

"Hold on." He turned his stallion in the direction of the stable.

As she wrapped her arms around his waist, Meadow liked the feel of his warm skin against her open hands. It somehow felt familiar, like she had held Colt, in this same way, many times before.

The trip back to the stable seemed fast, as though they'd set a new record, given Smoke's ground-eating canter. Colt brought Meadow to the stable yard, and she quickly slipped to the ground. She looked up at him, not knowing what to say, and not wanting the magic to end. Finally she blurted out, "Would you like to stay for dinner?"

"Not this time." He smiled. "Perhaps another . . . ."

He started to ride away, and then suddenly turned around and spoke one last time.

"I'll see you again when it's time to bring in the Sky Horse."

"Okay." Meadow didn't ask how Colt knew about that.

He seemed to know everything about her.

Chapter 38

The Barbeque

It was late summer in the mountains near Sedona, with shorter days and nights with a nip in the air. A promise that colder fall weather was on the way.

Rose put on a festive Mexican shawl Shep had brought back from one of his trading trips. It might get cool tonight, she thought, and this is perfect for the end of the season party. Linda had told them it was going to be a real Mexican fiesta, with all the trimmings, even a piñata. Rose was trying to see herself in Shep's small shaving mirror when he walked in. She turned to face him.

"Oh, Shep, how can I tell if I look presentable for the party?"

"You look beautiful as usual, Darlin'." He kissed the top of her head.

"But you know Mary Bowman always looks like she just stepped out of a fashion magazine."

"Mary Bowman couldn't hold a candle to you if she bought the whole darn waxworks. Now quit worrying."

Rose smiled. It didn't matter if she was wearing jeans and covered in horse dust, Shep always thought she was the most beautiful woman in the world. Just one of the things she loved about him.

On the drive out to the Bowman Ranch, Rose felt a pang of sadness about leaving the stable now that the season was over. She wouldn't miss all the hard work, but she would miss the singular beauty of this place. And so much had happened in so short a period of time, it was mind-boggling. Mike's accident for one. She glanced at her middle son sitting in the back seat, entertaining Monty with his latest dude story. He was happy to finally have the cast off his arm.

And Meadow. Rose shook her head a little. What would that girl be up to next? She had left early this morning riding Foxfire, according to Mike. The rest of them had all been asleep, but Mike said the mare showed up mysteriously and Meadow hopped on and took off. Shep said she was probably taking Foxfire back to the Bowman Ranch and would meet them there. He didn't seem worried, so Rose decided she wouldn't worry either.

The party was already in full swing when they arrived. The Bowman's had gone all out, with the gaily decorated patio and tables loaded with every conceivable type of Mexican food. All of Bill's employees had been invited. Many were drinking beer and she heard snatches of conversation about goofy requests from guests throughout the summer. Two musicians were strumming their guitars softly in the background. Rose's mouth watered when the delicious aroma of roasting pig wafted by her nose.

Shep guided her and the boys over to where the Bowmans, Chief White Horse, and Dave Redland were already gathered on comfortable-looking seats near the fountain. Bill promptly served her and Shep generous Margaritas from the outdoor bar.

Mary turned to her. "I must say, this has been a most eventful summer." She'd just returned to the ranch after the successful opening of a new gallery in New York City.

Rose wasn't sure if she was referring to her gallery opening, or all the excitement in Brighten that summer. In her mind, the gallery couldn't compare with what had happened at the resort.

Rose nodded. "Yes, it was a whirlwind." She noted that, as usual, Mary was beautifully turned out. She tried to like the older woman, but found her a little intimidating, with her picture-perfect hair and expensive high-fashion clothes. There was an awkward pause.

"I hear Linda is heading to ASU this fall. Is Brett going to the high school in Sedona?" Rose couldn't think of anything else to say. She knew nothing about art work.

"No, Brett is enrolled in Eaton Military Academy in New York, so I can keep better tabs on him. Bill usually spends the winter here at the ranch, or our place in Scottsdale, in between his business trips. I have to run the galleries, so I will be mostly in New York." Mary's face was cold as a flat iron.

Rose made no comment. The Bowman marriage was pretty peculiar. She glanced over at Shep. How lucky she was, in spite of his recent long silences.

"Where are you wintering?" Mary asked.

"We'll try to rent the same house we had last year in Scottsdale. The kids didn't care much for the school though."

Brett had been listening to their conversation and watching them both. His whole body seemed tense.

"Well, I don't care much for being shipped off to some stupid military academy, either." He scowled at his mother.

"That's enough, Brett," his father said sharply.

Bill and Mary didn't spend much time together, but they certainly seemed in accord with how their children behaved. Brett clamped his jaw and sank down in his seat. Rose felt a little sorry for him. Poor kid, being shipped off from his family. When she caught Shep's eye she knew he felt the same, and he turned to Dave to divert attention from Brett.

"What's new with the pot hunter case, Dave?" Shep asked. "I hear you found Rick's body—or some of his remains."

"That's right. Everything about the corpse fits Rick's description, and no one else is missing around here."

"I guess Meadow was right about that after all," Shep said. "When does the trial start for the rest of the scoundrels?"

"It's set for November. It should be an open and shut case, though."

Shep nodded.

"Paul has already confessed to everything and, along with Wally's testimony, we'll put Professor Schumer away for a long time. Paul made a deal and will get off pretty easy for testifying."

"What about Wally?" asked Rose. "I understand he's recovered from his injuries."

"I don't think Wally will even serve time. He's not particularly bright, and was totally controlled by his brother," Dave said. "It's just too bad that Wendell and Lucy seem to have gotten away scot free."

"Yes, it seems they were behind the whole thing." Rose shook her head, thinking about the harm they had caused her family.

"The professor said they went back to the Midwest— maybe Iowa or Nebraska," Dave said. "We are issuing new *Wanted* posters this week, but we don't have any photos of them."

"I'm still astounded that I was taken in by those shysters," Bill said. "Wendell skimmed a lot of money off the top, leaving me with virtually no profit on the resort this summer. And then he still tried to steal the Indian relics."

"That's why they call them con artists," Shep said.

"I'm glad we were able to make restitution to you, Shep. I would never have charged you twenty-five percent of the take. Why would I do that, when you're bringing in so many more customers for the resort? Next year should be even better."

"Especially without Wendell and Lucy around," Mary added.

"At least all the artifacts are safely back in the hands of the University to be evaluated. Except the medicine chest, of course." Linda glanced over at Chief White Horse. "I'm really sorry we never found that."

"The medicine chest doesn't matter." Chief White Horse waved his hand dismissively.

"It will show up when the time is right."

"Where did you finally find all the artifacts?" Rose asked.

"They were stored in a warehouse in South Phoenix. Paul led us right to them, once his confusion cleared up," Dave answered. "Professor Schumer had a buyer, but we arrested him before he was able to conclude the deal."

"That was fortunate," said Linda. "If he'd sold them, it would have been a great loss to understanding Native American history and culture."

Dave nodded. "Yes, it was really a clever scheme, and we might not have solved it if Meadow hadn't led us up there that day."

"It was good of you to give her all the credit, Dave. In the newspaper article, I mean," Shep said.

Dave smiled. "Well, she deserved it."

Brett suddenly perked up at the mention of Meadow. "Where is she, anyway?"

Mike smirked. "Taking her time bringing *your* horse back, Mr. Bowman." All eyes were on him now. "I saw her take off early this morning. It was all *very* mysterious."

"What could she be doing?" Brett scowled. "She knows the barbeque is today."

Mike shrugged. "You know Meadow, she's always up to something."

"Yeah, that's what I'm worried about." Brett jumped up and headed toward the corrals.

Rose watched him go, feeling the same way.

Chapter 39
New Beginnings

At that same moment, Meadow was racing like the wind toward the Lazy B Ranch with a huge grin on her face. She rode Foxfire at a gallop, with Arrow next to them, keeping pace and matching them stride for stride.

That morning at sunrise, before anyone else was up, Meadow had looked out the window just in time to see Colt trotting up on Smoke with her prancing mare by his side. She ran outside and buried her face in Foxfire's mane.

"Why do you have Foxy?" she managed to choke out.

"It's time to go bring in Arrow." His answer was simple, but spoke volumes.

"Does Mr. Bowman know that you took her?"

"No, but he won't miss her today. Everyone's busy with the big party preparations."

She broke into a smile.

"You'll be back with the stallion and Bill Bowman will be grateful," he said.

Meadow's reunion with Foxfire had been joyful for both of them.

"Foxy, you know how much I've missed you," she murmured against her neck.

Foxfire nickered softly, and rubbed her head against Meadow. Before swinging up onto her back, she crept in to wake Mike and tell him she was riding to Hidden Valley.

"Tell Mom and Dad not to worry," she whispered.

"Okay," Mike said sleepily and rolled over.

The ride to Hidden Valley was magical. Foxfire and Meadow were one again, with her mare anticipating her every wish. She rode side by side with Colt, who was quiet as usual.

But as they neared Oak Creek, her confidence started flagging. "Are you sure this is such a good idea?"

"You want to prove to everyone that you can bring Arrow in," Colt said.

She nodded. "Yeah."

"Today is the perfect opportunity. Everyone will be at the barbeque."

"You're right, I'm just a little nervous." Something else was filtering through—she couldn't quite capture it, like a butterfly that kept flitting away at the last moment.

Colt watched her, then asked, "What else is bothering you?"

"I'm not sure, I keep having little flashbacks about when I rode Arrow. . . ." Meadow frowned, trying to recall. Then it came clear.

"Go on, tell me about it."

It was as though he could read her mind. "It's just that I keep seeing the medicine chest," she mumbled. "I think I know where it is." She stole a glance at Colt, afraid of his reaction.

He reached across and took her hand.

"Remember, I told you to trust yourself," he said gently. "Let's go find it."

When they reached Oak Creek, instead of crossing, Meadow directed that they ride downstream. They traversed down the creek bed for a while until they came to a bend, and Meadow reined Foxfire in. She looked around, her heart pounding.

"This is it!" Her rush of excitement made her lightheaded. "Over there, behind that big tree."

She jumped to the ground, ran over to the tree and pushed aside branches. Colt was beside her in an instant and they both saw the edge of a crate buried in the drifted sand. They started digging it out, with Kelsey furiously helping. Before long, the whole crate containing the chest was visible. Colt removed his hunting knife from its scabbard at his waist and pried open the lid. The contents were unharmed.

Meadow breathed for the first time since they found the chest. "What are we going to do with it now?"

"Don't worry, I'll get it back to the cave. It'll be safe there for the time being." Colt looked into her eyes. "But for now, I think it should be our secret."

"Okay." She felt a thrill to be sharing a secret with him.

"You need to go get Arrow by yourself anyway. I'll take care of this."

"Won't you be coming to the barbeque?"

"No, I need some more solitude before heading back to college tomorrow."

Meadow understood, but still felt let down. He came and went so quickly. She could've spent every hour with him and never tired of his company.

After remounting and riding on to the edge of Hidden Valley, they went their separate ways. Colt needed to rig up a travois to get the chest back to the dwelling and she had to get Arrow.

Watching him depart, sadness pricked her heart, wondering if she would ever see him again. This was only the second time she had been with him, but she felt like they had always known each other.

Riding up the canyon trail, before losing sight of the valley, Colt stopped Smoke, turning to wave farewell, as if he knew she would still be watching. She waved back and he continued on his way. She gazed after him until he disappeared.

She sighed and turned her attention to the task at hand. Would Arrow come to her? It had been a month since she had been to the valley. But she needn't have worried. As soon as the stallion saw them, he trumpeted a welcome, and then came charging over to Foxfire's side, dancing and prancing around her.

Meadow laughed with sheer happiness at their reunion. She had missed seeing him and the stallion acted like he had missed them, too.

She hated the fact that she had to ask him to come in to the ranch and leave his mares and freedom, but there was just no helping it. She had to do it. She had to show them all. And strangely, when she gestured for him to come with them, Arrow seemed to understand. They started down the path, Foxfire setting a rapid pace, with the stallion close to her shoulder.

Finally, she sat back slightly, and Foxfire slowed to a walk. Why hurry? After all, once she was back at the Bowman ranch she would have to give up Foxfire again. At that moment, however, nothing could dampen her spirits. It had been a perfect day so far, just being with Foxfire, Arrow, and Colt again, not to mention finding the chest.

She felt the amulet warm against her chest, and Meadow reflected back on the day she had taken it in to a jeweler in Sedona to have the clasp fixed. The jeweler had exclaimed that he had never seen a more unusual and beautiful piece. He had even asked the name of the artist, but of course she didn't know. She could only tell him that it was an old Indian relic. She wasn't sure who made it, or when. The jeweler had given her a strange look, but didn't ask any more questions.

Meadow looked over at Arrow, prancing majestically beside them, and wondered for the hundredth time how she'd been picked as the keeper of the amulet. She took a deep breath, determined to live up to Meda's legacy. Especially now that she knew they shared a common Native American heritage.

When would her father tell his story? He owed it to them all to come clean. He must have an important piece of the puzzle so everything made sense. Meda must have lots of descendants to pass the amulet on to. Why her?

She felt the weight of the responsibility she'd been entrusted with, and knew she wasn't the same girl who had arrived at Brighten that spring. Sometimes she felt very old—not physically, but like she had lived in another time. It was a strange sensation. As she reflected back on the summer, Meadow was filled with amazement at all the events that had occurred.

Her attention returned to the present when they reached the ranch gate, and the stallion hesitated. He stopped and snorted loudly, obviously remembering the place where he had been held captive.

"It's okay, Arrow." Meadow spoke softly. "You can leave again whenever you want."

Foxfire touched her nose to his, and the stallion calmed down.

"Let's go," she said, riding through the ranch gate.

From her perch astride Foxfire, Meadow saw Mike and Brett down by the corrals. Mike waved to her as she got nearer. "You did it! I knew you could!"

Brett just looked dumbfounded, then yelled toward the house. "Come here and look everyone, Meadow is bringing Diablo in!"

Bill Bowman and Dad came out first, followed by the others. They all watched, as she talked to the wild stallion.

The stallion was not happy to see all those people, and reared onto his hind legs, pawing the air menacingly.

"Come on, Arrow. It's okay. They won't lock you up again." Meadow reached for the pendant.

As she touched the amulet, Arrow settled down again and followed Foxfire quietly. Meadow rode to the entrance to the pasture and leaned over to open the gate. She gestured to the stallion, and he hesitated.

"Come on, Arrow. It's okay."

The stallion shook his long silver mane, and then as if making an important decision, walked through the gate and into the pasture.

Meadow followed, and slowly slipped off Foxfire, removing her bridle in one swoop. Then, she walked over to Arrow who put his head down to her level. She stroked him fondly for a moment before closing the gate on the two horses. Meadow turned, took a deep breath, and walked right up to Bill Bowman.

"You see, Mr. Bowman, I can bring him in when you want him for breeding. He'll stay until he's no longer needed, and then return to the wild herd."

"I never would have believed it, if I hadn't seen it with my own eyes," Bill said.

She remained silent.

"And, I see that you borrowed Foxy for the job."

Her hands felt clammy. "I hoped you wouldn't mind."

"You know, young lady, I never really wanted to take Foxy from you," Bill said. "But I did want you to learn a lesson. You can't mess with other people's property."

Meadow shifted and looked down at the ground.

"I also wanted you to demonstrate your outlandish claim about having some strange power over Diablo—and you certainly proved that to me." He reached over and lifted her chin up until her eyes met his.

"You mean I can have Foxfire back?" She felt light as air.

"Providing I still get her foal next spring. Does that meet with your approval?"

"Oh yes!"

Meadow couldn't help but feel a little twinge about giving up Foxfire's foal, but she would have agreed to anything to get her mare back.

"Does anyone else have any reservations about this girl's abilities?" Bill looked around at the others in the group.

Dad put his arm around Meadow and squeezed her tightly.

Her mother looked on, smiling.

"Well, come on everyone, we've got roast pig to eat!" Linda took Dave's hand and led him back to the party.

They all followed, and the party began in earnest. Everyone had their fill of barbeque and Mexican food, and then a couple of blindfolded hotel employees whacked the piñata until it gave up the tasty treats inside. Laughing, Meadow and the rest of the young people scrambled after the candy.

After the feast, the party started to wind down, and most of the hotel staff left to pack their belongings for their departure the next day. The evening cooled, and the rest of the group found places to sit around the fire pit. Meadow sat with the others for a while, and then stole away.

She wandered over to a grassy knoll overlooking the pasture, where she lay down. Kelsey came and stretched out next to her, and she relaxed, watching the twinkling stars, and listening to the faint sound of guitar music behind her. In the pasture below, Foxfire and the stallion cropped grass companionably. She breathed deeply, happy that their world was now in harmony, with everything falling into place as it should be. She had Foxfire back and Arrow would be able to come and go freely. And Dad would tell them his secret before long. She'd make him.

After a while she spotted someone coming toward her. As he got closer, she saw it was Brett. Looking good in his jeans. She hoped they wouldn't have another fight. No, she was too happy to fight with anyone.

She sat up as he approached.

"I have something for you, Meadow," Brett said, almost shyly.

"What is it?"

Brett pulled the long forgotten stuffed carnival bear from behind his back with a flourish. "Ta da," he said, making her laugh.

"I'm so glad you found my bear. I wondered what happened to him. Thanks, Brett."

"You're welcome, little lady," Brett said with the Carny accent.

"Why, Brett, you're so gallant." Meadow mimicked Scarlett O'Hara's southern drawl, and took the bear from him.

She sat the bear next to Kelsey, who sniffed it curiously, then licked its nose. They both laughed at that.

"What are you doing out here?" Brett asked.

"Watching the stars—do you want to join us?" She patted the grass next to her.

"Sure." Brett eased himself down.

Several minutes passed, as they sat quietly watching the sky together. Brett finally broke the silence.

"I'm sorry I didn't believe you, Meadow." He fixed her with his deep blue eyes. "I should have known you wouldn't make up stories."

Whenever he looked at her like that, she felt shy and breathless all at the same time.

"It's okay. I know it sounded really crazy sometimes."

"I've had such a good time this summer, mostly because of you," he said. "I hate going away to military chool."

"Military school? Gee, that sounds pretty intense."

"Yeah, you weren't here when Mother made the announcement."

"Maybe it will be fun being away from your parents. You know, lots of freedom."

"Are you kidding me? Freedom at military school? That's a laugh!"

She felt dumb even suggesting such a thing and her mood plummeted. Shoot! Why did she always say the wrong thing?

But then Brett did laugh. "Listen, don't look so crestfallen. I'll be fine, if you write to me, and tell me everything that's happening back here."

"Okay," she said, feeling better. She lay back on the grass and gazed up at the sky. "Look! There's a shooting star."

Brett smiled. "It seems like wherever you are, exciting things happen."

"Quick! Make a wish," she said.

"I wish . . . that you will write to me . . ."

"Yes . . . I will."

"Promise?" he asked.

"Yes, I promise. But how exciting will it be? I'll be in school too, in Scottsdale—Snobsdale, I mean."

Brett laughed, and then took her hand, kissing it.

"I'm really going to miss you, Meadow . . . but then . . . there's always next summer."

"Yes." Her happiness soared, as if she were riding Arrow, the Sky Horse through the stars, his coat shining brightly in the night sky. "There's always next summer."

THE MYSTERY BOOK TWO

The story continues when the Shepherd family move back to Scottsdale for the winter, and Meadow finds her life in turmoil. In addition to being the new kid in school, she begins to receive threatening phone calls, and Arrow has disappeared. Danger lurks at every turn since the villains are still determined to recover the Indian Medicine Chest. The mystery of her family's heritage weighs heavy.

Will she ever find the answers?

THE LEGACY BOOK THREE

Back at Brighten, Meadow renews her quest to uncover her father's secret. She is tested to the limit as she bravely forges ahead, outwitting criminals who will stop at nothing to gain the treasure. Will she be able to protect Arrow?

The stunning revelations will forever change her life and the lives of those she holds dear.

About the Author

Melody Huttinger grew up with horses as her best friends. She learned to train them, tutored by her father, who rescued many so-called untrainable and neglected animals. Her family owned and operated various riding stables throughout the years, providing inspiration for Arrow, the Sky Horse series. Many of the characters in the story are drawn from the colorful collection of characters she met as a young dude wrangler.

From her family home in Northern Arizona, Melody has carried on the tradition of re-training Thoroughbreds off the track and has owned and trained various other breeds, including Arabians, Quarter Horses and wild Mustangs.

As a child, Melody read every horse story available, but at times became disappointed in the lack of knowledge that many of the authors displayed. She set out to write her own story depicting horses in a more realistic light.

Arrow the Sky Horse series, although partly fantasy, is based on her own experiences growing up with a family in the horse business. She hopes all readers, young and old, will be entertained and enjoy the stories about the animals so close to her heart.

Acknowledgements

First and foremost, I would like to thank my parents for providing me with a childhood chock full of horses, and the freedom to enjoy them.

In the beginning of the process, Dottie Moore gave me the encouragement to continue with the project by her unwavering faith in my story. I couldn't have written this book without the help of my critique group, Maura Dorn, Stephanie Jefferson, and Dougal Reeves. My good friend, Casey Knight provided immeasurable support in so many ways and helped to format the manuscript.

And last, but certainly not least, my wonderful husband, Jay, who listened patiently to all the revisions and rewrites.

A hearty thanks to you all!